Peter Sale was born in Liverpool to an Irish family and received his education at Saint Joseph's Academy of Hard Knocks. He left school at fourteen, ready for adventure, and, after ducking bombs with the American Red Cross in London, chasing Nazis in Hamburg, training with the New Zealand Air Force, writing country music in Nashville and appearing in Hollywood TV commercials, he settled down to write about his childhood memories in *Tom Kipper's Schooldays* and its sequel, *Tom Kipper: The Wartime Years*. Peter Sale lives with his wife Carmelisa in a town called Paradise, California.

Also by Peter Sale and published by Headline

Tom Kipper's Schooldays

Tom Kipper:
The Wartime Years

Peter Sale

headline

First published in 2007 by
HEADLINE PUBLISHING GROUP

First published in paperback in 2008
by HEADLINE PUBLISHING GROUP

1

Cataloguing in Publication Data is available from the British Library

ISBN 978 0 7553 3679 1

Typeset in Sabon by Avon DataSet Ltd,
Bidford-on-Avon, Warwickshire

Printed and bound in the UK by
CPI Mackays, Chatham ME5 8TD

Headline's policy is to use papers that are natural, renewable and
recyclable products and made from wood grown in sustainable forests. The
logging and manufacturing processes are expected to conform to the
environmental regulations of the country of origin.

HEADLINE PUBLISHING GROUP
An Hachette Livre UK Company
338 Euston Road
London NW1 3BH

www.headline.co.uk
www.hachettelivre.co.uk

From the Scouse heart of Tom Kipper
To the Gang of Hard Knocks:
Socks Kinneally, Betsy Braddock, Vange O'Malley,
Whacker Doyle, Sean Maloney, Conks Murphy,
Fred Magee, Gobs Flanagan.
An invincible army of miscreants, humorists,
Villains, knaves, scoundrels, scallywags and heroes.
And, oh yes, Carol Mattson, Camerawoman
  Extraordinaire,
And that Mexican Scouser, Carmelisa Azuara Sale.
May the Liver Bird deliver you a plethora of Mersey
  kippers.
And chips.
Amen.

Tom Kipper

Prologue

It was the best of times,
it was the worst of times.
It was the ominous drone, the clatter
of incendiary, the soft cry of the mother,
the laughter of Scouse kids; it was summer's
May fire that banished despair in Liverpool's
choir of humour and hope.
It was the kick of a can down an alley,
a pan of good scouse.
For Tom Kipper,
it was always 'the best of times'.

Chapter One

Last Year's Wet Echo

In those bleak but somehow comforting days of former glory, the news came by wireless, that magical instrument in antique wood, complete with valves and a potage of squawks, on a mantelshelf or dresser. It brought to the beleaguered island the news of the Axis powers dominating Europe, crouching in Normandy, peering through eyeglasses at the White Cliffs when it wasn't raining, which it mostly was.

'How can we,' enquired Oberleutnant Hans Kranken-hausen, 'invade such a gigantic sponge?'

'Keep raining,' breathed Corporal Charlie Fotherington of the Royal Engineers, in Dover. 'Is there any of that Guinness left?'

Crouched, sprawled in attentive position, families listened with cocked ear to the wireless, usually at six p.m. to Winston Churchill, or to their favourite, Lord Haw-Haw, for he was the predominant, obvious traitor, the sinister Brit who had betrayed King and Country. He had even had the temerity to take his wife with him. She didn't need a ration book. Daily they chomped down quantities of the finest liverwurst.

But wireless hours were sparse; in this year of forty-one the minutes were precious. What could possibly fill the void? Men, or mostly men, worked in deep subterranean pockets, eschewing Liverpool sunlight and fog, to rattle the presses of the *Echo*, that newspaper of great dimension and strength that smothered all Merseyside with its power and insight and print that came off on your hands and best shirt. The news was clean, the press a pot of carbon.

From tobacconists and grocers and newsboys, the *Echo* spilled out to all an avalanche of hot news of the doings of the malignant Axis, whether America would come into the war in their baseball pyjamas, if Liverpool or Everton would win the cup, whether hemlines were getting shorter. From comic to tragic.

Often the *Echo* would flop on to a middle-class doorstep while strato-cumulus hurried from Dee to Mersey bringing drizzle or bucket, which frequently inundated porchways. 'The bloody *Echo*'s wet! Look at this! It's just disgusting!'

'Cancel it, darling,' said Mrs Gladwyn Elderberry-Fyffe, sipping her tea, not looking up from her *Express*.

'How can you read that trash?' said Morgan Fyffe, throwing the blobbed *Liverpool Echo* on the dining table.

Thus from a million Merseyside throats issued the selfsame bewailing of the wet *Echo*, a tragedy of great dimension, so that in quieter moments, at elevenses time when ire was stilled and calm sipped with tea, the lone, disconsolate voice of a man caught in a web of dissolution cried out in fury, 'I wouldn't give you last year's wet *Echo*!'

His cry echoed across the estuary.

Thus when Rudolf Hess climbed into his Messerschmitt 109E and flew to Scotland, the hot news appeared in the *Echo* before it hit the air waves. He climbed out of his machine in bonnie Scotland, and immediately sent a message to Winston Churchill via the doughty Scottish constabulary suggesting terms of surrender, asking for peace between two noble nations. 'The Führer asks,' he is quoted as saying, 'that you give us peace.'

'Tell him,' said Winston, 'to speak to Herr Schikkelgrubber (that unemployed housepainter), tell him that I wouldn't give him last year's wet *Echo*!'

Thus, against all the odds, the wet *Echo* proclamation signalled the initial disintegration of the Axis powers.

'Was ist,' asked Schikkelgrubber, 'ein Wet Echo?'

'Mary and Joseph!' said my mother, which caught me by surprise for my ma never expostulated like that except in extreme crises. Evidently the letter she clutched in her worn hands set off the cry for she sat down and read it again before folding it up into its envelope and thrusting it into the pocket of her Kelly green apron.

'Pull yourself together,' she said to me for no obvious reason, so I knew it was going to be a bad day for everyone in the household. Put her in a Spitfire and the Nazis wouldn't stand a chance. 'Any chance of a cup of tea, Maria?' asked Dad. He brought 'Maria' back with him from Italy in World War One, or the Great War as they called it then.

'Your sister's coming in,' said Ma, stirring the pot.

'Winifred?'

'Who else?'

'Hmmn.'

'Here's your tea.'

'When is she coming?'

'Tomorrow.'

'Hmmn.'

'She's coming in early in the morning and spending the day with us.'

'Do I have to wear a tie?'

'She's your sister, not mine.'

'Can I go up to the Windmill with Charlie Sweeney tomorrow?' I asked.

'No, Tom Kipper, you cannot. You will stay here and keep your Auntie Winifred company.'

'You mean Old Winny?' I asked, for which I received a clip behind the ear.

And so a great foreboding hung over 213 Mary Lane, for an invasion was about to take place. It was not at all like the great invasion we were all waiting for from the coast of France by the Wehrmacht, but to us it appeared to be just as significant and the entire house seemed somehow to become cleaner and neater, and I was not allowed to throw dirty shoes and socks in the hallway as was normal tradition.

She arrived right on time. I thought they would need a large earthmoving machine to prise her through the front door. She was busty, overpowering and voluminous. She was also majestic, moving ponderously with massive power, smelling of perfume, cologne and lavender, filling the hallway and living room with her presence.

'Joseph,' she said to Dad, 'you're looking fine.'

Dad was smiling in a funny kind of way as they embraced; then she embraced Ma and kissed her on the cheek.

'And this is the part Tom Kipper loves,' she said as she overpowered me like a Sumo wrestler and kissed me on the lips. It was like being greeted by a friendly squid, or getting a smack in the mouth from Sullivan. I felt I was going into a coma before she released me. Nobody escaped.

Old Winny was given the largest seat to encompass her great, royal bulk and quarts of steaming tea with Eccles cakes through which she continued to talk of great Kipper traditions, their father having been a copper-plate engraver by day and a known violinist by night with the Liverpool Philharmonic Orchestra, so that most of us just shut up and listened to her. She was a great hive of information about Dad's family in outer Liverpool, which we had never visited because of the Blitz.

As she settled comfortably into her new environment she became less voluminous, her accent seemed less sharp and her demeanour more settled and gentle.

'Where's your husband, Auntie Winifred?' I asked.

'Harry has gone to the good Lord,' she answered. 'Before his time.' She sniffed.

'He was a lovely man,' volunteered Ma.

'Liked his beer too much,' replied Auntie Winny.

Then she enquired about all us tatty kids before, late in the afternoon, looking through the window at the sky, she announced it was time for her to depart. She was to catch a bus to the ferry to cross the river to Liverpool and Dad was to go with her to the bus station, so I volunteered to go with them. She held my hand as we walked.

'You're my favourite,' she said. She and Dad hugged at the bus stop and they both had tears in their eyes.

'Dad,' I said, 'I'm going to ride the bus with Auntie Winny to the ferry and then I'll walk back. It's not too far.'

'Well, all right,' said Joseph Prendergast Kipper, 'but be back before dark.'

It was when Auntie Winny and I stepped off the bus that a great wailing sound reverberated across the area, like something moaning in great distress.

'Air raid,' everyone shouted.

The ferry building shelter lay below ground, a spacious subterranean dugout for emergencies, now spilling with passengers hurrying down the concrete steps towards a narrow doorway leading into the roomy chambers.

Mr Morgan Elderberry-Fyffe, soured by his morning's Wet Echo and irritated by his wife Mrs Gladwyn Elderberry-Fyffe, who treated him with some contempt, pushed his bulk against Auntie Winny to ease her away from the doorway he wished to enter first. We were going downhill and Fyffe was well overweight and grunting, so he was successful in his aim. I thought I heard Auntie Winny say gently but distinctly, 'You bastard!' but the crowd grew thicker and it was some minutes before we found a pleasant seat with good light and plenty to read.

'We'll be all right here, Tom,' said Auntie Winny.

The sound of aircraft varied in intensity. No explosives seemed to have been dropped and it was all over in about ten minutes. The All Clear sounded.

As we stood up and proceeded towards the narrow doorway leading to the steps, Morgan Elderberry-Fyffe was immediately behind Auntie Winny and myself. The step leading up the stairs was quite high, and as we climbed the first step Morgan Fyffe said to me, 'Give me a hand, boy, up this step.'

The umbrella carried by Auntie Winy was hefty. It had belonged to Harry her husband, and they both used it as a walking stick. Winifred raised the umbrella way above her head and, aided by gravitational pull, brought it down on Morgan Fyffe's bowler hat, crying as she did so, 'I wouldn't give you last year's wet *Echo*!'

The hat parted like Vesuvius, spreading the main body over the eyeballs of Fyffe, who fell backwards into oblivion. There were cries of 'Hear, hear!' and 'Smack him again!'

In great triumph I saw Auntie Winny to the landing stage where she hugged me like a large cheese and onion sandwich and pressed upon me one large silver half-crown.

I loved Auntie Winny after that and watched as the *Royal Daffodil* peeled off from the stage and headed out into the fast-moving river towards Liverpool, and she waved to me all the way with her large umbrella.

And I smiled. Good old Auntie Winny!

And I thought I could hear my mother say, 'Pull yourself together, Tom Kipper!'

'I need,' I said, 'a long pair of pants!'

'To sell *Echo*s?'

'Ma, I am not going to sell *Echo*s or *Express*es.'

'And what are you going to do?'

'I am going to start my career. I am going to be an executive!'

She stirred the pot of scouse. It had a mouthwatering smell. It must be scouse. Across the fast-moving Mersey, over the frenzied wharves of shipping, the sand dunes of the Dee, the imperious Liver Buildings and the shabby tenements of outer Liverpool, with its bleak taverns of ale, moved the mysterious forces, heartwarming and spiritual, of scouse. Pots were being simmered and stirred in that ancient city, the benedictions of the aroma refreshing heart and soul.

'Do you want a bowl of scouse?'

'No, Ma, I want a pair of pants with long legs.'

Ma put back her head and shook with gales of laughter, which I had not been expecting. 'Eat your soup,' she said, wiping her eyes. I'm sure I heard her say, 'The boy's Irish.'

The following day, me and my brave mother, Mary Catherine Kipper, with her large purse, visited Atchinson's Men's Dress Shop on Sainsbury Avenue, which in quality was a degree or two, or even three, below Woolworths. But their trousers fit. I wanted a black shirt like James Cagney in the Roaring Twenties but ended up with white, which went well with a tie stolen from my elder brother Charles's collection. Charlie was sinking U-boats in the Atlantic and foaming pints of ale in every port so he did not resist.

'I was delivering chandlery to a lady on Dorrington Avenue and she told me to go to the Admin. Association on Water Street.'

'Who is this lady?' asked Ma.

'She's very pretty. Had on a pink dressing gown with lots of jewellery and smelled of perfume. I think she's a secretary.'

'Hmmn. Lots of perfume.'

'I want you to go with me.'

'You want me to go to Liverpool with you?'

'Yeah, Ma.'

'What?'

'Yes, Mother.'

There were thirteen of them. Thirteen merchant ships sunk in the river. The River Mersey. Funnels and masts stuck up like plants in a watery plot. Some not in the river were sunk at their moorings in Albert and other docks, spiralling smoke. All the ferry boats were sunk or waterlogged, thus denying passengers access to and from Liverpool. Thus was my career brought to a cataclysmic halt before it even started.

'You could swim across,' said my best mate Sully, hefting his capacious bag of *Echo*s. He left me and ran across to a busload of passengers arriving from the Wirral hoping to reach Liverpool that day. But it was two whole days before we all poured on to the ferry and eventually tramped up the gangplank to Water Street.

It was an impressive block of white buildings sliding down towards Victoria Street from Dale and the front door was a grand entrance. The steps leading up to it were wide, almost imperious, and made of a stone that carved the initials of all who trod upon her, for the steps had been hollowed out by the shoes of those who had ascended through the years. My shoes fitted perfectly into the contours as I jogged upwards.

The swing door had a large brass plate for pushing inwards into the darkened interior, in which I found a counter and absolute silence except for the gentle clacking of typewriters far in the distance. Time seemed to stand still. It was a comfortable building from another century; I tried to imagine how many other people had trodden these floors and looked up at the high ceiling as I was doing now. The brass bell on the counter was polished by many palms summoning attention.

I rang it. It had a pleasant sound, gently bonging into a Victorian age.

It seemed like a long time before heavy footsteps sounded down the hallway, bringing with them a huge man of portentous appearance wearing a black serge suit, moisture on his brow, breathing heavily. 'What can I do for you, young man?'

My chin came to the top of the counter and so did the middle button of the giant's serge suit.

'Please, sir,' I said, 'I've come for the job.'

'The job?' He smiled.

'The office junior job.'

'You mean the office boy?'

'Yes, sir.'

'Who sent you?'

'The Administration Association on Water Street, sir.'

'Oh.' I handed him the card the Association had given me. He scrutinised it very carefully. 'Where are you from?'

'The Wirral.'

'Oh, across the water.'

'Yes, sir.'

'You came a long way.'

'The ferry boat brought me.'

He gave a huge guffaw. 'What school did you attend?'

'St Joseph's.' I did not know why but I added: 'It's called the Academy of Hard Knocks.'

Oh, how my interviewer smiled at that. 'How old are you?'

'Fourteen.'

'Hmmn. Can you do anything special?'

'Well, I was editor of the school magazine and I can type forty-two words a minute.'

'What?'

'I can type forty-two words a minute.'

He was startled. And I think delighted.

'You just stay there, young man. Let's see, your name is Tom Kipper, right?'

'Yes, sir.'

'Stay there.'

He manoeuvred his bulk down the hall and I could hear him say, 'There's a young boy down the hall looking for the job of office boy and he says that he can type forty-two words a minute.' I heard typewriters cease to function and women's voices say, one after the other, 'Forty-two words a minute', and some laughter, and then, 'Well, bring him on down.'

And so I was greeted by, it seemed to me, a swarm of secretaries and men in suits with ties and executive demeanour, but all of them seemed to be smiling.

'Put the typewriter over there,' said one of the secretaries. I had never seen so many workers in one room.

I sat down at the typewriter, a very posh Smith-Corona, and fed in one white page of typewriting paper. One of the older secretaries, the one with the large horn-rimmed spectacles, said, 'Tom, we are going to time you. Are you ready?' She held a watch.

'Ready,' I said.

'Go,' said Mrs Bridget Smythe.

'Now is the time for all good men to come to the aid of the party,' I typed, and again, and again and again.

'Stop,' shouted Mrs Smythe.

The sheet was taken from the typewriter. Ladies' heads grouped around the completed document. 'Forty-one, forty-two, forty-three, forty-four ... He did forty-four.' Two mistakes.

I was patted on the back. All of the secretaries wanted to know where I was from. 'Oh, across the water.'

The treasurer said, 'Let me talk to the lad.' So the ladies went back to their machines chatting away about me and happy for a respite from Smith-Corona.

'You shall start on Monday,' said Mr Hocking, 'at fifteen shillings per week. Don't be late.'

'Before you go,' said Mr Jones, the original interviewer, 'you have to see the Chief Executive Officer. Don't be afraid of him as his bark is worse than his bite.'

It's too good to be true, I thought.

'Come through here,' said Mr Jones.

I stood before his desk, oak or teak, massive, ponderously magnificent, stately, no bigger than St George's Hall, indeed quite similar. In awesome fact very similar to the extra-large executive seated behind it.

He wasn't Henry the Eighth, although he looked ready to torch the monasteries.

Unless you were mesmerised by his bulk, his oily, shifty eyes, his withering sneer and the big black bowler hat on the hat stand that was split down the middle with guillotine precision by Auntie Winny.

'Ah! Last year's wet *Echo!*' boomed Mr Elderberry-Fyffe.

Thus I was born into the world of commerce.

Chapter Two

*The Last Cup of Tea
in the World*

At El Paso Corned Beef Inc. in the Liverpool business district in the Fox Building (solid, three floors, constructed in the 1890s, important, complacent, across from the white-storeyed post office, magnificently central) there was on the second floor, in a corner, a storage space for musty files, cobwebs, spiders of different hues, a strange silence, a bulwark against this valley of tears, and the office boy. Tom Kipper. That's me.

I was sent there for lunch. This was a lunch I brought from home, 'across the water', in the capacious pockets of a dark blue, voluminous overcoat which was more or less a Merseyside necessity when the fog came creeping up the Mersey from the Irish Sea, bringing Gaelic mystery and an understanding of life that defied human explanation, for it was haunting and mystical.

St Patrick (who was a Scouser) knew about it. His father, Gianello di Fato from Corsica, and his Welsh mother, Eleanor Rhys from Penrhyndeudraeth, helped in some ways to construct what is now Liverpool, the capital of Ireland.

Where was I?

The view from my 'office' encompassed, through the large window, a fine view of the other side of the narrow street built for horse and cart to visit the warehouse. On the second floor of the opposite building was a beautiful secretary in lace; that's how she seemed to me.

I took a rubber band and a paper clip from the musty shelf. The window was large, pushing upwards from the sill. She typed with great concentration, light flowing in from the narrow Chepstow Avenue, zinging the typewriter carriage with great élan, smiling at her finished product.

Which was when I snapped the rubber band to ricochet the paper clip off her window and drew my Scouse face back into the shadow as she jumped, looked all compass points, and went back to her machine.

After three more paper clips she declared war, shaking her charming fist at an enemy she couldn't see. So I munched down on Ma's sandwich, which contained greens I didn't want and what was left of last week's rationed bacon and Cheshire cheese. It was quite delightful; I had destroyed the enemy across on Chepstow Avenue with paper clips and was munching down on a WWII banquet. What more could a tatty teenager need?

'Tom,' asked Miss Dorothy from the doorway, 'if you go to the Mad Sandwich Shop today can you get one for me?'

'Yes, Miss Dorothy, I'll be going at twelve.'

'Thank you, Tom.'

She was a shorthand typist and had been all her adult life except when having a beautiful brood of four boys who all loved her. Her expertise with shorthand and machine were first class, her speed at delivery gently slowing down in her golden years, although her facility and skill with port and sherry kept good pace with all the other widows at the Crown and Horseshoe.

It was time for her to retire. Everybody at El Paso Corned Beef knew of the impending departure of Mrs Dorothy Cruikshank, a sad yet joyous occasion. Everybody called her Dot. I always called her Miss Dorothy.

Before she left my doorway she gave her charming smile and said, 'Have you fired any good paper clips lately, Tom Kipper?'

'Apart from the grave crisis facing the British nation as we stand alone against the Axis powers is a second most serious matter of crucial concern for all of us,' said Mr Churchill.

'I told you he'd mention it,' breathed Auntie Chrissie.

'Shush!' everybody said at once.

We were all crowded close to the radio on the mantel. His voice was coming through loud, clear and Churchillian, even with the Havana clutched in his pudgy grip. 'I am referring, of course,' said he, 'to the matter of tea.'

'I told you,' said Auntie Chrissie.

'Sheeesh!'

'Two vessels, the SS *Bletchley* and the SS *Gossamer*

Thread have been severely damaged by U-boats at undisclosed locations and are tied up in foreign ports with their cargoes of tea. We have some coffee from our American friends, but tea will possibly be in short supply for a while. There may be none. So I urge all of you out there in this brave island to ration your tea ration. Make it much weaker, perhaps use it twice. Sad news. However, we shall prevail!'

A great, audible groan went up, exploded. No tea! We can prevail without tea?

Absolutely impossible!

Never in the field of human conflict had the British nation faced such incredible odds. The Blitz they shall survive, but . . . no tea! No Pekoe and Black with a dash of rationed sugar and milk?

Impossible odds!

Faces were grim on the ferry boats, conversation at a minimum, tight-lipped passengers groaned and seethed, absolutely un-teaed, bereft of slurps of this salvific beverage.

'I bet Winny's got plenty in his bunker,' grouched Captain Wilshire Scott. 'This coffee's bloody lousy!'

And so the nation groaned.

All except the worthy officers of the police station in Chipton Downs.

Mr Dylan Evans from Llanfair-Newydd occupied a most significant post at the *Liverpool Echo*. He was not the editor or a sub-editor or an executive officer, janitor, doorman or general manager. But his job encompassed an area of the human psyche which ensured he was the very first person read in the *Liverpool Echo* just as soon as it was picked up from the wet porch or obtained from Socks Kinneally at the Pier Head.

And that area was *gossip*.

It was juicy gossip to set thirsty people salivating on the ferry, in the office, at the hearth, in the pub, in the restroom. But there was one subject that predominated in those awesome times of the Blitz, and that was *tea*, or, rather, the lack of it.

The pen of Dylan Evans, Welsh scribe, was never still, and he penned awesome stories of the bleak conditions of the tea tragedy with the utmost skill.

Always on page four.

All subscribers to the world's greatest newspaper (except the *Chipton Downs Post*) immediately turned to page four.

This was war . . .

His column was entitled *Fable and Fantasy by Dylan Evans*. On Monday, it read:

She was a modestly dressed, middle-aged lady, seemingly of some substance, who went into a rage in Mildred's Olde Tea Shoppe on Lime Street.

'This is a tea shop,' she shouted, 'and you have Eccles cakes and cream tarts and blueberry muffins and you have *no tea*! What kind of tea shop is this?'

Wielding her bag on its strap she delivered several blows to the tea counter and then started to devour her hat, which appeared to be made of felt.

One of the attendants tried to comfort her but the modest lady, who refused to divulge her name, snatched the cap from the attendant's head and began to chew away on that also, shouting 'Tea, tea' between mouthfuls of felt and cotton.

She disappeared into Lime Street railway station before the constabulary arrived.

There is still no word on the steamers bringing in tea from the Colonies . . .

The girl in lace was standing at the front of the small queue when she saw me coming through the doorway from Victoria Street with a stack of envelopes to post.

Her eyes lit up and she stomped across in my direction as soon as she completed her business at the post office counter.

She was so pretty, with a small, upright figure, well dressed but with eyes flashing.

'What is your name?' she demanded.

'Tom Kipper,' I answered, awed at her style, one hand clutching papers, the other on her hip.

'Well, Tom Kipper,' she ground out, 'you ought to be ashamed of yourself!'

'Oh, I am,' I stuttered, wondering why.

'Do you know that you have cost me my job with your tomfoolery!'

'I have?'

'Oh, yes, Tom Kipper, you have. Is that your real name? Are you Irish?'

'Yes, miss.'

She seemed to stamp a foot. 'Aren't you ashamed?'

'Of my name?'

'No, not of your name. Of me losing my job.'

'Yes, miss.'

She was suddenly quiet.

'Miss,' I ventured, 'may I ask a question?'

She was biting her bottom lip 'What is it?'

'May I ask how I lost your job?'

'With those damn paper clips, Tom Kipper.'

'Paper clips?'

'I was holding a stack of papers when you fired a clip. I tripped and dropped the papers just as Mr Wentworth walked in, so he fired me.'

'Wasn't it an accident?' I timidly ventured.

'Yes, it was.' There was a tear in her eye.

'Can we sit on this bench over here, miss?' We sat on the bench and she cried.

'He's just damn jealous,' she blubbered in her handkerchief.

So I waited a while till the spirit of peace descended and said, 'May I help you. Miss . . . ?'

'Wendy,' she said, straightening up. 'I'm not supposed to leave till Friday but I want to leave this very damn minute. The trouble is I have so much to cart away.'

'I have an idea,' I said. 'We could carry your belongings over to El Paso Corned Beef. Store some in my room – it's a filing room – and pick them up some other time.'

'Oh, could I, Tom?'

'Of course, Miss Wendy.'

I went with her into the Grimshaw Building, clattered up in the old lift, swept into her offices, passed a tall man in a herringbone suit with his mouth open and perplexed, tealess staff members.

'Can you carry these two file boxes, Tom?' asked Miss Wendy.

'Yes, miss,' and out we went.

'Where are you going, Miss Winters?' shouted Herringbone, obviously Mr Wentworth.

'Out of your life for ever,' hollered back Wendy Winters. All the staff cheered.

We walked upstairs at the Fox Building and into my spidery office. Wendy looked through the window, across the narrow alley to her old window. Tears formed in her eyes again.

'Oh, I'm sorry, Tom,' she blubbered, sitting down at my Victorian desk.

'I'd get you some tea, Miss Wendy, but there isn't any.'

'What's going on here?' It was ponderous Mr Jones. 'Why is this lady crying?'

Before I could answer he said, 'Tom, you'd better see Mr Crisp as soon as possible. He needs something at Customs.'

And that was how I left them, with Mr Jones being very solicitous and Miss Wendy sniffing away.

'It's true, Ma,' I said on Tuesday. 'It's on page four of the *Echo*, by Dylan Evans. Let me read it to you.'

It read:

He was a fairly stout man from Wigan. He stood on the pedestal that normally houses the Liver Bird on the river side of the building, threatening to jump off unless someone brought him a cup of tea, half a teaspoonful of sugar, dash of milk. Spectators and officers of the Fire Department were begging him to come back down but every time they moved in his direction he moved closer to the edge.

The tea lady of the Old Liver Complex was hurriedly summoned to the president's office, and ordered to make what the man wanted as soon as possible.

She whispered in his ear, 'Very well, sir, but there's only enough Pekoe left for your own next secret cup of tea.'

'Oh, give it to him,' he wept, slumping forward across his desk. *'It's the last cup of tea in the world.'*

Mrs Gloria Fossinger, the tea lady, brought it on a tray, through the spectators, in a silver teapot accompanied by an English bone china cup and saucer and a digestive biscuit, beckoning the man down and telling the police and foremen to clear off. On a park bench near the pedestal she spoke to the Wigan man soothingly and he did, indeed, calm down.

Which was more than you can say for the Fire Department, who wanted tea themselves.

And so the Tea Drama continues.

Police Constable Wilkins O'Shea was heading respectfully towards his retirement years and unlike many of his calling had become unfazable, hardly ever angry, and unmindful of advancement in rank, preferring to remain a PC all the law-attending years of his dutiful career.

Other members of the force, superior in rank, openly sneered at his gentle, compassionate style.

'He doesn't even spit,' derided Inspector Fossdick O'Dwyer. 'What kind of cop is that?'

A depressing man was Fossdick, even with tea. His wife, Penelope O'Dwyer, shook her head over him. 'Did your mother never teach you how to smile? Look, my darling, this is how you do it. You see, you open your mouth, spread your lips. No, Fossdick, not like that. You look like King Kong gargling scouse!'

PC Wilkins O'Shea never married, for his intended ran off with a man of action, a party man, a shallow fellow who showed her a splendid time for twelve months before scarpering off to Ballykinlar with another woman.

Should Wilkins ever feel a touch of loneliness he would visit his widowed sister, Minnie, who lived alone in a red-bricked cottage on Marmalade Drive where they would take tea and crumpets and sometimes quite delicious sausage rolls. It was on one of these visits to his sister that he gave my Grandpa Finnegan the shock of his life, for Wilkins stepped through the door in his uniform, buttons sparkling, bobby hat under his arm. 'Hello,' he said.

'Oh, Wilkins,' Minnie murmured, 'I wasn't expecting you. Come in and have some tea. Put your hat over there. Sit down. This is Mr Finnegan, my neighbour from next door come to visit.'

Grandpa and Wilkins shook hands. 'Finnegan. Finnegan. I think I've heard that name before,' said Wilkins.

' 'Tis indeed a fine name from the ould country,' said Grandpa. Every copper down on Grinch Street knew him. A policeman, he thought, a policeman in uniform. Her brother a copper. Seems like a nice feller. I wonder if she tells him about the coal.

'You only get one cup of tea,' said Minnie to her brother Wilkins. 'I have enough left for tomorrow before England dies of thirst.'

'No tea, hey,' said Wilkins. 'Well, well, well, let me see what I can do about that tomorrow.' PC Wilkins leaned close to his sister in conspiratorial fashion. 'I know,' he confided, 'of a substantial cache of confiscated tea – Pekoe and Black, I think – doing nothing but employing space.'

Minnie's grey twinkling eyes lit up. 'Perhaps tomorrow?' she asked. He nodded.

'Yes,' he answered, 'but don't tell you-know-who,' looking sideways at Grandpa.

Grandpa's hearing had partially dissolved into blissful years of creative listening to race results and Gaelic mysteries beyond belief told in the Dirty Duck, so it was much later, when Wilkins departed for home, that she told him. He smiled his Finnegan smile.

That same evening as twilight descended graciously on the River Mersey, Grandpa, at O'Brien's Horse and Crown, told my uncle Bart Finnegan. It was not until the following night at the Bird in Hand that Bart told his brother Aloysius, and they grinned that Finnegan grin, like freebooters and pirates of the Caribbean.

Much later that night, as light rain fell on Grinch Street, two shadows crept through the back door of Chipton Downs police station – finding, strange as it may seem, the door unlocked – and crept out again with a large green suitcase.

'Shall I get the other case?' whispered one shadow to the other.

'No. Let's not be greedy.'

On Wednesday, Dylan Evans wrote:

We have yet to receive validation of the report from outside sources that a Liverpool fan, name of Melinchor Jones, from Prestatyn, became unhinged because of lack of tea, kicking at inanimate objects on Tithebarn Street – postboxes, lampstands, pictures of Winston, etc.

This tealess man was last seen heading towards Liverpool Cathedral muttering Welsh oaths, saying that he was indeed going to take the matter up with the head man.

Reports suggest that a damaged freighter, loaded with Pekoe and Black, is being guided by the Royal Navy into the Crosby Channel.

Downing Street is being deluged with mail. Some of it quite unseemly.

Security is tight.

It was brought to Ma in a sugar sack, a rich bouquet of Ceylonese tea surrounding the bearer, Bart the Crusader.

'It'll keep Karl Marx brewed up for a few weeks, Mary.'

'Bart, I don't know what to say.'

'Well, Mary, a couple of half-crowns might help a thirsty man from Tipperary.'

The Mince Pie Gang of Clara Garrity, Zilda Sweeney, Maureen Mulvaney, Cathy Sullivan and Aunties Madge and Florence were delighted when Mary Catherine Kipper invited them over that evening for tea and chocolate dumplings.

'But, Mary,' protested Zilda, 'there is no tea in the whole of England.'

'I was mailed some from Tipperary,' she said. 'Hurry on over now. Bring some sugar.'

'It's Orange Pekoe,' declared Clara, breathing the glorious aroma.

Dylan Thomas, page four, Thursday:

Jason Brevington, MP for Chipton on the Wall, had a serious altercation with a fellow MP in the Commons Tea Room, which had no tea, accidentally jabbing him rather sharply in the paunch with his tea tray (minus tea).

Mr Aston Fulbright, MP for Yettington on Avon, the recipient of the smack in his protruding corporation, accepted Mr Brevington's apologies before accidentally kicking Brevington in the shin.

The arrival of the Prime Minister, smiling and full of tea, in the room excluded any more jollity.

'Did you bring any tea with you?' enquired a weak voice from the MP for Brodgitter under Lyme.

It was at nine o'clock one sunshiny, splendid Monday morning that I swaggered into the El Paso Corned Beef emporium to a tealess staff of morose individuals.

Well, Miss Fiona Healey was morose. Gloria Wainwright was churlish, Mr Dobbs was grouchy, Lydia McLaverty was melancholy, Mr Crisp was crabby, tongues were hanging out, lips were cracked, muscles were twitching, someone was moaning, 'This is our finest hour!'

Strangely enough, Miss Wendy was right in the middle of the El Paso clan, just as unteaed as everyone else. What was she doing here?

I think Ma Kipper put show-biz in my beige, Irish legs for I tangoed the last few steps into the main office.

All bleak eyes bore down on me. Was I mad? Had lack of tea done this to the boy? Why was I not morose like normal people?

'Ladies and gentlemen,' I said, 'it is a long way from Tipperary but those Tipperarians have sent us . . .' and with an elegant gesture I reached into my brown paper bag and pulled out a large package, followed by another,

'Tea!'

Oh, what a party we enjoyed!

'Long live Tom Kipper,' Wendy shouted.

'Miss Wendy,' I said, 'what are you doing here?'

'I work here, Tom Kipper,' she said, 'thanks to you,' giving me a smacking kiss. 'I'm taking Mrs Dorothy Cruikshank's place.'

'Wait till I tell Ma!'

It was then that the main doors sprang open and Mr Elderberry-Fyffe fell through them in his daily drama.

Putting his manicured fingers on top of the entrance desk he viewed the entire El Paso Corned Beef troupe smiling at him in grand array.

Taking a deep breath he said, 'You've all been drinking tea, haven't you?'

Chapter Three

Amapola Cortez

'Old girl, you're going bloody crackers,' said Elderberry-Fyffe.

'It's loaded with onions. Spanish onions.'

'And where did you get this information from, Mrs Fyffe?'

'That flawless piece of newsprint, the *Echo*. It's on the table, right under your nose.'

'Oh, well, let me see.'

Page Two read:

A Spanish steamship, the *El Torrero*, loaded with onions has docked at Liverpool. Even though our gardens have managed to produce some lively crops of Spanish onions for the war effort, this import is of great significance to the world of food.

For what is a stew without Spanish onions? What

is a ham and cheese and tomato sandwich without the rich flavour and aroma of Spanish onions? The people of Merseyside, indeed the whole of Britain, look forward to this rich harvest from our Spanish allies. Prices will probably exceed domestic values. These most splendid Spanish onions will bring relish to the English table.

'How did they escape?'

'Escape?'

'Spain is almost occupied by the Germans. If that ship tries to return the U-boats will get it and the Gestapo will have an ice cream party with the captain.'

'I can taste those onions already. I wonder if Chester the grocer has any,' said Mrs Elderberry-Fyffe.

'London will get them,' said Fyffe. 'Winston is already tucking into liver and onions.'

Bart Finnegan was already pondering on onions with similar constructive objectivity, though hoping to omit the exchange of coin of the realm from his calculations.

'What do you think about those onions, Bart?'

'Hard to tell, Charlie.'

'Would bring a good price. There's none left in England.'

'Aye.'

'Can I introduce you to a pint of Guinness, Bart?'

The radio in those endearing years may have been a squawkbox of unintelligible drama at times, but out of nowhere clarity occasionally zoomed into high relief, which is what happened when Charlie Bancroft said 'a good price', for Bart Finnegan knew immediately that his honesty was being tapped, assaulted, impugned.

He smiled. 'A pint of Guinness you say, Mr Bancroft?'

'Listen, Bart, I have an idea.'

'Do you have the exchange, too?' enquired Bart.

Further up the Wirral peninsula, not far from brooding dockland, lay a pub of more than dubious reputation, the Broken Promise. When the landlord was stabbed to death with an oversize dagger in 1810, his assailant said, 'He'll never break another one!'

The men who occupied its chambers were workers such as stevedores, sailors both Royal and merchant, unlicensed plumbers, bartenders, unemployed painters, ex-con bookkeepers still trying to balance their ledgers, and one, just one, scroungy, hairy-faced Captain of the Sea, Seamus Rafferty.

The local constabulary called them 'bilge rats'.

'Ah, me boy,' said Rafferty to Bart late that day. 'You don't look any older. Well, not too much.'

Two very fine Guinnesses later, Bart chased foam from his lips and said, 'Have you still got the tug?'

'I have. And have you got the exchange, Bart Finnegan?' said Rafferty, lubricating his thumb and forefingers with gooey spittle.

'Aye, Rafferty.' He paused. 'It's about Spanish onions,' he said.

Rafferty is almost as fast as Bart.

*

'Your Uncle Bart has invited you on a trip in a schooner?'

'Well, Ma, it's more like a yacht.'

'Tomorrow night?'

'Yeah, Ma, I mean yes, Mother.'

'What about your job in Liverpool?'

'Well, this boat trip is just, kind of, late in the evening.'

She battered the pot of scouse. 'I'll speak to your Uncle Bart about the matter.' Ma ruled the Kipper roost.

'Is there any tea, Mary?'

'Can you take Karl Marx with you?'

Security seemed to be at a low ebb at West Sail dock.

'I'll wait for you here, Uncle Bart,' I said as I trod the boards of the ancient structure.

He was dressed like a merchant seaman the world over, the same baggy trousers, heavy jacket and big collar, a roll to his gait as though he was still looking out on vanishing horizons. The only difference was that he wore a beret, a beret of the Basque peoples which signified to the balance of the foreign world that you were from a Spanish vessel and that you were looking for revenge for a scuttled Armada.

Two seamen were in front of him as he trod up the gangplank leading to SS *El Torrero*. In his hand he held a clipboard clipped with papers and a large pencil nestled behind his right ear.

The two seaman in front passed ahead into the vessel. A large man on deck spread himself before Bart, arms folded.

'*Quien es usted?*'

'Who are you, señor?' interpreted a dwarf of a man by his side.

'Good evening,' said Bart. 'Customs inspection.'

'*Usted tiene sus documentos en orden, no es asi?*'

'You have papers, perhaps?' said the midget.

'These are all the papers I need,' said Bart.

'Oh, no, señor. This is a private vessel. You must show papers,' said the wee man for the giant.

'Then I ask you the same question, mister,' said Bart. 'Where are your papers?'

The man looked startled.

'*Espere aqui, ya regreso.*'

'Stay here. 'I shall return,' said the short chap.

The man went aft. Mist was seeping up from the river; the sky was darkening, Bart could see Kipper on the other side of West Sail dock. The big man waved to Bart to come up further on to the upper deck.

'*Yo lo presentare a usted al capitan.*'

'I shall introduce you to the captain,' supplied the midget.

Then he stepped back and motioned Bart to enter the cabin. Even Bart Finnegan, wry, smiling professor of Confidence Trickstering, went into shock. She was statuesque.

'A foin figure of a woman,' said Bart later in the Dirty Duck.

She was dressed in men's clothes, which made not one iota of difference to her femininity, her charm, her command, her style and grace. Mischief was on her lips. She was in spirit a second Bart with that elegant smile, twenty years younger, non-crustaceous, almost swashbuckling, not quite a pirate.

And she was the captain. She extended a hand, warm and inviting. 'Please sit down,' she said in fine modulated English, heavy with Castilian. 'I am sorry, but I have no tea.'

He took her hand. 'Bart Finnegan.'

'You are Eengleesh?'

'Irish.'

'You are Irish living in Eengland?'

'Living in Liverpool, the capital of Ireland.'

'How is that possible?'

'It's hard to explain,' said Bart. 'Perhaps one day my sister, Mary Catherine Kipper, will explain it all to you.' Little did Bart know how true this was to be.

'Her name is Keeper?'

'She married an Englishman.'

She smiled: 'And now, Bartholomew Feenegan, what are you doing aboard *El Torrero*? What can I do for you?'

'First thing, captain, is you can invite my nephew, Tom Kipper, aboard and then I would like to speak to you about money.'

Her eyes lit up, for, as Brinsley O'Connor so sapiently points out, matters of financial security always give you a glitch in the clutch.

'Tell me more about this Spanish woman,' said Ma, ironing an ancient shirt for her husband, Karl Marx.

'She's beautiful, Ma,' I said.

'Oh, is she?'

Tom was silent.

'Go on.'

'Well, she just is. She has red hair, and she kind of shimmers as she walks.'

'Shimmers?'

'Kind of wiggles.'

'Wiggles?'

'Well, yeah, Ma. Like sometimes you do.'

Oh, how Ma smiled.

'How was she dressed?' She tested the iron with a spit-wetted fingertip.

'In men's clothes, but with jewelled sandals on her feet, and she smelled heavily of perfume.'

'Perfume? What kind of perfume?'

'Gosh, Ma, I don't know, but it was delicious.'

'Delicious?'

'Well, it kind of made your head swim.'

'Swim? Go on. Go on.'

'Well, she kept flashing her eyes at Uncle Bart.'

'What?'

'At me, too, Ma. And all the time she was smiling.'

'I bet she was. Then what happened?'

'She and Bart lowered their voices and talked quickly about some project.'

'What project?'

'I don't know. I was looking through her cabin window at the Liver.'

Tom had absorbed every word but revealed not one iota of the *El Torrero* Chamber of Commerce Inscrutable Intelligence regarding what was to take place the following night without notice to the chamber.

'And Uncle Bart took you on this foreign ship?'

'Well, I was invited aboard by Captain Amapola Cortez. I was on the dock when the captain and Uncle Bart signalled me to come up the gangway.'

'Great merciful heavens! Wait till your father hears about this!' Again she tested the iron.

'Is there any tea?' asked Karl Marx.

'And,' asked Ma, 'where did you get that beret?'

'Did you order some Spanish onions, my dear?' said Elderberry-Fyffe to his wife.

'Ten pounds, but all I got was one.'

'One pound?'

'One onion. Let me show you.'

'How do you know it's Spanish?'

'It smells.'

'Smells?'

'Smells Spanish. Look at the size of it.'

'Probably contraband. Don't order any more.'

'Why?'

'The ship was raided last night by gangsters. Probably American. Carried off half the cargo. I do not want to see any in this house!'

'The Americans stole Spanish onions?'

'Yes, and kidnapped the captain, a Spanish woman.'

'Where did they take her?'

'Probably to some seedy tavern. That's why you only got one onion.'

*

Seamus Rafferty nudged the tugboat *Priscilla* to starboard, roped her to the *El Torrero*.

There was little conversation.

'Bart,' she said, shaking his hand and then signalling to two sailors waiting on the lower deck, who began to unload boxes on to the tugboat. I helped Bart and Captain Seamus Rafferty to move the boxes into uniform formation. It was fast and easy. Even the Wehrmacht would have been impressed. Not to mention the denizens of the Bird.

Then money passed from Bart to Captain Amapola Cortez; she counted the notes and then took me by great surprise by hugging me.

'When are you going back?' asked Bart.

She looked out across the Mersey, that incredible stretch of historic water, at the Liver Building rising nobly like a cathedral through the mist.

'I'm not going back,' she said. 'I'm coming with you.'

Bart grinned. I cheered for reasons not known to me. Sailors never ask why. She spoke briefly to her two Spanish seamen, handed them some of Finnegan's largesse, and climbed down with me into the aged tugboat. A large lorry was waiting at the deserted pier to unload the Spanish onions.

'The Spaniard pub,' said Bart to Captain Amapola, 'is just down the Esplanade. It will be still attending deserving clientele at the back door.'

The *Priscilla*, now the *Roach*, moved silently away from the pier, scruffy Captain Rafferty grinning a Scouse smile with a handsome bundle of pounds in his pocket, back to the Broken Promise for an investment in ale.

'Well, well, well, Bart Finnegan,' said Hugo Castillo, handsome black Irish, confirmed bachelor, 'who have we here?'

'You'll be surprised,' said Bart Finnegan, 'very surprised. Captain Cortez, meet Hugo Castillo, owner of this scruffy tavern.'

Love is blind. But even I felt the magic. Captain Amapola's black Moorish eyes caressed Hugo Castillo and put her Spanish seal on him. Thus is history fulfilled. 'I'll have a small beer,' I said. Which I didn't get. But all smiled.

Into later years Cortez never left the side of Hugo Castillo, although she beat him occasionally because she was Spanish and a woman into the bargain. After two or three Spanish sherries, Merseyside could hear her singing 'Ramona'. They were married a few Scouse moons later at St Joseph's next to Hard Knocks. The bells chimed with Hispanic reverence.

Black-eyed gulls wheeled over the morning ferry.

Most of the ships sunk in the May blitz had been salvaged so the way was clear for the *Daffodil* to clunk into the stage at Liverpool. Well-dressed office workers swarmed upwards for the tide was low; the streets were still wet from last night's storm.

I didn't see Mr Elderberry-Fyffe on the ferry or the landing stage so he must have caught an earlier boat, or the train through the Tunnel.

I could hear Mr Jones saying 'The Yanks are coming' as he swung through the doors meant for cheeky office boys.

'Old Winny must have given Roosevelt a kick in the backside, then.'

'When are they coming?' asked Gloria Wainwright, secretary to Mr Dobbs.

'Good morning, Tom.'

'Good morning, Miss Wainwright.'

I went immediately to my messenger basket to pick up any orders for the coming day. Not all the office staff had arrived so I moved dexterously into Mr Elderberry-Fyffe's office to place a large object in the middle of his polished desk. It glowed with a soft gloss in contrast to the black inlay of the desk. I left softly.

Mr Jones arrived soon after, heaving his ample frame in from Victoria Street, followed by the financial controller, Mr Hocking, and Lydia McLaverty. Bone china teacups were rattling at eleven when the doors were swished open by Mr Elderberry-Fyffe who had been delayed at the Chamber of Commerce for bureaucratic nonsense purposes. He looked flushed, annoyed, perturbed, rattled, ready for war, like a Liverpool supporter sleeping during a game, even shaking his knobbly stick at no one in particular. The staff ducked its head. Pushing open the door to his elegant suite he shouted for his secretary, Miss Fiona Healey, whom he was going to eat for lunch.

But Miss Fiona had not made it to his side before Elderberry-Fyffe let out a massive roar. 'Who put this blasted object on my desk!'

All mouths dropped open. All eyes swivelled at each other and away to the ceiling. And then everybody broke into a wave of laughter at the sight of the dignified Elderberry-Fyffe framed in his doorway with a stick in one hand and a most splendidly proportioned Spanish onion in the other. Which is when he smiled. 'Gladys will be so pleased,' he said.

I grinned.

Chapter Four

Flannery's Foo-Foo

'Ma, what is scouse?'

'You eat it almost every day and you don't know what you've been eating?'

'Ma, I know what I eat, but somehow I feel there is more to scouse than meets the eye.'

'Tom Kipper, you have been blessed.'

'Blessed? How's that, Ma?'

'Not many people understand the mysterious, Irish qualities hidden in scouse.'

'Do you, Ma?'

'No. Nobody does. It's as mysterious as the autumn mists hovering over the Mersey. Some historians try to tell us it was brought over by Scandinavians three hundred years ago made of corned beef and cabbage and cucumbers. But that's a lot of foreign nonsense. It was originally Irish stew, the Welsh threw in leeks and the Lancastrians threw in swedes.

The vegetables, not the people. The mystery was most probably from St Patrick himself.'

'Wow, Ma.'

'Ask your father. If he's awake.'

'Natural phenomena,' said my dad, without stirring, 'are merely shadows, according to Plato.'

'What does that mean, Dad?'

'It's called Eros.'

'Eros?

'Well, it's self-explanatory. Is there any tea?'

So that was Irish and Greek philosophy for the day.

Joey Flannery was a scruffy kid, about a year older than me at St Joseph's Academy of Hard Knocks, with a permanent sneer and a Scouse accent that was different from that of the rest of us. His spitting prowess was beyond reproach, grunting adenoidally, sneering afterwards. Yet I didn't dislike him. Betsy Braddock did. Said he was disgusting. But Francine Quigly didn't.

He never hit anybody except in self-defence, which is also when he used his unique vocabulary. 'Wassabluddymarra wit you den, la'?' and 'Shuturgob' were favourites.

He was also sharp at maths and history, I was told by my cousin, Mickey Flaherty, in the same class. The kid, Flannery, was mean but he was sharp. I always thought he would have made a good Chicago gangster. It was a year after I quit Hard Knocks that a voice behind me on the ferry boat said, 'Hello, la'.'

At first I couldn't absorb what was different about him,

then I realized it was his hair, for the great, stubbly, red forest he sported at Knocks was slicked and creamed back from his forehead so that it shone, glinting brassily, in the bleak Mersey sun.

He still had the sneer as though he knew something nobody else in the universe did, which always made me wonder what it was.

'Hi, Joey,' I said weakly, dazed in the face of such Flannery mystique.

'I've seen you on the boat before,' he grunted.

So we strolled the upper deck as the imperious Liver Buildings edged closer, swapping yarns about days of yore at Knocks, about the football scores.

'Listen, Kipper,' he said, as we disembarked, 'd'ya wanna make a bob?', which is Scouse parlance for 'How would you like to increase your revenue?'

I nodded my Kipper head in acquiescence, so he said, as we ascended the gangway, 'Nobody has any men's hair cream these days. The only people who have Brylcreem these days are the RAF, the Brylcreem Boys. Any other hair cream you get is bloody tacky; sticks to your hair like paper glue at Knocks.'

'So?' I enquired on Water Street in the shadow of the Liver.

'I'm a chemist,' he said. 'I work for Bracey's the Chemist up on Seymour Terrace. I make hair cream.'

'The chemist or you?'

'Me.'

I had to let go a good chuckle. 'You make hair cream, Joey?'

'It's easy,' he said. 'The reason why there's a shortage is because there's a shortage of ingredients. But I have them, Kipper.'

I was going to ask if he bought or appropriated but I didn't want to chance a smack in the kisser. Hey, I was dealing with a giant in the men's hair cream industry.

'How do you make it?'

'Simple. One part a secret oil, one part lime water, add one drop perfume, shake and it emulsifies. Voilà! Hair cream!'

'Wow!'

'The expensive part is the perfume.'

'Which you get free.'

'Almost.'

'How may I join your industry?'

'I need someone to sell it. You meet a lot of businessmen in the city, but I don't.'

'How much?'

'Sell it for a shilling, you get twenty-five per cent.'

'Make it fifty.'

'Forty.'

'It's a deal.'

'See you tomorrow. Bring a bag, Kipper.'

Joey Flannery brought supplies the following day. Four flasks. On a park bench at the top of the stage he took one from a string bag. 'This one has the ingredients but it is not emulsified.'

It was amber, the bottom half oil, the top white lime water, giving off a strong smell of perfume. 'It's smelly without the scent,' he said. 'Now watch.'

He shook the flask, and the ingredients mixed to a whitish emulsion. The label on the front had the words 'Men's Hair Cream' printed in gold lettering (I was expecting 'Flannery's Foo-Foo').

'Take the bag. Kipper. That'll be two shillings.'

'Pay you when they're sold,' I answered, which I did, for they sold like nobody's business, customers eagerly asking for further supplies.

'It's hard to get flasks,' said Flannery a few days later as I gave him the two bob. 'See if your ma has any of those antiseptic containers.'

'Tom,' said Mr Crisp, 'I would like you to go to Gossingham Traders down on Victoria near North John and deliver this letter personally to Mr Gossingham. It's very important, Tom. Look smart. Can you straighten your tie and perhaps,' he whispered, 'comb your hair again.' Smiled, he did.

Betsy Braddock liked my hair like this, almost unkempt.

It was a greystone building set back from the street with acacia trees arranged modestly before the swinging brassed oak doors. On the second floor Lily Henderson, aged sixteen, going on seventeen, said, 'Hello, Tom Kipper,' for I had visited Gossingham's the month before.

'Miss Henderson,' I said in an aloof fashion, 'I have a letter which I must personally hand to Mr Gossingham.'

'Give it to me, Tom Kipper, and stop acting like the Duke of York.'

'I can't, Lily, I have to give it to Mr Gossingham himself.'

'No way,' said Lily.

'Then I shall report to my superior that he refused to accept the correspondence.'

'You are annoying me, Tom Kipper.'

'You know, you look Irish and you're not!'

'My mother is.'

'Everybody's got an Irish mother!'

'Including you, O'Kipper!'

'What is it, Lily?' crackled stentorian tones behind the receptionist.

'It's Tom Kipper from El Paso Corned Beef, Mr Gossingham. Says he has a letter he must personally deliver to you.'

He didn't look too old, fortyish, pale skin, black black hair, somewhat snotty (imperious) black Errol Flynn moustache, high collar that was choking him. Wife must have been slowly increasing the starch. Lifting his eyes from the letter he said, 'So, you're Tom Kipper.' He edged to the counter. 'Tell me, Tom, do you have any of that hair cream available?'

'I have one in my pocket, sir,' I whispered.

'One and six?'

'Yes, sir.'

I handed him the carefully wrapped flask. 'Shake it well, sir,' I said.

He was smiling quite delightedly as he gave me the one shilling and sixpence.

'Good show, Tom.'

As I left, Lily said archly, 'You are sly, Tom Kipper!'

'And you are beautiful, Miss Henderson.'

She was happy.

So was I. I had made an extra tanner.

But the story did not end there. Drama such as Willy Shakespeare never dreamed of entered my life, and when it happened I kept it all locked away in my heart. I was a changed being, a chastened kid in the grim city – how could fate deliver me such a cruel blow, shatter my self-esteem, scatter my fortune? My cup ran over, downhill like a river of scouse, and stars fell from the sky.

'Tom,' said Mr Crisp, 'I have a special package for Mr Gossingham at "Traders". You know where they are located now.'

'Yes, sir.'

'See him personally, now!'

'Yes, Mr Crisp.'

I whistled down North John, for in my pocket I had snugly encased a flask of Flannery's slick hair cream. Tonight I was going to attend St Alban's Club with the gang from Knocks so all was well with the whole wide world. If there wasn't an air raid.

Lily wasn't at the desk. Must have gone for lunch at Lloyds.

'I have to deliver this to Mr Gossingham personally.'

The girl gave me a very cool, protracted stare. One of those.

'Mr Gossingham,' she called.

'Don't shout, Clara,' said Gossingham.

I looked at him over the counter, fortyish, pale skin, imperious black Errol Flynn moustache, high choky collar.

And no hair. Not a touch of thatch clutched at his bald, shiny pate, bleak and barren, a stark, naked scalp. And I had done this to him with Flannery's Foo-Foo!

'You all right?' asked Clara.

'Yes,' I answered weakly.

'Do you take medication?' she enquired with furrowed brow.

'Only toffee.'

After I delivered the package I staggered down Victoria Street with the flask still in my pocket. No wonder Flannery had said it was a secret formula. With this product we could wipe out the Wehrmacht in Africa!

It was not far from quitting time when I reported safe delivery to Mr Crisp at El Paso. I don't remember the ferry and the bus home to Mary Lane.

Ma immediately said, 'What's wrong?'

'I can't tell you,' I muttered.

But I did, later on, after cod and chips.

'You mean he turned bald?' she enquired.

'As a coot.'

'Hmmn. Have you spoken to the boy, Flannery?'

'No, Ma, he's in Kildare visiting family.'

'Well, you'd better speak to St Joseph.'

'Is he bald, Ma?

'Tom Kipper! What a thing to say. He may have a receding forehead but he must have been pretty sharp to get the Blessed Mother. Gracious, child. St Joseph, bald indeed!'

I hardly slept that night. Nightmarish dreams of bald heads shining on me filled me with foreboding.

But the worst was to come. The following morning I had hardly disembarked from the *Royal Iris*, it seemed, when Mr Crisp said, 'Tom . . .'

'I won't go,' I said.

But I took the letter.

'Are you all right, Tom?' People kept asking me if I was all right. Yes, of course, for the loony bin. 'You look pale.'

I dragged my feet down North John, each shoe weighing five tons, up to the second floor, through the doors. Lily was on duty.

She had such a nice Tuesday morning smile for the condemned man.

'Put a blindfold on me and light my cigarette.'

'Tom Kipper, what are you talking about? You see too many Humphrey Bogart pictures. I suppose you want to see the boss personally again?'

'Yes, please.'

'Who is it?' crackled the stentorian tones.

'It's Tom Kipper from El Paso.'

'Oh. I wonder if he has any hair cream?'

He stood before me, magnificently arrayed in black black shiny Flannery-creamed hair, magnificent. He shone brilliantly.

'Oh, I'll take that, Alfred,' said another voice from within the glassed enclosure, and there stood another Mr Gossingham, as bald as a large, juicy, pink melon.

'OK, Stanley,' said Alfred, smiling at me. 'Well, Tom, do you have any?'

'Yes, sir, Mr Gossingham,' I said. He gave me eighteen pence.

'Hey, Tom, just great hair cream!'

Lily was looking at me humorously when he left. 'There are two of them, Tom. Twins. Didn't you know?'

I shook my head weakly. Again the world was worth living in. I danced down Victoria Street.

Lord Mayor James Fitzgerald-Pilkington had arrived early in his chauffeur-driven Bentley, but he was keeping a low profile until Royalty presented itself. He rubbed his hands together for better circulations, while his wife, the aristocratic Mrs Gloriana Pilkington, bathed in the publicity, the spotlight of the moment, dressed in an immaculate two-piece pink suit from Harrods and brimming over with the official Pilkington smile, which held up her face.

Pale, anaemic Merseyside sunlight was filtering weakly through Irish clouds on to the steps of Liverpool town hall. At this time of the year it was considered a benefaction by the small gathering of Liverpudlians lining the entrance, sniffling in fine Scouse fashion.

I stood with Betsy Braddock on the steps at the entrance from Water Street. The crowd of Scouse peasants and visitors was quite thin at first but was now increasing at a fast clip, so that Betsy and I were being pressed forward so that I could wink at Princess Elizabeth when she walked up the hollowed-out sandstone steps.

'She's coming,' shouted an Everton peasant. The polished grille of the Rolls glinted in the sun. Lord Mayor Fitzgerald-

Pilkington trod sedately down the steps with his wife. As the chauffeur opened the rear door for her highness, the mayor stepped forward to greet her, taking her gloved hand. She gave a Royal Windsor smile, and preceded him up the steps with her security guard into the town hall.

The procession of dignitaries stopped for a moment. The Lord Mayor, wearing his massive gold chain, stopped right by me. I could smell his aftershave. He turned slowly towards me, bent down slightly and said, 'Are you Tom Kipper?'

'Yes, your majesty,' I replied, not knowing what I was saying.

'Do you have any of that hair cream left?'

'Oh, yes, sir.'

'Would you be kind enough to drop one off at my secretary's desk in the town hall?'

'Yes, sir. Two bob.'

'She will provide you with the necessary currency.'

'James, we must go,' said his missus, Gloriana Smythe-Fitzgerald-Pilkington, shooting poisoned Pilkington arrows at me, Tom Kipper. They moved sedately to the interior.

'Did you hear that?' I asked Betsy Braddock, who was grinning like a gargoyle with gout.

The Lord Mayor just made it. He received almost the very last flask of Flannery's emulsion, for, at seventeen and a half years of age, Joey Flannery volunteered for the paratroopers and the last we heard his regiment was dropped into Greece. Where, it is commonly rumoured, he is manufacturing Grecian-formula hair cream.

Calls it Flannery's Foo-Foo.

*

'I was talking last night at the Ladies' Guild,' said my ma, 'to Mrs Joyce Flannery.'

'You mean Joey's ma?'

'Aye, the very same.'

'Did she hear from him, Ma?'

'Yes, she did, and he's doing well from what she can gather. They made him a sergeant.'

'Joey Flannery – a sergeant!'

'It seems he was very brave.'

I was laughing. It was ludicrous. Tatty Joey Flannery a sergeant. Even Ma was smiling.

'However,' she said, 'the police were looking for him.'

'The coppers?'

Ma poured three cups of tea from her large brown pot, which was dressed in a Kelly green woolly cardigan with a hole for the spout. 'It was to do with Bracey's the Chemist up on Seymour Terrace.'

'Oh?'

'It seems there was a mysterious depletion of valuable perfumes and a very rare skin emollient, which was discovered only after he left.'

'Is there any tea?'

'Ah, Aristotle has arisen. Give this cup of tea to your father. Better give him a buttered scone, too.'

'So what happened, Ma?'

'Well, Joey was wanted for questioning in the matter.'

'And he's not here.'

'You don't know anything about this, do you, Tom Kipper?'

'Me, Ma?'

'Am I speaking to two other people?'

'Ma, I work for El Paso Corned Beef.'

'And sell hair cream on the side.'

'Aw, gee, Ma.'

'Fortunately,' she said, banging the scouse pot with her outsize wooden ladle for Irish emphasis, 'when they discovered he had won some sort of medal in Greece, they dropped the case. They think he's a hero.'

Joey Flannery, he of the elegant sneer and great spitting prowess, a hero?

'I have to go, Ma.' I gave her a kiss.

Dad stirred in the depths of his great sunken armchair. 'Did you say the boy's in Greece? Tell him he should study Plato, Socrates and Aristotle.'

At the door I said, 'Who do they play for, Dad?'

I think he was smiling.

Chapter Five

The Spaniard

They say he looked like a Spanish Main pirate with two good, watery eyes and two good legs, not one of them made of pine, captain's hat leaning rakishly to starboard on his rusty head.

He was before Tom's grandparents' time, back in the previous century; didn't need a compass, was born with one inside him. Some Scousers said he was Irish, a Cork man, but how could he be with a name like Standish? He was and still is a ghost.

He captained a vessel, they say, a stout ship in fine seaworthy shape, enough room for maybe twenty passengers; sailed the very first ferry boat 'across the water' to Liverpool. If they didn't pay he never brought them back, left them feeding the Liver Birds at the Pier Head. Old Jack Hassock who crewed with the *Iris* tells that he overheard Standish one foul night telling his captain how to steer the ferry when fog clung to the Mersey like Tories with Scotch. Rain lashed the bridge; waves lifted the vessel like cork. This was between the wars. 'Right, full rudder, Captain, bring her about into the tide.' And the ship locked to the gangway like a cat to a canary.

'Aye, 'twas Standish brought me in,' the captain murmured.

'What was he like?' asked a *Liverpool Echo* reporter.

'Ugly, and mean as sin, like a scurvy bilge rat.' The captain shuddered. 'Wouldn't like to meet him ashore.'

'So, Mr Kipper,' boomed CEO Elderberry-Fyffe, 'you have been with us less than one month and have somehow managed to fall through the roof!'

No one so far had called me Mr Kipper. I was either Tom or Tommy, which I didn't care for. All of the secretaries smiled delightedly upon me, Mr Jones barked when he spoke but I heard him say to sniffy Miss Penelope Matthews that he was 'tickled pink' they had at last acquired an office boy.

'I'm sorry, sir,' I said to Elderberry-Fyffe, who snorted and motioned me to the door. Mr Fyffe's *Liverpool Echo* had arrived in impeccable condition on his doorstep this morning so he was almost in balance with the world. It was the day before that we had heard the droning and the office staff had looked apprehensively skyward and then towards each other, not uttering a word, waiting for something.

I had already discovered the spiralling flight of steps curving towards the roof and the curiosity that killed the cat and the Hard Knocks kid ached in me, so that at the sound of the droning I fleet-footed upwards to find a heavy door opening on to the flat roof which gave a splendid view of many more rooftops, spires, motor traffic and massive spaces of bombed ruins from the Blitz. To me it was just magnificent. My Irish eyes caught the high-flying planes droning across the city, in a blue-grey sky for a change, and then the air raid sirens wailed in agony. The black extension, stretched in oblong fashion across the roof, was a mere stepping stone for me and this is what I used it as, like an Olympic hero. My right foot went through the plate glass, then my left, then half of my skinny Irish body.

Holding on to the frame I lowered himself through the roof to the gentlemen's lavatory below where I found better accommodation seating on the seat. The cubicle door was open. And then Mr Elderberry-Fyffe walked through the main doorway and said, 'Ah, good afternoon, Mr Kippah – so nice of you to drop in.'

Miss Penelope Hawkins put a bandage on the gash in my left hand, smiling and laughing all the while as I narrated the story, which she passed on to all the other secretaries, a most grateful audience. They loved Tom Kipper all the more afterwards, calling it the Kipper Caper.

Miss Emily was the only one of the secretaries who looked apprehensive through her giggles, as though an inmost thought troubled her gentle nature.

'I think the boss likes me, Ma.'

'You mean even after you jumped through the roof?'

'He even calls me Mr Kipper.'

'He didn't fire you?'

'No, Ma, and Miss Penelope Hawkins bandaged my hand. By the way, didn't the siren go off here in Chipton Downs?'

'Yes, it did. Your father kept sleeping in the arms of Das Kapital. The cat never moved and the All Clear went off five minutes later.'

'What did you do, Ma?'

'I just sat in this chair, sipped a cup of tea and dreamed about Ireland.'

The common warehouse street in Liverpool is a narrow one-way alley seemingly chopped between tall buildings towering to the mostly foggy sky. Canned comestibles are for the most part stacked in these warehouses, brought in by old, leaky, stinky lorries but also by horse and cart from a previous era, for petrol is scarce, needed for the most part by Spitfires to shoot down Heinkels.

The Lancashire men manning these towering warehouses are noble creatures armed with charming Scouse accents, large clunky black boots, cloth caps pulled rakishly across the forehead, trousers baggy across the knees, a friendly demeanour – and a weird sense of humour.

Matthew Maginnerty said, 'So, you, Tom, are the new office junior they are talking about.'

'Yes, Mr Maginnerty.'

'Tom, don't call me Mr, I'm Matt. Come and have a cuppa tea.' His voice boomed in the cavernous interior like God summoning Moses, echoless, as though echoes were forbidden. Cases of El Paso Corned Beef were stacked floor to ceiling like an American armada. His office, a minuscule space crammed with one desk and two ancient chairs, was tucked in a corner of the massive warehouse. The charred kettle with the saucy spout stood on a metal plate at the edge of the desk. Matt had it boiling merrily in a couple of minutes.

'Who's down at the office?' he asked.

'Mr Jones, Mr Fyffe and a lot of typists.'

He laughed. He knew everybody 'down the street', had inventoried them for many years.

'What do they have you doing?'

'Well, I have to bring written orders to you every day. Mr Crisp says I must go down to Customs at the Harbour Board once or twice a week and I have to pick up sandwiches for various people at the Mad Sandwich Shop most days.'

'Hmmn . . . You'll get trampled to death at that place. How's Miss Emily?'

'Sometimes she looks sad.'

'Does she now. Here, have a cuppa. Do you know why?'

'I really don't know, Mr Maginnerty, I mean Matt. She always helps me to seal the envelopes at the end of the day and put stamps on them.'

'Is she a good secretary?'

'Well, she types a lot faster than me.'

Matt laughed.

I said, 'She has a few conversations with Mr Morgan during the day which must be serious business.'

'Oh?'

'That's when she looks a bit sad.'

An iron chain hauling a massive hook rattled on the outside of the building.

'Gotta go,' said Matt. 'See you tomorrow, Tom.'

He screwed his cap on sideways, de rigueur, and moved swiftly for a man of his bulk.

Would make a good Father Christmas, I thought.

'You need a haircut, Tom Kipper.'

'Yeah, Ma.'

She glared at me with blue Connemara eyes.

'I mean, yes, Mother.'

'Hmmn, that's better. You'd better go on over to see Timothy Drake, Drake's Haircutting Salon down on the Esplanade.'

'Uncle Bart says he's a sissy.'

'Just because Mr Drake does women's hair as well as men's does not make him a sissy.'

The front door knocked.

'Speak of the devil,' said Ma.

It was Bart. It was always a matter of perpetual wonder to Tom Kipper: how did his mother know it was her brother Bart? She didn't see him. She couldn't smell him. He had uttered not one syllable. Yet she knew it was Bart. I had heard many times of the mysterious forces within scouse, had never believed the fable, but here it had happened again.

'I have no money, Bart,' said Ma, tight-lipped.

'Ah, Mary, so wonderful to see you, and to see young Tom Kipper. How are you, young man?'

'Smashing, Uncle Bart.'

Bart was short on cash. The casual observer didn't see the almost imperceptible shifting from right to left and back again, as though challenging gravity, but Ma knew him the way a pot knows scouse.

'Tom is going to Drake's for a haircut,' said Ma.

'I'll walk with him,' said Uncle Bart. 'I need a trim myself.'

Mary Catherine Kipper slipped him a silver florin.

'That's for a haircut,' she told Bart, knowing in the recesses of her female reasoning that it would end up in another drawer.

Timothy Drake hairdressed and barbered on the far edge of Kirby Avenue, still a single man at forty-five, accomplished in his occupation, absorbed in character analysis and an atheist to boot. He and Bart trod on each other's toes with all-consuming grace, Bart always blessing himself before settling in the chair and Drake flashing a sharp pair of scissors in rapier-like response.

'This is my nephew, Tom Kipper,' said Bart. 'You can execute me first, then Kipper. I'll pay.'

'Is he a Christian, too?' queried Timothy Drake, smiling.

'Aye, a fine lad. Will most probably be a priest or a barber one day; might hear your confession or charge you double for a haircut.'

'Or, perhaps,' said Drake, 'he'll be in the Diplomatic Corps like his Uncle Bart.' Thrust and parry.

'Let me tell you,' said Bart, 'about the barber who was always insulting his customers.'

Timothy Drake just loved jousting with Bart. 'Tell me, Bart.' He smiled.

I listened, too, for when Uncle Bart was not hungover or chasing the Old Lady of Threadneedle Street, he was a fascinating teller of truth, but mostly fiction. So with dramatic gesture he told the story of Charlie who entered his barber's shop and said, 'Well, I'm off to Rome to see the Pope!' Charlie's barber snorted. '*You* see the Pope! Only important people get to see the Pope, like the King of England or Stanley Matthews or the Archbishop of Canterbury. You'll never get to see the Pope!' So he gave Charlie a haircut and Charlie went away smiling, to return one month later.

'Well,' he said, 'I went to Rome and I saw the Pope.'

'Oh, yeah,' said the barber, 'you and two hundred and fifty thousand other people in St Peter's Square in Rome!'

'That's true,' answered Charlie, 'but shortly afterwards two members of the Swiss Guard escorted me into the Pope's private chambers.'

'Oh, yeah.' The barber laughed. 'And what did he say to you?'

'He said to me, Charlie, who gave you that lousy haircut?'

Timothy Drake and I laughed together.

'Good story, Bart,' said Timothy. 'I'll get you next time.' He handed Bart his coat after brushing him off.

'I'll just walk up the street for some cigarettes,' said Bart. 'Back in a moment.'

But Bartholomew Finnegan never returned for the sky was blue, seagulls wheeled over the Liver, kippers fried in the pan. Scouse did mysterious things to people. In his pocket he had Mary Kipper's florin and the Spaniard inn lay snug on the Esplanade breathing vapours of good, healthy ale.

'Ale, Mr Castillo, if you don't mind, from that tap.'

'Which school did you attend, Tom?' asked Timothy Drake as he brushed me off.

'Hard Knocks,' I said.

'Oh, St Joseph's.'

'It's Our Lady and St Joseph's.'

'I know. I went there myself. Still got the bruises and the blessings.'

'Shall I give you this shilling?'

'No, Tom, keep it. Your Uncle Bart Finnegan said he would pay.'

'He's not coming back.'

'You know him as well as I do, Tom.'

'What shall I tell him?'

Mr Drake opened a small drawer at the top of a pine bureau and extracted a pair of horn-rimmed spectacles.

'Tell Bart,' he said, 'his glasses accidentally fell out of the top pocket of his jacket into this drawer. Tell him he can have them back just as soon as he brings in two shillings and another joke. And, oh, yes, Tom, say one for me.'

'Uncle Bart said you were an atheist,' I said.

'Would you believe a robber?' asked Mr Drake.

I trod off down the Esplanade in the direction of the Spaniard. Bart is lost without his glasses for reading or for darts. Now he needed another two shillings. The great, great mystery always challenging the great Finnegan tribe was where did he get his finances from. The Bird in Hand received a steady portion, and the Spaniard from time to time, of his somewhat illusory wealth.

But even the Bank of England didn't know where it came from.

I trod across a short lawn to the big, green doors of the Spaniard. Even on the lawn I could smell the healthy odour of ale and Woodbines and hear Scouse voices clashing in Mersey dialects.

'Hey, you can't go in there,' said a large man with an apron wrapped round his bulging middle.

'Please, sir, I have to speak to my Uncle Bart.'

'You mean Bart Finnegan?'

'Yes, sir.'

The name was magic. 'Hmmn. OK. Go on in. He's at the bar. Where else?'

'Uncle Bart,' I said, pulling his sleeve.

'Yes, Tom?'

'Mr Drake has your glasses and says you can have them back for two shillings.'

Bart screwed up his face, took off his cap and scratched his head, which is when Tom Kipper looked over the beer-washed bar into the blue eyes of Emily Magginerty from the offices of El Paso Corned Beef Inc. She was pouring Guinness.

What is Miss Emily doing here? I thought. She's a secretary at El Paso.

She wiped her hands on a bar towel and came round the bar through the smoke to me. She's so pretty, I thought.

'Tom Kipper,' she said. 'How's your hand?'

'OK, Miss Emily,' I said.

'Tom,' she said, 'I'm pretty busy here right now as you can see. I want to ask you a favour.' She paused. 'Would you please not tell anybody at the office that you've seen me here.'

'Of course, Miss Emily. I promise.'

'Thank you, Tom. When I have more time I'll explain to you why. OK, Tom?'

'Yes, Miss Emily.'

She went back behind the bar, disappearing into the blue smoke.

'I'm going home,' I said to Uncle Bart.

'OK, Tom. Regards to your mam. You don't have any spare change, do you?'

I shook my head, hanging on to the silver shilling in my pocket. As I left through the green doors I saw Miss Emily handing Bart a free pint, which brightened his eyes even without his horn-rimmed spectacles.

They say the building was once known as the Chipton Downs Hotel and that it almost floated on ale, not to mention cider and wine. The Romans had a place there, according to local Irish chatter, before the Dark Ages. The Saxons probably watered their horses there with a quart of ale per nag, and in the Middle Ages everybody, regardless of age, slurped ale, even housewives, who couldn't witch about their husbands staying out all night for they, too, were locked in its embrace.

It changed its name in the eighteenth century to the Nagging Horse, and still in the same century to the Hole in The Wall, which was certainly accurate, for multiple supplies of grog were smuggled without licence from *la belle France* to a most thirsty and rebellious clientele. It was all quite jolly. Until the Law arrived. Its name became the Crumble in the following century. It still sloshed in ale.

To give the activity some grace and charm, the Chipton Downs Hotel hung up its sign, tearing down 'The Crumble'. Between the wars, men of common cloth frequented its chambers, referring to its sanctuary as the Spaniard, for the new owner said he was black Irish, a Castillo from the Gladdach, Galway.

He looked quite fierce did Hugo Castillo, with his raven-black hair and moustache, while his wife, Amapola, had dazzling red tresses. Their offspring, Pedrito, couldn't make up his mind between black and red, although he mostly preferred Liverpool Red.

The Spaniard is perched on a slight rise from the Esplanade looking out on to the sometimes turbulent River Mersey, an absolutely choice spot from which to watch Liverpool burning from end to end as Lord Haw-Haw had predicted.

The pub had, and still has, charm. Good ale. And not one Hun incendiary burned its structure. The only thing that burned were its fish and chips.

Before Hugo Castillo took up ownership of the Chipton Downs and changed its name to the Spaniard, Captain Standish was a frequent visitor to its interior, slapping his silver crowns, acquired in the Spanish Main, ferociously on the bar for it was early in the century and most men were swashbuckling and crooked. The ghost of Standish still haunted the ancient inn, according to Mersey legend and the crews of the ferry boats that joined Wirral and Liverpool in harmonious industry.

It was in the evening, as the shadows lengthened along the Esplanade and the black-eyed gulls settled on the sandy shore, that the time-honoured phrase rang out in the Woodbine smoke of the Spaniard: 'Time, gentlemen, please!'

The bright murmur of wise chatter was stilled for one brief moment as honest men slurped a final pint of honest ale to prepare the lies they would tell their wives. Cries of 'See ya later, Charlie, Jim, Bill, Matthew' rang out as the cream of Merseyside shambled through the green doors towards the grey Mersey.

'Tidy up, Emily,' said Hugo Castillo, smiling his Spanish Armada smile and giving her the keys. 'See you tomorrow.'

She said, 'OK, Mr Castillo,' and started to rinse glasses and swab the mahogany counter, occasionally glancing through the generous windows at the ever-flowing river and the imperious Liver Birds poised on that impressive building.

A pleasant silence descended on the bar, broken only by the gentle ticking of the pub clock. She straightened chairs, mopped the floor, polished a mirror. A sense of quiet peace descended upon Emily, the peace that oft-times comes when least expected. It is handed to you, freely given. It only reached perfection when you accepted it.

On impulse she took a glass and poured cold beer into it, turning to look at herself in the mirror.

Coins crashed heavily on the counter.

'Give me a pint of your finest ale, lassie,' croaked a voice.

Emily froze. In the mirror she saw him, gaunt, a wild beard smothering half his face.

'We're closed, sir,' she managed to squeak.

'I said give me a pint of ale, shiver me timbers – and hurry!' Saliva drooled on his lips. 'Don't tarry with a thirsty man!'

She filled a pint glass and tremblingly placed it on the mahogany counter, spilling froth.

He wasn't so tall, but wide, dressed in a coat of many dark hues, a leather strap crossing one shoulder to his waist, which was bound by a leather belt adorned with an oversized brass buckle. His hat sat seemingly sideways on a shock of red hair; black pock marks adorned his face.

'Who are you, sir?' bleated Emily.

'Who am I?' he ground out. 'Who do you think I am?' Leaning forward: 'I'm Standish. Captain Standish, lassie!'

He drank half the glass as she watched, fascinated, terrified. Ale dripped on his beard.

'And now,' he said, 'Oi've come to tell you something.' He wiped his mouth on his sleeve. 'You've got to tell him,' he said.

'Who? What? Sir?'

'Morgan,' he roared. 'Your Mr Morgan. You have waited long enough.'

'You mean my Harry?'

'Of course I mean your Harry Morgan. Keeping this job a secret from him must cease, do you hear me? I knew his great-great-great-grandfather well. Now put the money in the till!'

She scooped up the coins, turned to deposit them in the open drawer, and then he was gone. Tugs hooted out on the river. The tide flowed, and Captain Standish, spirit of river and tide, was gone. Goose bumps crawled across her skin.

She must tell Harry, her dear, dear Harry Morgan. Too much time had flown by. She slammed and locked the big green doors and headed to the ferry. Seagulls wheeled overhead.

Chester Kilpatrick, the editor of the *Chipton Downs Post*, a newspaper of remarkable insignificance, sat bolt upright – which is a very difficult thing to do – when he was alerted to the latest sighting of Captain Standish, who he knew didn't exist. But this was red hot news, that the ghost of Standish not only had been seen, but had conversed with a Miss Emily Maginnerty, the young barmaid of the Spaniard, an almost sleazy pub tottering down on The Esplanade. This had been shored up with bricks and mortar for well over two hundred years, so that its exterior, upon reasonable examination, looked enhanced by sticking plaster. The decided opinion by the Expire Construction Company was that it would one day crumble gently to a holy ruin.

But the mediocrity of the Spaniard's outward shell was far exceeded by the history of its people, drenched in fable, for good and for bad – mostly bad if it were possible to review court records written by gentle folk who had long passed through this valley of tears and ale.

'It's a front page job,' said Chester Kilpatrick. 'Let the presses roll!'

Chipton Downs read its *Post* with great relish. Even Mr Elderberry-Fyffe considered visiting the historical edifice, slurping, perhaps, its common ale. 'It's history, Gladwyn,' he said.

The common bar of the Spaniard was jammed with common and uncommon people whirled together like scrambled eggs, most of them wishing conversation with Emily Maginnerty, whose wages had doubled.

Hugo Castillo rubbed his financial hands with great glee, for coin of the realm was flowing into his fingers like the Mersey at high tide. So overwhelming was his good fortune that he hired Bart Finnegan as extra help behind the bar. Thus did Bart pay back his two-shilling debt to his generous barber, Timothy Drake.

I took the ferry to Liverpool every morning now, the very first down the gangway and up into the mainstream with the daily commuters, treading with light step past the Liver Building, along Water and Dale Streets, up the well-worn steps of the Fox Building, and through the side door for office boys and a clerical staff who greeted me with smiles.

Down at the warehouse on Basingstoke Street that day I took a sheaf of orders to Matthew Maginnerty who gave me a cup of tea in a chipped mug.

I knew what he was going to ask. 'How's Emily?' he said.

'Absolutely fine, Mr Maginnerty. She's very happy. Mr Harry Morgan is, too, I think.'

'Oh, so you noticed.'

I just nodded my head.

'You're a sharp man, Kipper,' grinned Matt.

For Emily had taken the swashbuckling advice of Captain Standish, and after she had quit the Spaniard at closing time and was hurrying to the ferry with her heart in her mouth, a figure approached her on the Esplanade heading in her direction.

'Harry,' she cried as they hugged each other. She found herself crying, blubbering away.

'It's all right, Emily,' he said.

'I've something to tell you.'

'I know,' said Harry. 'Let's go over to O'Reilly's Chippy. It's quite comfortable inside.'

And so she unlocked her story, about gathering enough money for 'Emily's Floral Boutique' at the Market Place in Chipton Downs. 'It has a most pretty cottage in the back, Harry, my love. I wanted to keep it secret and tell you when we eventually became engaged. That's why I kept putting it off.' She wiped away a tear.

'No more,' he said, slipping the ring on her finger.

'Oh, Harry, Harry. Let me tell you what just happened to me at the Spaniard. And what are you doing here, my love?'

'I'll tell you next door at the Finder's Keepers pub.'

'It's closed, my darling.'

'Just a moment,' said Harry Morgan, turning to O'Reilly. 'Do you have any liquid refreshment, even beer, old chap?'

'Against the law,' said O'Reilly, 'but if you'll follow me into the private kitchen I may have a glass or two of vino. Bring your fish and chips.'

The Cabernet Sauvignon was inspirational. They raised glasses, chomped down on cod and mushy peas. 'Tom Kipper,' said Harry, 'worked out that Matt Maginnerty was your dad. So he told him about you working at the Spaniard.'

'I'll kill him!' said Emily.

'No, no,' said Harry. 'He was worried about you.'

'I'll kiss him,' said Emily.

'And then your dad told me. I love you, Emily.'

'How d'yer like the chips?' asked O'Reilly.

Hugo Castillo and his raven-haired wife, Amapola Castillo, shouted in unison, 'Time, gentlemen, please!'

'You can leave now, Emily, if you like. Hugo and I can lock up.'

'Oh, thanks, Amapola.' She would be able to see Harry sooner.

'We hope you haven't been bothered too much by all the riff-raff ploughing through here ever since the *Post* told your story about the ghost of Captain Standish.'

'But he wasn't a ghost, Amapola,' said Emily.

'Hey, let's have a beer on the ghost.' Hugo poured the glasses. 'You can read his history in the Brooks public library,' he said.

Emily found herself laughing. 'I'll tell him that next time.'

'Here's to Standish.'

Emily rinsed her glass. 'I'll go home to Harry now,' she said.

The river flowed evenly on the tide. A thin mist hung like silver cobwebs over the wharves and the large ships moving ponderously upstream with cargoes from the Americas and Australasia. Life teemed across in Liverpool city even in those fragile years. A silver sliver of moon jockeyed between ragged clouds.

'Hugo,' said Amapola, 'I've been tidying up the bedroom and I've put away your Captain Standish uniform until you need it again.'

Hugo sighed, smiling at his good fortune and the excellent drama classes he had received at the Academy of Hard Knocks.

Chapter Six

Two If By Sea

They arrived in very large ships, berthing at close but very different locations with heavy showers of good Liverpool rain to bring them in.

The *Echo* and the BBC broadcast their imminent arrival in order that the Axis powers might have superior intelligence. After several days of walking the deck under glowering skies the entire company of American troops was assembled in a cavernous warehouse near West Sail dock. The noise between gum and Camels was deafening until the commanding officer arrived, Lieutenant Colonel Morris Hamilton.

His uniform bristled with ribbons and gongs and his cap was pulled so far over his eyes you couldn't see them.

'Men,' he said from the podium, 'this is a very special day, an historic day in the annals of American history.'

'He's crackers,' whispered PFC Tony Volenti.

'Pots for jars,' volunteered Sergeant Carl Schultz.

'Men,' said the decorated colonel, 'we all remember Valley Forge.'

'Where the Sam Hill's Valley Forge?'

'Beats me.'

'History,' said Colonel Hamilton, 'is repeating itself. When we hurled cases of tea into Boston Harbor, it was for the sake of freedom, not democracy!'

'What's he talking about?' whispered Staff Sergeant Willis.

'He was a history major back at both Yale and Harvard,' whispered back Corporal Radivitch.

'He's loco in the cabeza,' said PFC Manual Lopez.

'We all remember,' said the colonel, 'the cry "The British are coming". Well, men, we shall this day be uttering a new cry! For we remember Bunker Hill and Lexington and the Boston Tea Party!'

'He's pots for jars.'

'I thought we were fighting the Joymans,' said Schultz, straight out of Brooklyn.

'And we remember the ride of Paul Revere. One if by land, two if by sea! For today, men, we shall cry out in a loud voice, the Yanks are coming! The Yanks are coming! Let me hear it now; all together: The Yanks Are Coming! The Yanks Are Coming!'

Nobody uttered a word.

A lone seagull flew into the cavernous structure and out again. Tugs hooted on the Mersey.

'That's an order!' he shouted.

They responded feebly.

'Louder!' And they did.

'He's bloody daft.'

Water Street leading up from the waterfront was awash with office workers from city buildings, crowding the pavements, awaiting the invasion. Barrage balloons floated overhead and there was even a hint of sunshine. At the juncture of Water and Dale Streets at the town hall, the audience jostled for a better view.

'The Yanks Are Coming,' suggested a lady dressed in stars and stripes to nobody in particular. She smiled at me and I smiled back as they came, treading eight abreast up Water Street, trampling with precision on the cobbles, looking in awe, mouths agape, at the vacant spaces left by the Blitz.

'They look hungry,' said an aged Liverpudlian, waving his stick.

'They're not hungry, they're looking at the girls.'

'I like that one over there.' A scantily attired young woman in rope-soled sandals and not much else indicated a blond-haired PFC smiling a broad grin in her direction.

'They've got no music.'

'What happened to Tommy Dorsey?'

It was a silent army for they were shod in rubber-soled boots, not crashing on the deck like the Brits.

'They're for sneaking up on the girls.'

Lieutenant Colonel Morris Hamilton rode at the head with almost military bearing, for The Yanks Were Coming to invade Liverpool, avenge Boston.

He had received a messagegram from his wife, Gloria, that very morning, reading: 'Have you taken any Redcoats prisoners yet, my darling? Blessings, Gloria.'

'Great, great sense of humour, that woman,' chuckled the lieutenant colonel. The horse that he was riding agreed with him.

'He was riding a bloody big nag,' I told Ma later on.

'A nag?'

'A white horse. Up Dale Street.'

'Glory be!'

'Will probably be in the *Echo* tomorrow.'

And so they marched up and around until they reached St George's Hall where they were brought to a halt, ordered uniformly in line.

Lieutenant Colonel Hamilton dismounted, handing the reins to an aide. 'Stand at ease,' he ordered, adding, 'Men, The Yanks Are Here.'

He stood imperiously before them, smiling. 'The city is yours; take the rest of the day free from duties; have a good time. Don't drink too much of that foreign whiskey, Scotch. Be back in barracks at the appointed time. Attention! Dismiss.'

A white Jeep with a chauffeur was waiting for him.

'The Hotel Adelphi,' he told the driver.

'Where's that?' the driver asked the British WAAF sitting beside him, who had been designated as the British aide.

'Almost across the street, sergeant.'

'Better come with me, Corporal Heather, for security purposes,' the driver said.

She did.

She ended up in Boston.

*

82

Mr Elderberry-Fyffe fell through the doorway into the reception area of the main office.

'That damnable doormat,' he expostulated, 'should be replaced or removed!'

His large grey eyes under his large grey eyebrows caught sight of Tom Kipper – that's me.

'Mr Kippah,' said Fyffe, 'fix that doormat or destroy it. Get rid of it. We have enough problems with the war, without inanimate objects causing our downfall. Humph!'

All eyes were upon him, either directly or surreptitiously, for the occasion of his falling through the doorway of El Paso Corned Beef was precipitated by Johnnie Walker Red, by appointment to His Majesty the King, by courtesy of the Chamber of Commerce.

Similar incidents were happening to chief executive officers all over Liverpool city as they fell through doorways after heavy lunches courtesy of the Chamber. Mr Fyffe's navigational system brought him eventually to his desk.

'Miss Healey,' he called in stentorian tones, 'bring me please some of that cheap American coffee and take a letter. We need more of that damn corned beef from Chicago.'

Tears formed in his bloodshot eyes, and he dozed off.

Great-Aunt Charlotte was sister to Grandpa Francis Finnegan. Her husband, Cuthbert, had expired in her arms some ten years past. She never forgot his last words: 'Charlotte, are the kippers fresh?'

Uncle Cuthbert and Grandpa Finnegan had got along together like bread and jam, Socrates and Aristotle,

Guinness and Mild. Granny Smith, as we generally referred to her, lived in a most comfortable white cottage from another era, with a sprightly garden of foxgloves, dahlias, bluebells and a very happy birch tree in the centre of her minuscule lawn, all of this within a stone's throw of the ferry landing stage.

Back in my days of chandlery duty I had delivered firelighters, paraffin and furniture polish to her doorstop so we knew each other very well.

'That Tom will be a priest some day,' said Auntie Maud.

'Priest, my backside,' said Granny Smith, 'he'll be a plumber or a pope. I know because he once fell down the cellars steps and he used some choice holy expletives picked up from his grandpa.'

She was often referred to as a 'sprightly old dame', but she was much more than that, for she was as sharp as a tack, colourful, invested with a promotional personality, and a snappy dresser carrying a most splendid mahogany cane, which she didn't really need for locomotion, but to imperiously rap or tap people with.

She took the ferry quite often across the Mersey to Liverpool, then boarded a tram to the shopping areas around Whitechapel. The conductor always guided her to a seat; if he didn't he would either get the beady eye or a rap with the infamous stick.

On the very day of The Yanks Are Coming Granny Smith was sprightlily walking up Whitechapel from Lord Street as PFC Walter Wendorff was sauntering down. It was one of those rare, precious days of sunshine when flower and leaf fall in blessed togetherness, and he was smiling the huge smile of servicemen on Liberty.

The stick rapped gently on the buttons of his tunic.

'Young man,' she said, 'we are going to lunch.'

'Yes, ma'am,' he grinned, taking off his hat.

'Take my arm,' she said, which he did. 'Now we are going to T. J. Hughes department store.'

'For lunch, ma'am?'

'They have a café, not splendid, but adequate, and you look hungry.'

Well, she made his day.

The eyes of all the young women in the place swivelled to this brand-new import from America. Well tailored, handsome, and with his grandma from Florida.

'We'll take that table,' she said to the waitress, pointing her cane to the window.

'It's not yet cleared away, miss.'

'Then clear it!' The stick waved.

By the time PFC Wendorff and Granny Smith reached the table it was cleared.

'Good,' said Granny, 'it looks down on Lord Street. Here, put this cane on the window ledge. Now, young man, what is your name? Before you answer that, I am Charlotte.'

'Yes, ma'am, I mean, Charlotte. Well, I'm just plain old Walter. Walter Wendorff, at your service.'

'Ah, here comes Tom now.'

'Sorry I'm late, Grandma,' I said, 'I had to take paper to Customs down near the Liver.'

'Take that seat,' she said, 'and let me look at you.'

'Howdy,' said Walter.

'Oh, this is my grand-nephew, Tom Kipper. He lives across the water in the same town as I do. And, oh yes, you must come to visit us. Tom, this is Walter; he's American.'

'The Yanks Are Coming,' I said as we shook hands.

'Charlotte invited me to lunch,' said Walter.

'Would you like to order?' asked the waiter.

'Yes,' said Grandma, 'we're all going to have the same thing: leek soup, sausage rolls and ice cream with chocolate cake. And tea, of course.'

Walter and I looked at each other and laughed.

And so they talked as if there were no Wednesdays, non-stop, Grandma wielding the teapot.

It was after the ice cream that Wally asked, 'Who do you work for, Tom?'

'Oh, a company up on Victoria Street, El Paso Corned Beef Inc. I'm the office junior.'

'Would you repeat that, Tom?' Wally Wendorff's eyes glowed like illuminated saucers, history and geography enmeshed.

'El Paso Corned Beef Inc.'

'I'm going,' said Granny Smith. 'Been here in Liverpool since ten o'clock. Come on, you men, help me down to the tram.'

Everybody cleared the way for Charlotte Smith and her male escorts. The tram conductor helped her aboard.

'What's your telephone number?' asked Wally.

'Ask Tom. He'll give it to you.'

The tram slid noisily towards the Pier Head.

'Tom,' said Wally, taking me by the arm, 'I have something that just might interest you.'

'Why don't you come up to the office? I'm past my lunch break and it's just up here past Paradise Street.'

So I took Wally up the wide, well-worn flight of steps, through the office boy swing doors and up to the mini-office-storeroom in the back.

'This,' said Wally, 'is what I've got to tell you.'

And when he reached into his golden treasury, I jigged, pirouetted, whooped, yahooed, while all the world wondered.

'Can you,' I said to Wally Wendorff, 'come up here to the office tomorrow morning? Do you have time off?'

'Only on one condition,' answered PFC Wendorff.

'Name it.'

'That you introduce me to that blonde dame down there in the main office.'

'You're fast, Wally.'

'A Yankee,' said Wendorff.

'I'll introduce you,' I said, 'to the whole blooming staff.'

'Hey, won't that get you into a scrape?'

'Not with the information you've just given me!' I took his arm. 'Follow me.'

All eyes looked up at the mysterious stranger with his neat uniform, jaunty hat, and Chicago smile.

'Hi, everybody,' he said, 'I'm Wally.'

They all came forward to surround him. Even the blonde, Penelope Hawkins.

'We heard The Yanks Were Coming,' said Mr Jones.

'Have a seat,' from Miss Fiona Healey.

'Would you like a cuppa tea?' Gloria Wainwright.

'A cup of tea would be nice.'

So he settled in. Telephones rang and staff went slowly back to machines and ledgers as Wally Wendorff edged closer to Miss Penelope Hawkins, picking up some papers she had accidentally dropped at his feet, and Miss Penelope, normally of shy disposition, did not discourage this bold Yankee.

That is, not until Mr Elderberry-Fyffe burst from his cell and into the cavernous main office, still with Johnnie Walker Red fandangoing his inner self, saw the uniformed stranger and pronounced, 'What are we doing with the armed forces in this establishment?' Which was tantamount to expressing in American, 'Throw that bum outta here!'

'I'll see you tomorrow, Miss Penelope. Perhaps we can have lunch together.'

She found herself nodding.

I saw Wally to the door. 'See you tomorrow.'

'You bet.'

'And Miss Penelope seemed to like Wally Wendorff.'

'Tell me again,' said my ma, Mary Catherine Kipper, banging crockery around, 'about your Grandma Charlotte in the café.'

'Well, she was great.'

'How did she get the Yankee soldier into the café?'

'I think she hit him with her stick.'

Ma smiled. Oh, this was most valuable information to be imparted to the T&C (Tea and Crumpets) gang tonight at Clara Garrity's house. Nazi intelligence never had it so good.

She shook the mine of information; that is, me.

'Tell me more.'

'Well, Ma, we had leek soup, sausage rolls and ice cream.'

'Did your grandma say anything about the family?'

'Well, Ma, she did but she said it was confidential.'

'Confidential?' she screeched. 'Just let me tell you, Thomas Kipper, in all of your life there has been nothing confidential. Do you understand?'

'Yeah, Ma.'

'So tell me.'

'Are you sure you're ready, Ma?'

'Time is running out, Tom Kipper!'

'She said Grandpa Francis Finnegan had a secret love affair going with the widow next door, Mrs Maggie Malone.'

'She said that?' screeched Ma.

'I shouldn't have told you.'

'Oh, yes, you should. What else did she say?'

'Better keep stirring the pot, Ma, the scouse is getting cold.'

'I don't want any of your lip, young man! What else?'

'Well, she said that when Grandpa surreptitiously transferred supplies of coal from the LMSR to her coal bin he never left without a cuppa tea.'

'And what's wrong with that?'

'You mean the free coal or the tea?'

'Tom Kipper, you're going too far.'

'Grandma Charlotte asked me to give her telephone number to the Yankee soldier.'

'Well, I never! Wait till the ladies hear about this tonight.'

'I gotta go to confession, Ma, it's getting late.'

Ma banged a pot. 'Don't forget to tell him any inexactitudes you may have thought up.'

I said to myself, I think she means lies.

On Wednesday morning I barged out through the famous swing doors on my way to the Mad Sandwich Shop on Chesapeake Street with list in hand and assorted change in pocket. The crowd fronting the glass cases was not its usual barbaric size so it was with some ease that I offered my list to none other than my old friend Conks Murphy of Hard Knocks.

'Conks!'

'Kipper!'

'What are you doing here?'

'I was about to ask the same question.'

'Is there any chance of getting a sandwich, young man?' asked an imperious bureaucrat in a black suit and a trilby hat.

'Not much,' batted back Conks, 'but you're next after Kipper.' Conks was fast. Faster than The Yanks Are Coming. I took the package. 'See ya later, la',' said Conks.

'Ta-ra.'

Wally Wendorff was sitting on my stool in the storeroom office when I returned.

'Come down and have some tea,' I said. Miss Penelope straightened from her Royal typewriter as white sunshine streamed through floor to ceiling Victoria Street windows to fall on her face and figure. I could smell her perfume, a cloying eminence that would knock any man's socks off, a rich bouquet that seemed to surround her. It could do more damage than the Panzer Corps.

She immediately seated Wally to bring him tea in a bone china cup brought that morning from home.

'Hi, gorgeous,' said Wally. The staff stayed at a distance, sensing a Shakespearean drama unfolding. Penelope lowered her eyelids like the portcullis on Glamis Castle. I found myself blinking. They stirred tea together, clinked teaspoons in saucers. The Liverpool Philharmonic Orchestra was not too far away.

'It's Antony and Cleopatra,' said Gloria.

'Romeo and Juliet,' muttered Lydia McLaverty.

'What's that damn Yankee soldier doing in my office?' snarled Elderberry-Fyffe. 'Get rid of him.'

A door slammed. The spell was not broken.

'Stay there,' I commanded, taking from my pocket a card, four by six, which I had typed up that very morning.

I knocked on Miss Fiona Healey's glass-embossed door and went in. She pulled a mouth.

'What is it, Tom?'

'It's a secret message from Chicago, miss,' I said, handing her an envelope with the card inside.

'Is this a joke, Tom Kipper?'

'No, Miss Healey, and it's urgent. Mr Fyffe should receive it immediately.'

'Very well, Tom.' She adjusted her spectacles and smoothed her skirts before venturing into the Inner Sanctum, the Valley of Death.

'What is it, Miss Healey?' Sometimes, thought Miss Healey, he looks like Benito Mussolini.

'It's most urgent. sir. From Chicago. A top secret message.'

'A what? What is this farce? Who gave it to you?'

'Tom Kipper, sir.'

'Ah ha, Mr Kippah! I might have known. Well, Miss Healey, now he has gone too far. But first, let us read it before we fire him!'

Saliva was glistening on his jowls. And so, with great Scouse melodrama, Mr Elderberry-Fyffe read the card:

Dear Mr Fyffe,

The American soldier in the main office is PFC Wally Wendorff, stationed in Liverpool for a short period of time. His father, Bertrand Q. Wendorff, is Chief Executive Officer and part owner of El Paso Corned Beef Inc. in Chicago. Wally says that if you have any problems with his pa he would be willing to sort them out for you.

Respectfully, Sir,
Tom Kipper.

'Are you all right, Mr Fyffe?' asked Miss Fiona Healey.

'Water,' cried Fyffe.

With the imposing skill of a true executive he pulled himself together as Miss Fiona sponged the water off his lapels.

'Come with me, Miss Healey,' he commanded, striding towards the door. Like a massive thunderstorm from the North Sea he descended.

'Mr Kippah,' he boomed. 'How wonderful of you to bring such a distinguished guest to our chambers.'

Fyffe wrung my hand till my Connemara eyes popped, and then pumped Wally Wendorff's.

'Have you had tea? Where are the crumpets? Miss Penelope, bring them to my office. All of you come into my office. Why, that such a great friend of ours should visit.'

Wally grinned like mad. 'He's worse than my dad,' he whispered in my ear.

Miss Penelope brought more tea with crumpets as we surrounded Fyffe's desk, a mini-*Ark Royal*.

'You should visit us more often, Mr Wendorff. Where have you been? How is your wonderful father?'

'He's well, Mr Fyffe. Never off the golf course.'

'A fine game, Wally. From Scotland, you know.'

'Yes, Dad has been to St Andrews.'

Within half an hour Miss Fiona said she had letters to type and Miss Penelope slipped through the door.

Wally said, grinning that Chicago grin, 'Mr Fyffe, why don't I give my dad a call on your phone so that you can speak to him, too? It's about ten in the morning Chicago time. A good time to shake him up.'

'Well, well, Wally, are you sure?'

'You bet your boots! Now, tell me, is there anything special I should beat him around the head and ears with?'

'Well, there is this terrible, terrible shortage of corned beef.'

'It'll be on the next ship!'

'Miss Healey,' bellowed Fyffe, 'get me Chicago. Mr Bertrand Wendorff, Chief Executive Officer.'

Fyffe glowed. The phone rang.

'Dad,' said Wally, 'the Yanks have invaded Liverpool.'

'How are you, my boy?'

'Smashing, Dad, as they say in ye olde country.'

'What's the weather like?'

'Like a Republican dinner: lousy. I mean bloody lousy. I'm picking up the language.'

'Well, my boy, what's happening to you? Your mother and I and the family talk about you constantly and pray to St Joseph for your good health.'

'Thanks, Dad. Right now I'm in the Liverpool offices of El Paso Corned Beef Inc.'

'Good Lord, how did you arrange that?'

'A freak of circumstance. Now listen, Dad, I'm going to hand you over to Mr Fyffe who's the CEO here, but before I do I have a most urgent request.'

'Name it, my boy.'

'Dad, you gotta ship, as soon as possible, a very large consignment of corned beef to Liverpool.'

'What?'

'Yes, Dad, the people are starving. They're living on fish and chips. Chips. It's another word for French fries. When they can get them. They badly need corned beef.'

'I got it, my boy. I had a large supply going to Los Angeles which I shall divert immediately. Don't worry. Your mother and I love you. Now, let me speak to Fyffe.'

'Bertrand, my dear fellow,' said Fyffe. Then Bertrand

took over. It was a long time before Fyffe spoke again.

'Oh, yes, Bertrand. No, Bertrand. How very wonderful, Bertrand. Very funny. Yes, God save the king. Your father wants to speak to you, Wally.'

Wally spoke. Fyffe gleamed at me. I think he was pirouetting.

'Yes, said Wally, 'there's a wonderful girl right here in this office. Her name's Penelope. Yes, Dad, it doesn't take long for a Wendorff. Love you. Dad. Oh, yes, cheerio old chap – that's English. Bye.'

Fyffe rubbed his hands together. 'Fine father you have, Wally. I gather he's expediting the corned beef, which is great news for the country. And yes, you should take Miss Penelope to dinner, all expenses paid by El Paso, Liverpool.'

She was in the doorway, shining, ready to go.

'There's just one thing more,' said Wally, leaning across the desk. 'Dad said you should give Tom Kipper a large raise in pay.'

Fyffe glowered.

I grinned.

'Tom Kipper's Grandma Charlotte poked me with her mahogany cane on my broad Yankee chest,' said PFC Wendorff, 'and ordered me to take her to lunch, or the other way around.'

'On the main street?' asked Penelope.

'Right in the middle of Whitechapel.'

'And you offered no resistance?'

'It was to no avail.'

'Let us sit on this park bench.'

The moon jigsawed like a silver galleon through ragged clouds on the Spanish Main. The Liver Building was its destination as stars pinpointed crystal at eventide.

'She lives on the other side in the Wirral, according to Tom Kipper, at this address, and here is her telephone number.'

'My, you move fast, Mr Yankee,' said Penelope Hawkins.

'I have decided,' he said.

'You have decided what?'

'I have decided to fall in love with you.' A gentle breeze swept leaves across the flagstones.

'Don't you know,' she said, 'Rome wasn't built in a day?'

'Yeah, I know that, honey. And it took ten thousand years to build the Suez Canal!'

'It did?' She moved closer to him on the bench. 'Tell me more.'

Gently they embraced.

'I have an idea,' she breathed.

'Is it a good one?'

'Let us,' she said, 'take a ferry across the Mersey, and take tea with Grandma Charlotte. Perhaps I can borrow her mahogany cane and beat some sense into that presumptuous Yankee head.'

'One if by land, two if by sea,' said PFC Walter Wendorff. 'I've always wanted to take a ferry 'cross the Mersey.'

Chapter Seven

The Chipton Downs Post

'Hello, Tom Kipper.'

The voice was softly behind me in my left ear, swimming over my shoulder.

She looked sixteen.

'You're taller,' she said. Wow, I thought, to Ma I was still the same size.

It was Betsy Braddock. Not the superior Besty Braddock of Hard Knocks days. There was a faint hint of eau de Cologne, pale-hued colour on her lips, arched eyebrows, bemused at the change in tough guy Tom Kipper of yard days.

'Betsy Braddock,' I found myself saying, 'Oh, gosh!'

'I'm working at T. J. Hughes,' she said, smiling. 'I saw you one day in the store with an American soldier and your grandma.'

'That was Granny Smith,' I said. 'The PFC is a friend stationed with the PX on Dale Street.'

The eau de Cologne seemed to be getting stronger, weaving something you couldn't actually see, so that Betsy Braddock in her simple English cotton frock seemed in a frame all by herself on Paradise Street.

'Are you all right, Tom?' She smiled.

'Oh, yes, OK, Betsy.' How could a sixteen-year-old girl knock your cotton socks off, weave such a magic spell? Dad said grown-up ladies do the same to old age pensioners.

'I'm in Perfumery,' she said. 'Drop by and say hello some time, Thomas.'

'Pop' Maguire was gracefully reaching the age of retirement. A thatch of white hair crowned his head, offset by thick, springy, black eyebrows hovering over his steely blue eyes like a heavy mortgage. He always wore a waistcoat with his suit did Mr Maguire, putting fingers in its pockets when musing or speaking with authority.

'Tom Kipper,' he said to me on the steps of St Joseph's after Mass, 'your editing of the school magazine was quite exceptional,' fingers in waistcoat pockets.

'Thank you, sir.'

'I was wondering, with you job in Liverpool, whether you might find time to help out a new editor, who, frankly, doesn't know what he's doing. What do you think?'

'Smashing, sir.'

'Well, look here, Saturday morning would be the best time if you can make it. Say ten o'clock?'

'May I bring an assistant, Mr Maguire?'

'But of course.'

When I told Ma she said, 'Who's the assistant?'

'I'm going to ask Betsy Braddock.'

'Mrs Braddock's wee lass?'

'Aye, Ma. She's a great typist.'

'She's pretty.'

'Aye, Ma.'

'Do you like her?'

'I'm leaving now, Ma.'

I leaned across the glass enclosure of the Perfumery at T. J. Hughes. 'Betsy, I have been asked by Pop Maguire to help with the *Josephian* magazine on Saturday at ten o'clock. That's tomorrow. Can you do some typing and stuff with me?'

'Of course. See you over there at ten. Must go. Here comes Genghis Khan, the grungy boss.'

It was easy. A large quantity of submissions had been collected but they were all over the Gestetner printing room without any organisation, like the Dirty Duck on free beer. The editor, Wally Flanagan, was a pretty sharp kid but disorganised, so we went eagerly to work, and order came out of chaos as the sun was sinking down behind the church spires. Shadows grew tall and skinny.

'Let's get some fish and chips at O'Reilly's Chippy,' I said. 'Pop Maguire's paying for it.'

But what I kept top secret, never revealed to Betsy Braddock, was a page I gave to Wally Flanagan.

'It's the last page,' I said. 'Don't tell Pop Maguire. Just slip it in.'

Wally Flanagan was delighted. It read:

> The pile of bricks on Switchcross Lane,
> They call it old Saint Joe.
> It never rose to fortune's fame,
> Because the kids are slow.
>
> The students seem to come and go,
> Never one a hero.
> Horizons were so very low,
> Attainments then were zero.
>
> Its occupants are saints and sinners,
> Trying hard to win.
> Some have failed and some are winners,
> Giving life a spin.
>
> But all return as life slips on,
> To see this pile of rocks;
> It's where they built their character
> This place they call Hard Knocks.
>
> > Betsy Braddock
> > Former student

The *Chipton Down Post*'s readership was minuscule by comparison with that of the all-consuming giant, the *Liverpool Echo*, but Chipton Downers were more faithful to the *Post*'s news and gossip-bearing nonsense.

The captain of this industry was Chester Kilpatrick,

Chief Editor, inspired for life to bring a veritable plethora of news to eager readers athirst for exposés, gossip, rumour, scandal, hearsay, good and bad tidings; particularly necessary on the ferry boats to Liverpool in the morning when they weren't being sunk by the Luftwaffe. Mr Kilpatrick would venture to all compass points, scouring clubs, guilds, fraternities, even seedy pubs for hot news.

Thus it was that he took his fine wife, Cordelia-Isela, down cellar steps dating from pre-Victorian times into the smoke of the Portcullis, owned and managed by Jason Moriarty, a man with a dark past from County Antrim, where, it was rumoured, the Moriartys had ties to the IRA and Guinness, all fine Irish fable.

People talk in pubs. Aye. Particularly after generous portions of Guinness, assorted ales and gin. Tongues wagged. Chester Kilpatrick listened.

'I can't see,' said Cordelia-Isela, parting Woodbine smoke with painted nails.

'Over here, darling,' said Chester, indicating a small, circular table away from the jocular Irish clientele crowding the bar, but close enough to absorb absurd informative conversation, if you knew Scouse. Over vodka and tonic for Cordelia-Isela and a pint of good pale ale for Matthew they glued their middle-class ears to the dialogue.

'They say there's a U-boat in the Irish Sea.'

'Don't worry, Mahoney, the Irish navy will get it.'

Mahoney sipped his brown ale. 'Tell me, Murphy, how can the Irish navy get it when Ireland remains neutral? This war is between the English and the Huns.'

Murphy screwed his lips around, meditating deeply after three Guinnesses.

'Let me tell you a story,' he said. 'I was once in a Finnegan pub on O'Connell Street in Dublin and I happened to overhear a conversation between two visitors from Cork.'

Mahoney waited. Murphy held his Irish tongue.

Mahoney said, 'Are you going to continue the story you started at three o'clock, now?'

'Ah, yes, where was I?'

'In Finnegan's bar listening to a private conversation.'

Murphy finished his pint. 'It's a terrible thirst I have now on this hot, hot day.'

Mahoney signalled the barman. 'He's dying of the thirst,' he said.

The foam slithered down the glass on to the wet bar and Murphy's tie. 'Ah,' said he, placing the glass back on the counter. 'One of the heavy drinkers said to the other, "He's the only man I know who can put his right hand into his left hip pocket and lift himself two feet off the floor."

' "Ah," said the companion from Cork, "sure no man can do that!" And the first man, also from Cork, said, "It's O'Flaherty I'm talking about!" His companion thought awhile, not too long for Cork men can't think too long, and said, "Ah – *he* could!" '

Mahoney looked at Murphy's half-empty pint. 'Now tell me,' he said, 'what has this hairy tale got to do with the German U-boat in the Irish Sea?'

Murphy finished his pint. 'Listen,' said he, tapping Mahoney's chest, 'if you will just give it considerable thought in your thick head, you will balance a fine relationship.'

'Ah, Murphy, you could be just right. Let me think a moment.'

'You don't happen to have the price of another pint, do you?' asked Murphy.

The woman's voice was shrill in the corner bar of the Portcullis. Her dress appeared to have been borrowed from a smaller sister, buttons having popped off the top so that she modestly covered her upper torso with one hand while gargling stout with the other, the hem of her skirt edging quickly north from knee to hip.

'You've just got to read it,' she said, sucking on a Players-Weight. 'I went to that school, St Joseph's, and we received cane and Catechism every day. The stuff in that magazine is hilarious. I think it's edge-ucational, too. Wish I was back there sometimes.' She dabbed at her eyes with a pink lace handkerchief.

'We're going home, luv,' said her male escort. 'By the way, O'Brien said there's going to be a raid tonight.'

'How would he know? Did he get it from Connemara?'

The magazine lay on the floor where it had fallen so that Chester Kilpatrick retrieved it quite easily after O'Connahy and Considine had creased it with hobnailed boots.

'It's called the *Josephian*. Quite interesting.' He turned a few more pages before folding it into a jacket pocket.

Cordelia-Isela said, 'Chester, we're either going home or to the Rose and Crown.'

'Isn't that the pub,' enquired Chester, 'where you can't speak without a licence?'

'Sarcasm, Chester, is not your strong point.'

Chester smiled. In his pocket he had all he wanted.

'Hold the editorial,' shouted Chester Kilpatrick, 'we have a Special.'

'The presses are already humming, sir,' said Patrick Kilgooley.

'Then stop them,' commanded Kilpatrick.

What he wrote occupied the entire editorial section of the *Chipton Downs Post*, not large in physical dimension but all-consuming in intent:

> Chipton Downs [it read] may be a modest backwater of Merseyside but it has a quality much desired by other locations.
>
> It has a plentiful supply of first-class schools. These schools were not erected by the Board of Education just to teach the three Rs and then discard its pupils to the world of commerce, the industrial scrap heap, for there is another consideration. I am referring, of course, to character.
>
> Now let me quote from the latest issue of St Joseph's magazine, the Josephian: *The pile of bricks on Switchcross Lane . . .*'

And Chester Kilpatrick quoted the entire dedication.

This piece of literature, wrote Kilpatrick, was written by none other than an old student, Miss Betsy Braddock, who was at present working in an executive capacity at

T. J. Hughes department store in Liverpool.

'She is an inspiration to all of us in Chipton Downs,' he ended. 'God bless her and St Joseph's.'

The YWCA – the Young Women's Christian Association – met monthly in the gym on a Friday, late in the afternoon, going into the evening.

The YMCA – the Young Men's Christian Association – stood guard and, in some cases, escorted them to their various doorsteps after they slammed the doors of the gym, a meeting place for all and sundry, particularly sundry.

On the steps, before parting, Maggie Quigley said to Betsy Braddock, 'That poem of yours in the *Josephian* was silly and sloppy!'

Patsy O'Halloran said petulantly, 'It was wet, Betsy.'

Valerie Kilgallon said coyly, 'It was plain hogwash!'

Tom Kipper, genuine one hundred per cent author, said, 'Hi, Betsy.'

Betsy Braddock, a whole fireball of all-consuming female anger, rage, fury, passion, vexation and wrath, said slowly and distinctly, 'Tom Kipper, you wrote that poem in the *Josephian*, you put my name on it; never, ever speak to me again!'

My 'Shall I see you home?' was shot down in flames.

'That's what she said, Ma,' I said.

'Girls are like that,' said my dad from his Karl Marx armchair. 'Something like capitalists.'

Mary Catherine slithered the pot of scouse to another gas

ring. She was smiling. Connemara stardust glittered in her blue eyes. She wiped her hands on her apron.

'St Joseph,' she said, 'has always a different way of bringing things right.'

'Ma, what are you talking about?'

'Now let me ask you: isn't Betsy Braddock normally a nice person?'

'Well, she's a good typist.'

'I'm talking now, Tom Kipper, about her character.'

'Well, yeah, Ma, but she was plain bonkers, daft, crazy as a loon.'

'All women are like that,' said my dad. 'Is there any tea?'

The armchair creaked. Both the occupant and the chair needed an oil.

Mary Catherine said, 'Tom, sit down on the dining chair. Now read this.' And she handed me the editorial of the *Chipton Downs Post*.

I shut up. My paralysis started with my eyeballs and travelled down to my knobbly ankles.

'Would you like a cuppa tea?' asked Ma.

'Yes, Mother.'

'Better get the door,' she said, 'the bell's been ringing three times.'

Like a giant sloth full of succulent bugs, I dragged myself to open the front door.

'Hello, Thomas,' said Betsy Braddock. 'I was passing so I thought I would bring these mince pies to your mother. May I come in?'

She was already in, giving Ma a hug. 'Mother sent these over, Mrs Kipper.'

Under one arm was the Saturday *Chipton Downs Post*.

'Thank your mother for me, Betsy. How is she?'

'Looking forward to your next meeting, which I think is tonight.'

'Tom, see Betsy to the door.'

'I was wondering,' said Betsy, arching sixteen-year-old eyebrows, 'if Tom would like to go walking with me up to the Windmill. There's something in the *Post* that's interesting.'

'Of course he would,' said Ma.

I was halfway up Windmill Hill before I realised I hadn't said a word.

'That's the way they are,' said Pa, 'just like capitalists.'

Sunday morning, walking down the hallowed steps of St Joseph's, next to Hard Knocks, I said, 'Hey, Ma, I've got something to tell you at home.'

At home on Mary Lane I told her, 'I had a dream last night about a U-boat in the Irish Sea.'

'Really, Tom, and how did it go?'

'Like this, Ma':

First Engineer Wolfgang Mueller said, 'We have surfaced, Captain Heinschenkel.'

Heinschenkel said, 'Zen open ze conning tower for I must look at Ireland, that mythical place I have heard so much about from meine grandmother, Izelda.'

'Better hurry, Captain.'

'I, Herr Mueller,' said Heinschenkel, 'vill decide if I must hurry.'

He climbed the metal rungs into the conning tower, adjusted the glasses round his neck. 'It looks green,' he said.

'You must look to the west, Captain. You're pointed east. That's Liverpool.'

'Vell, yes, I know that, Mueller.'

'English destroyers are heading our way, Captain.'

'Are any Schottische warships in sight?'

'Scotland has no navy, Herr Captain.'

'Vot kind of country has no navy?'

'Scotland.'

'Very vell. I must talk to the crew.'

Assembled, they looked like the Everton soccer team after a night out at the Cottage Loaf.

'Men,' he announced, 've must abandon ship. The Royal Navy is coming. Inflate the boats quickly. I vill pull ze plug. A storm is coming in from the Atlantic.'

Two inflated boats pulled out from the sinking U-boat straight into the eye of the storm.

One boat was washed ashore at Wicklow with a veritable flotilla of empty Guinness bottles.

The other, commanded by Heinschenkel, pulled into a sandy beach, near a pier. The beach was covered with sea shells and bore a lone occupant, Seamus O'Hara.

Looking across the river they had washed up on

they saw a massive city with elegant buildings, seagulls crying messages of welcome.

'Was ist,' asked Heinschenkel of the man, O'Hara, 'das magnificent township?'

'That,' said O'Hara 'is the capital of Ireland.'

'Dublin?'

'Och, no. Liverpool.'

'Liverpool in England is the capital of Ireland? How can zat be?'

'Ah, now,' said O'Hara, 'that's a long story. You'll have to ask Tom Kipper's mother.'

Chapter Eight

Camilla

Camilla Finnegan was second in line to Bart Finnegan's throne; that is, she was number two out of a total of six sisters. If she should accede to the Finnegan throne there would be no jewelled crown and no wealth lodged in a vault at the Old Lady of Threadneedle Street. Bart had it heavily invested in multifarious breweries, headquartered at the Dirty Duck.

She had style, did Camilla. Perhaps precocious as a teenager, she became a trainee nurse, graduated to Liverpool University, and was received into the world of medicine as a clinical psychologist.

She had an occasional man friend and seemed somewhat different from her sisters, for she was less 'Irish', although the spark remained.

'All psychologists,' said Bart, when Camilla refused him the price of a pint, 'need psychiatry.'

Then she met Charlie Forsyth, a painter of houses who referred to himself as an Estate Decorator, his abilities reaching to fences and bathrooms.

Women fell like the Roman Empire for him, his charm magnified by stunning blue eyes and a boyish grin. But he hung on to Camilla for she oozed security versus his wayward philosophy which sparked in taverns and with the ladies. History was writ one evening at Flanagans Apple when Camilla Finnegan, her hand upon that of Charlie Forsyth, suggested a ring might be in order. 'I just rang the bell for the barmaid, my sweetheart,' smiled Charlie.

Camilla smiled back. 'I'm not talking about that kind of ring, Charlie.'

The conundrum puzzled Forsyth. For about ten seconds. 'Oh, you mean a ring on a finger!'

'Yes, Charlie. After all, we have been seeing each other for some time now. Perhaps our association should be solidified.'

'You're beginning to sound like a clinical psychologist,' said Charlie.

A frown was beginning to venture on to the usually serene face of his female escort. 'Have I said the wrong thing?' she enquired.

'Not at all,' said Forsyth. 'It's just that you and I are in the prime of our lives and having such a good time. Why upset the rhythm of our spontaneous beings?'

Camilla gawped. He's said this before, she thought.

'The world,' said Charlie, after three ales, 'is something like a playground.' He paused for breath.

Psychologist Camilla Finnegan leaned forward and tapped him on his hairy chest in her best clinical manner. 'Marriage is also about having a good time, Charlie, but if you are not interested in such an intimate union between you and me then you can take your irresponsible, idle, feckless, smug and sanctimonious playground and stick it. Do I make myself clear?'

'Aye, love.'

'Furthermore, I am leaving Chipton Downs for ever. Should you change your creative mind tell my father, Bart, and I just may one day return. If you're lucky!'

She scattered silver coins on the table. 'Goodbye, Charlie,' she spat and the swing doors of Flanagans Apple propelled her away.

'All alone, Charlie?' asked the barmaid, gathering glasses.

'She'll be back,' said Charlie.

'Could I pour you a Guinness before I go, love?' asked Florrie.

'Aye, 'twould be nice,' answered Forsyth. 'Better make it two.'

Ah, confidence is such a trickster.

Camilla Finnegan vanished.

Into which dimension had she translated? She left her flat on Throgmorton Avenue one sunny morning to catch the ferry, the *Daffodil*, to Liverpool and had now been absent for a fortnight. Had she been killed in an air raid? It had been known for people to vanish. Even Sherlock Holmes himself once vanished. And there was the strange case of Tatty O'Toole and his missus, Fionna, whose house was next door to Jim Fortune, Jewellers. The house and the jewellery store collapsed into each other when the bomb dropped, while the occupants were safe in backyard air raid shelters.

The O'Tooles vanished. There were tales, perhaps fables, that they were seen in Connemara, well dressed and affluent, whereas before the bomb they lived on scouse, jam butties and kippers. Idle speculation at the Dirty Duck concluded that the entire contents of the Fortune jewellery store had been destroyed, for the shelves were empty. So the jewellery also vanished.

But rumours, conjecture and speculation join hands, for shortly afterwards Bart Finnegan bought more than one round of ale for the clients of the Dirty Duck and the source of Bart's finances was also invisible.

When Bart assisted Tatty and Fionna O'Toole on board the seaworthy vessel to the dear Old Sod, the Ould Country, Dublin, he hefted large suitcases full of heavy woollens, they said, for the cold weather ahead; not necessary, of course, for the elegant quarters they would occupy. Bart stayed. They vanished.

Loaded with insurance, Jim Fortune smiled. So did Tatty O'Toole.

The radio sounded tinny, loaded with static.

'With great accuracy,' said Lord Haw-Haw, 'the gallant Luftwaffe again rained massive destruction upon the English Midlands and Liverpool. Oh, you foolish people in Britain, without food, or light, or even beer, why not surrender now to the ever-glorious Reich . . .'

Static drowned him out.

'A pint of pale ale,' said Clancy Donovan, 'and one for the missus.' The occupants of the Dirty Duck had one ear cocked to the radio and one to Liam Herlihy telling a bunch of lies.

The static broke. 'This is the BBC News and this is Alvar Lidell reading it.' His well-modulated tones told the inhabitants that all was still well in Westminster. 'There was scattered bombing last night,' read Alvar, 'not heavy. No casualties reported. Four Heinkels shot down. Mr Churchill, the Prime Minister, said the Secret Service is investigating rumours that Axis agents have been dropped somewhere on Merseyside. Now, the cricket . . .'

Static drummed in from the North Sea.

'Did you hear that?' said Herlihy. 'Spies have been dropped down right here. There just might be one right here in this pub. Did I tell you the story . . .'

Over in a little town just outside Hamburg, Lord Haw-Haw's wife, Betsy, said, 'William, when are we getting out of here, darling? These Hun maidens are giving me a large pain in the gluteus maximus. All they do is drink lager and sing something about Horst Wessel. Any chance of Berlin?'

'I'll ask the Führer tomorrow,' said Haw-Haw. 'That fellow Alvar Lidell gives me a pain in the neck.'

Chipton Downs was replete with its designated classes of society, which were easy to distinguish because the upper crust had two surnames. The lower crust also had two, the one at home and the one at the local constabulary. The middle class were in a mess but that was because they couldn't go up and they couldn't come down so they broadcast it with their accent which was a peculiar mixture of Scouse and BBC English in which you had to say lots of nonsense and make it sound erudite, which is not an easy thing to do when you're short of money.

Mrs Frobishire-Byrke, genuine upper crust, said, 'Whatever became of those people from 707 Plato Drive? The pretty woman, if you like large noses, and the fellow with the almost Irish brogue?'

'Quite short of change, those two,' answered Mr Blankenforth-Angles. 'Went to the Fatherland and became Nazis.'

'Surely you josh?'

'Not one bit. If you still listen to BBC radio, the fellow, chap name of Joyce, became Lord Haw-Haw.'

'Oh, is he the one we listen to during the bombing?'

'The very same.'

'Great merciful heavens. You mean to say,' said Mrs Frobishire-Byrke, 'that this club, this club, the most famous and fabulous in the entire Wirral peninsula, the Ash-Willows, allowed those traitors to enter its gates? What made them do it?'

'Money.'

'Theirs or ours?'

'Good thought, Mrs Frobishire-Byrke. Must ask the committee tonight. Would you care for another Scotch?'

'Oh, Mr Blankenforth-Angles, you are a charmer.'

And it came to pass that Uncle Bart's most beautiful daughter, Camilla, his second out of six, became a member of the Ash-Willows purely by accident.

So they say.

Mr Willie Bossington-Harforth bumped into Camilla Finnegan on the upper deck of SS *Daffodil*, the ferry from Liverpool, turning into the tide on the other side of the water. 'I say,' he said, which is what all young men use as a leader into a much deeper relationship, 'the roll to starboard caught me unawares. Are you all right, Miss . . . ?'

'Finnegan,' she replied, not knowing why, because under normal circumstances she would have given him the British elbow. But there was something about the man. Perhaps it was his trilby. Or that smile. Something hidden. They walked the upper deck until the ferry bumped into the stage.

'Would you care for a cup of tea,' he asked, 'before boarding the jolly old bus?' He seemed harmless. Nice manners, although his moustache needed trimming.

'Yes, I would,' she found herself saying, much to her surprise and the delight of Mr Bossington-Harforth.

An hour later he said, 'I say, I have a car at home. Would you like me to pick you up for dinner at my club, the Ash-Willows? Not much of a place, really, but rather smashing food. Don't need any coupons.'

The club faced out on to the River Mersey, glittering darkly at night in the meagre lighting of the sprawling dockside and a yellow moon edging out from Connemara across the Irish Sea. It was quite poetic and, she had to admit, she liked his style.

'Where did Camilla Finnegan vanish to, Ma?'

'Nobody knows. One day she was here and the next she was gone like the wisp of Irish mist.' Ma continued to roll the dough, then bash it, suck on her lips, roll the dough again with a cross between fury and resignation. I stood just looking at her. I knew that she knew something; Kippers have radar, a subject which had been much in the news recently, the *Chipton-Downs Post* as well as the *Liverpool Echo*.

'But, Ma,' I said, 'you know everything.'

She didn't answer immediately so I knew I would strike paydirt soon if I played my cards right.

'Your mince pies, Ma, are the best in the Wirral, in fact the best in the world!'

'You think so?'

'You know, Auntie Flossie makes scrummy mince pies but they don't have the same flavour as yours. Of course I wouldn't tell her that. I shouldn't, should I, Ma?'

'Of course not. Your Auntie Flossie tries very hard.'

The threat of rain was hanging over Merseyside like a Tory promise, making Liverpudlians rush to the shelter of the taverns for liquid sustenance. She bashed the lump of dough one last time with the Connemara Kiss, a karate chop which gave it a blessing.

'I have something top secret to tell you,' she said, sitting down at the kitchen table. 'Pull up a chair.'

I sat across from her with my very finest innocent look, which I had copied from my brother Vincent, the teenage confidence trickster. 'You have heard and read recently about radar, the secret device used by the Allies to detect the Luftwaffe as they head towards Britain?'

'Yeah, Ma. I mean, yes, Mother.'

'Well, your Uncle Bart has confided in me a secret which has to do with the disappearance of your cousin Camilla.'

'Eh?'

'According to Bart, the Germans have invented a similar device and the Secret Service is just beginning to catch up on it. The enemy has infused – I think that's the word Bart used – a sensitive power of some sort into their bombs so that when they rain down on England and explode, the pieces of shrapnel send coded messages back to Berlin. They call it Abschlunker, I think.'

'You mean, all the shrapnel in my shoe box is loaded with information?'

'No. This is a recent development, according to Bart.'

'What has this to do with Camilla?'

'Well, she has been recruited by the Secret Service to ferret out this information. As you know, your cousin Camilla is a clinical psychologist at the Exchange Hospital in Liverpool, so her profession will help her to winkle out German agents who are working secretly in Merseyside.'

'You mean spies?'

'Yes, I suppose so.'

'Uncle Bart knew all this, Ma?'

'Yes. Apparently Camilla confided in him, said she was

just going to vanish for a while so as to keep under cover,' Bart said.'

'Wow!'

'Tom Kipper,' she said, peeling a turnip for the scouse pot, 'what I have told you is top secret. You can always trust your Uncle Bart.'

'Did he borrow a florin for beer?'

'How did you know that?'

'Top secret, Ma.'

It was on Whitechapel going up towards the Old Haymarket that I saw her, Camilla Finnegan, my cousin, the undercover woman, walking quite purposefully towards an unknown destination. Then she swung right in the direction of Lime Street station.

I speeded up to catch her, for I was in the footsteps of a secret agent, a beautiful, seductive secret agent, a clinical psychologist working for Whitehall, Churchill and Scotland Yard versus Nazi agents in a cell right in the middle of Liverpool. I felt exhilarated by feverish excitement.

Then I lost her in Lime Street station. A mélange of uniformed people crossed my path. She disappeared. I stopped.

'Tom Kipper.' Suddenly she was at my side. 'Have you had lunch?' she asked, taking my hand.

'Yes, Camilla.'

'Would you like another one?'

I nodded my head and smiled.

'Oh, you silly Tom Kipper. You are in your lunch hour, I

presume?' She was radiant and beautiful, like her mother, Auntie Annie. Not at all like Bart.

'Yes,' I managed to say.

'What about,' she said, 'you and I taking a walk?'

The base of Queen Victoria's statue still stood in the rubble just south of Lord Street.

'Imagine,' said Camilla, 'she ruled the British Empire for over sixty years.'

'My dad said she used to drink heavily.'

'Drink heavily of tea, Tom.'

'The Luftwaffe really gave us a thrashing last May, didn't they, Camilla?'

'Yes. This is all they left of this area, but Liverpool shall rise again.'

I kicked some rubble with my shoe, and bent to pick up a bit of shrapnel. 'Your dad told Ma the reason for your disappearance these last two or three weeks. We all wondered where you had gone to.'

'He did?'

I spoke softly, for I was referring to the disclosure that Camilla Finnegan had been recruited as a British Secret Service agent. 'Yes, we all wondered where you were living; but you don't have to say anything if it's top secret.'

'Oh, no, Tom,' she laughed, 'I'm just teaching him a lesson. A friend of mine from Chipton Downs has loaned me a flat in Ainsdale, just up the coast.'

I wondered who she was teaching a lesson to but kept silent for her security.

'Willie is such a nice person.'

Another clue. 'Willie' must be some kind of password. 'Operation Willie'. Top Secret.

'Forsyth is out,' she said. Wow? Willie and now Forsyth. 'Operation Forsyth'.

I wondered if she meant to take him out. I looked at her in amazement. How quickly she had become absorbed into International Espionage.

'Is there any element of danger, Camilla?'

She laughed out loud among the rubble. 'Danger? No way, Tom, he's a pussycat. Hey, what are we doing here?'

'Taking a walk after lunch.'

'Let's walk down Lord Street before we go back to work, Tom. It's been lovely talking to you.'

A policeman with an impressive bobby's helmet was moving towards us rather quickly, face perspiring, buttons gleaming, boots clomping. 'Just a moment, people,' he said.

We both just stared at him.

'Did you pick up something off the ground?' asked PC Clarence Kinneally.

'Yes,' I said, 'a piece of shrapnel. It has markings on it.'

Camilla said, 'Why do you ask?'

'I am not at liberty to discuss the matter,' answered the PC. We gawped at him. As soon as the constable saw the movie of Arthur Conan Doyle's *Hound of the Baskervilles* he wanted to become Sherlock Holmes.

'He hasn't a clue,' said his mother, Esmerelda.

'If he had, he wouldn't know what to do with it,' said his father, Jack Kinneally.

But fate works in strange ways, for Clarence Kinneally

bombarded police HQ with requests to be admitted into the bobby ranks, sitting all one night on the doorstep of the town hall bearing a sign, 'I want to become a policeman', until he caught the sharp eye of Senior Inspector Willard Quigley, who said, 'You know, we are short of recruits.'

'Not that short,' answered his partner against crime, Junior Inspector Fogelton. 'So far he's failed all the tests. He can't even spell constable. On the last one he spelled it constabull.'

'Well, give him another try.'

'Cutting Corners' Fogelton was a yesman. He gave Clarence Kinneally another try; personally marked his paper 'Passed. A unique applicant' without looking at the answers. Kinneally's passion became his heaven, and every night he could be found polishing his helmet emblem with Brasso.

The emblem now reflected into our eyes its great sheen.

'Then I am not,' snorted Camilla, 'at liberty to answer your tomfool question.' Her Irish zoomed to one hundred per cent; eyes that her forefathers had battled the English with at the Post Office in Dublin flashed.

PC Kinneally shook his helmeted head. 'Answers like that, miss, aren't going to get us anywhere.

'Excellent,' said Camilla, 'now get the blazes out of my way!'

'I'm sorry, miss, but I must continue my investigation.'

Tom Kipper, that's me, said, 'I'm late getting back from lunch.'

He looked at me. I thought he was going to ask what I had for lunch.

'Why did you pick up the shrapnel?'

'What's your name?' I asked. That shook him.

'PC Kinneally.'

'I picked up the shrapnel because I collect it.'

'Hmmn. You'd better both come with me to the station.'

'What?'

A small crowd of onlookers, pedestrians, nosy parkers, eavesdroppers, aunties with children in prams, and grandpas in cloth caps had gathered as witnesses.

'Shame,' said a robust lady in a red hat.

'The station's just over the street.'

'Let us,' said Camilla, 'follow this hare-brained nincompoop across, because I've never been in a police station. Have you, Tom?'

'Never,' I lied.

One or two of the nosy parkers followed us, including a fellow whose face looked familiar from days at Hard Knocks. He had a Brownie camera on a strap over his shoulder and books under his arm. He came with us into the station room but stood in the background.

'Will you please sit down while I call Inspector Fogelton.'

'Constable,' said Camilla, 'just answer me one question before you go.'

'Yes, miss.'

'Fundamentally, why are we here?'

'Well, miss,' said the PC, 'you have probably heard on the wireless and read in the *Echo* that the enemy has invented a device known as Abschlunker, which they are dropping with bombs. It is rumoured that there is a top secret cell of Nazi agents perhaps here in Liverpool, so we must be on constant alert.'

'You're bloody crackers,' said Camilla.

'My cousin,' I burst out, 'is in the British Secret Service.' A camera flashed. A boy ran. It was the kid with the box camera, the Brownie, from Lord Street. 'And you think we're enemy agents?'

Camilla started laughing. So did. I. The PC managed a wry smile before he clomped away to an outer room.

Camilla couldn't stop laughing.

The inspector stood in the doorway listening to PC Clarence Kinneally, his eyes widening. The inspector's, that is. Junior Inspector Fogelton put his two hands on the PC's chest.

'You what?' he spluttered.

'I think he's going to strangle him,' I said.

The inspector slowly removed his hands from Kinneally's neck. Shaking his head, he came slowly over to us, wiping his brow.

'Would you like some tea?' he asked weakly.

The boy, Filbert Joshua, sped with great alacrity down the ramp and on to the *Daffodil*, thence up the ramp, breathing hard, and eventually up the steps of the *Chipton Downs Post* where he was accosted at the desk by Gloria Murphy, she of the coy but large Irish muscle. 'What do you want, boy?'

'It's most urgent,' breathed Filbert Joshua, 'that I see the editor immediately.'

'Would you like a chocolate-chip ice cream, too?'

'What's going on,' said Editor Chester Kilpatrick, who was standing in the doorway.

'Sir,' said Filbert Joshua, 'I have the most fantastic story to tell you.'

'Oh, yes?'

'And I have a picture you will not believe to go with the story.'

'And where did you take the picture?'

'In Liverpool police station.' Editor Kilpatrick's ears twitched. The kid could be crackers, but he needed a good story; his blood was boiling for exotic, dangerous, exhilarating news.

'Come into my office.'

And Filbert Joshua unfolded the drama, the intrigue, while the editor wept for joy, particularly after the beautiful picture was developed.

'Good boy,' said the editor, giving Filbert half a crown.

'I want two of those,' said Filbert, smiling.

'Give him three,' said the editor, crying.

The headlines ran: NAZI AGENTS FROM CHIPTON DOWNS ARRESTED IN LIVERPOOL. COUSINS POSING AS BRITISH SECRET SERVICE PERSONNEL ROUNDED UP ON LORD STREET.

Due to the valiant efforts of PC Clarence Kinneally, two Chipton Downers were taken into custody today. There was no struggle, and they submitted peacefully. Our own special agent, Mr Filbert Joshua, happened to be present at the scene of the arrest and photographed the interrogation inside the police station, the picture below confirming his testimony. He said the female suspect broke down into uncontrollable tears or laughter, he wasn't quite sure, as she was being interrogated. Further details of this amazing incident in our lives here on Merseyside are still to be revealed. Meanwhile let us thank PC Kinneally for his diligence, and the *Chipton Downs Post* for this International Coverage. Stay alert.

'So,' said der Führer in his Berlin bunker, 'was ist diese secret agents in Lifferpool, Herr Goebbels?'

'Mein Führer, two imbecilic Scousers tried to imitate our Nazi special agents and failed.'

'One of them,' said Schikkelgrubber, 'is called Tom Kipper. Am I not right?'

'Ja. Ja.'

'Is not kipper a kind of fish?'

'Ja, Herr Führer.'

'Describe it to me.'

'Mein honourable leader, words fail me.'

'You mean you don't know.'

'Ja.'

'And you are in charge of the propaganda of the Third Reich?'

Other inhabitants of the bunker heard the voice and rolled their eyes.

'Nobody, but nobody, can tell me what a Scouse is, and now nobody can tell me what a kipper is; not even a Tom

Kipper. Was ist das Reich coming to? Bring me more Schnapps, quick. Ve must send more Heinkels to Lifferpool!'

The Mince Pie Gang looked at Ma in awe.

'You mean to say,' said Clara Garrity, 'that your own brother, Bart Finnegan, lied to you about his own daughter?'

'He did indeed.'

'Have a touch of this sherry, Mary.'

Ma sipped the sherry and looked heavenwards for a moment. 'And I practically brought him up.' Nodding her head. 'I was the oldest, you know.'

'Shame on him,' grouched Zilda Sweeney.

'What did he say?' asked Cathy Sullivan, who couldn't remember the time of day.

'He said,' said Ma, 'that she was a spy for the British Secret Service.'

'It says here,' said Zilda Sweeney, tapping the *Chipton Downs Post*, 'she could have been a Nazi agent – and Tom Kipper for that matter.'

'The only thing Tom Kipper spies on are the mince pies.'

'How is dear Camilla now, Mary?'

Ma's eyes shone. 'Well, as you know, she was almost engaged to that house painter fellow, Charlie Forsyth, who almost lives at Flanagans Apple.' She lowered her voice an octave into espionage. 'The reason she vanished was to teach him a lesson. No engagement ring, no Camilla!'

'Now, what kind of man is that?' queried Clara Garrity.

'But St Joseph looked after her,' sad Ma.

'He did?'

'Coming home on the ferry from Liverpool she met Mr Willie Bossington-Harforth, who practically owns the Ash-Willows club in Chipton Downs and the Liver Building.'

'Yes? And?'

'So she sent Tom Kipper down to Flanagans Apple with a note for Charlie Forsyth inside which was wrapped a large squishy raspberry!'

'So she gave him the old raspberry!' said Zilda.

Ma smiled. 'Now her accent is changing.'

'How can that be, Mary?'

'Well, she spends a lot of time in the Ash-Willows with Mr Willie Bossington-Harforth and calls me "Arnt" Mary instead of "Ant" Mary.'

'Sounds bloody peculiar,' said Zilda, tippling a heavy glass of port.

'And what happened to Bart?'

'He vanished,' said Ma, 'just as Camilla vanished, Tatty and Fionna vanished, Charlie Forsyth vanished.'

'Will Bart return, Mary?'

'Yes, of course. Just as soon as the great thirst starts to consume him and he needs a florin.'

'Will he get it, Mary?'

'I wouldn't give him last year's Wet Echo!' But she knew she would.

At El Paso Corned Beef Inc. Victorian desks made of oak had been fitted at a 45-degree angle against the walls of one of the offices, the edge furthest from the occupant facing exceedingly tall windows that allowed daylight to flood the desks. The staff member at the desk was seated on a stool, fully cushioned, with sturdy legs. The stool, not the member.

Two characters from a Dickensian novel occupied the stools when I said, 'Do you think there are enemy spies in Liverpool, Mr Crisp?'

'But of course, Tom,' replied Crisp. 'We have the busiest port in England; more shipping than London. Even Winston visited us in the May blitz.'

'Don't forget the king and queen,' said Mr Watson, and added, 'Spies are everywhere.'

It surprised me. How safe was Camilla Finnegan? Could Sherlock Holmes do something, find clues to the state of affairs? Although nothing was missing, speculation was rife that a nest of foreign espionage agents was adrift in the city.

It was three o'clock. The big Victorian clock on the west wall of the main office bonged. There was something terribly reassuring about that bong. In the spacious office five people worked with a most quiet precision in the afternoon, a pale anaemic sun slanting through the large windows from over the white post office building. Each person was assured of his space. Peace reigned.

At three o'clock there were twitches of elbows, an ever so gentle breathing-in, a modest movement of four pairs of eyes in one direction, not too obvious, knowing smiles.

Mr Jeremy Watson, owner of the fifth pair of eyes, put down his pen, took off his horn-rimmed spectacles, opened his top drawer and took out a white napkin for the leathered top of the desk, a package of digestive biscuits from which he extracted one, a two-ounce whiskey glass and a bottle of

Johnnie Walker Red by appointment to His Majesty the King.

He poured a libation.

'Doctor's orders,' said he in a reverent voice; 'a wee drop of the creature.'

The staff nodded, smiling benignly.

I was fascinated. I had a desk of sorts for sorting the mail, folding invoices, gluing envelopes, and sticking stamps, just inside the doorway of the next office, by the white-haired office manager who didn't seem to do anything except straighten up his desk, mumble and snooze. At three o'clock (the Three O'Clock Gun) I'd sneak into the main office with papers in my hand to watch as Mr Watson raised his glass to the window and said, 'Sarah'.

'It must be his ex-wife,' said Gloria Wainwright, 'who left him for a sailor.' Gloria read a library of romantic fiction.

Mr Jeremy Watson saw me that day and beckoned me over with a crooked finger, so I went over to his leather-topped desk as he put down the glass.

'He is barmy about Sherlock Holmes,' Miss Lydia McLaverty had confided in my ear, the ear lengthened by Christian doctrine at Hard Knocks.

'Tell me again,' said Mr Watson, 'what happened yesterday at the police station.'

So I did, and Mr Watson listened, partly because of the story and partly because of 'the creature'. So he dropped his pen and embellished the tale I told with Sherlock-Holmesian elan, developing his theme, so that the staff, although indoctrinated into El Paso Corned Beef discipline, moved closer; shortly thereafter, it seemed, producing two bottles from out of nowhere, one of fine, tawny port and the other a Spanish Red, glasses appearing apparently from mid-air. Typewriters and ledgers were deserted, a *grande bonhomie* tempered the atmosphere.

The sun sank but spirits didn't.

Then Mr Elderberry-Fyffe walked in and thundered, 'What the deuce, Miss Healey, is going on here?'

A glass of Spanish Red was almost thrust into his hands. It brightened his dull day.

'Tom Kipper,' said Miss Fiona, 'is telling us about Nazi spies and the British Secret Service.'

'Ah, Kippah, I might have known it!'

'So,' said Jeremy Watson, 'you were arrested as a Nazi spy?'

'Yes, sir,' I said, 'and my cousin, Camilla, is with the British Secret Service. But please don't tell anyone.'

There was a grand chorus as they all raised their glasses: 'Don't tell anyone.'

I was even given a wee sip of port.

'Sherlock Holmes,' said Mr Jeremy Watson, 'would have sorted out this mess in five minutes. So, tell us, Tom Kipper, how did *you* sort it out?'

I could not resist it. I raised my port glass as Gaelic mischief coursed through my Irish veins.

I said, 'Elementary, my dear Watson.'

Chapter Nine

The Chamber

He was a changed Elderberry-Fyffe. He was no longer bombastic, spilling over with importance, oppressive mannerisms, demonstrative, imperious. It was all gone. It was a distressed CEO who fell through the doorway at ten o'clock GMT.

His gestures to the staff were feeble, fragile and entirely lacking in Elderberry-Fyffe character. Normally, when not barking or blustering at Miss Fiona Healey, quite often to close a conversation with an underling he would pronounce, 'I have spoken!' and metaphorically we would all fall on our bony Scouse knees and mutter, 'Amen!'

But he was in disarray and so were we. Where is an army without a general? Where is England without Winston? Where are the Blues without Dixie? Where is Liverpool without scouse?

Our morale was crestfallen.

When asked by a member of the staff – I think it was Miss Wainwright – about his condition, his secretary of ten years, Miss Fiona Healey, said, 'I think he's crying.'

'Are you going to the Mad Sandwich Shop, Tom?' timidly asked Miss McLaverty.

'Yes, miss,' I whispered.

We crept around. Coughing or sneezing was not allowed, almost forbidden.

Mersey fog seemed to sneak through cracks from Victoria Street to enclose El Paso Corned Beef Inc. in monastic isolation. I thought I heard a male voice choir intoning, 'Omnes gentes, omnes populi.' We should have all worn gowns with hoods.

'What shall I get for you, Miss Lydia?' I whispered through the monks' choral chant.

'Whatever's available, Tom,' she breathed back in Whisper Canyon. Doom and Gloom did a very slow fox trot.

'What's wrong with Mr Fyffe?' I asked.

'No one knows.'

'No one?'

'Well, it is whispered that it has something to do with the Chamber of Commerce on Bootle Street.'

Chamber of Commerce. That's where Tessie Salisbury works as an office junior, I thought. Hmmn. I would be passing Bootle Street on my way to the Mad Sandwich; so I just walked in as though it were St Joseph's Academy of Hard Knocks to find Tessie efficiently filing on a back desk.

'I'm hungry,' she said.

'Girls are always hungry.'

Tessie was the same age as me, but sharper, that woman sharpness, sharper than a good potato peeler in the hands of Ma Kipper.

'I am going,' I said, 'to the Mad Sandwich.'

'An egg sandwich would be nice.'

'A tanner,' I said.

'Aren't you going to treat me, Tom Kipper?'

'It all went at the club last night.'

'Bring it back here.'

'OK, Tessie, I'll pay. See you about one o'clock.'

'Hurry.'

The dining room of the Chamber of Commerce had pleasant, laced windows looking out on to Bootle Street from which one could survey Liverpudlians stumbling by on mysterious Scouse errands.

'Good sandwich, Tom,' she said as she munched.

'Do you go to any youth centres, Tessie?'

'I think about once a week,' she answered through a mouthful of egg and cheese. 'What about you, Kipper?'

'About the same. Maybe twice. I like St Thomas More.'

'Going this Saturday?'

'Only if you go.'

Her eyes lit up like Irish blarney. 'Are you Irish, Tom Kipper?'

'Ma is, so she insists I'm a hundred per cent.'

'My ma is too. She's a Considine from Clonmel. That's what she says, anyway. Who can believe an Irishwoman from Clonmel?'

I burst into Irish laughter. 'That's exactly the way I feel about my ma.'

Ah, she was a breath of fresh Irish air, bursting with freckles, rusty thatch for hair, a feminine swagger, a look of history, a precocious Clonmel smile, and no money.

'Do you ever,' I asked, 'see my boss, Mr Elderberry-Fyffe?'

'Most days,' she said, 'for the CEO business gathering. Why do you ask?'

'He looks depressed.'

'No wonder. Would you like more tea, Tom?'

'Yes, please.' It was a good cup of tea with the white-breaded salmon sandwich. 'You know why he is out of sorts, Tessie?'

'Yes, I do.' But she wouldn't tell me. 'I can't tell you. It's a trade secret.'

'A what?'

'A trade secret. There are certain matters of a confidential nature which are not to be divulged to people outside the Chamber.'

'Eh?'

'You heard me, Tom Kipper.'

'That's bloody daft!'

'It's moral conscience.'

'Which school did you go to?'

'St Theresa's.'

'That accounts for it.'

'What?'

'You entering into the secret service of the Chamber.'

'You are annoying me, Tom Kipper.'

'Goodbye, Tessie Salisbury.'

'You're going?'

'My lunch break is over.'

'You have another ten or fifteen minutes.'

'See you at the club on Saturday.'

'Tomorrow.'

'Don't forget to bring your moral conscience with you.'

'Tom Kipper!'

Members of the Chamber of Commerce met three times a week at headquarters on Bootle Street off Victoria for the obvious purpose of discussing business and the not so obvious of patronising the minuscule pub in those panelled chambers where secrets were revealed. It is still historically uncertain to this very day which was more significant.

Fionna O'Neill was the bar lady, bright, cheerful, honest – except for the petty cash.

Mr Elderberry-Fyffe was president, the finest they ever had, it was frequently ventured.

Miss Roxanne Delaney, spinster, forty-fivish, was secretary. Devoted to duty, she never broke a Chamber law, her once pleasant mouth becoming tight-lipped as another autumn's leaves fell by her window and she still awaited her ten thousand pounds.

For services above and beyond the call of duty a member could, probably would, receive a bonus of ten thousand pounds after twenty-five years of good service. Unfortunately for Miss Delaney she had served but twenty, but she wanted the gratuity right now, this very moment, growing at measurable speed in her bank account. Without it she could not fly to the Côte d'Azur to look for a French prince when this beastly war was over, which she estimated was far better than a Scouse prince at the Pier Head in Liverpool, fishing for fluke.

So she devised a plot. It wasn't quite as historic as the Guy Fawkes debacle, and she would substitute the Chamber for the Houses of Parliament.

Big Nose Wentworth entered the plot.

He was a tall, angular man, a most superior executive. Some of his staff thought he should have the initials P&C and BS after his name, the first denomination being Pomp and Circumstance. However, he was a good, standing member of the Chamber, never missed a meeting or a snifter at the pub bar.

Miss Roxanne Delaney ensured that she bumped into him in the corridor, removing her glasses and shifting her hips, both gestures being cordially noted by Pony Face Wentworth.

'I have some papers to be signed, Mr Wentworth.' She smiled. 'Would you care to step into my office?' He did.

'Miss Roxanne, it is a signal honour,' he said. Miss Roxanne simpered.

The plot commenced to unfold, for Wentworth was Vice President of the Chamber and second in line to Elderberry-Fyffe. What she was about to disclose to the VP would either ensure her bonus immediately or cost her the secretaryship, for it was a falsehood, but the utter despair of twenty years' slaving in Bootle Street without her French prince put paid to all caution.

Wentworth sensed the drama and sat down.

'Speak,' he said.

'You know, Mr Wentworth,' she said, edging closer, 'I have always held you in high esteem.'

'No bull,' said Wentworth. 'What is the impending revelation, Miss Delaney?'

She breathed an inch closer. 'Mr Elderberry-Fyffe made a pass at me.'

'What?'

She put a hand to her mouth and sobbed.

'There, there,' said Wentworth, 'all will be well. Tell me more.'

'I have always thought, Mr Wentworth,' she said, laying a hand on his chest, 'that you would be a much finer president, should the occasion happen to present itself.'

'True. True.'

'He pulled me close to him and kissed me on the mouth.'

Wentworth put an arm round her for comfort. 'The swine,' he muttered.

They both sat down. 'Now,' he said, 'how much of this is fiction?'

'All of it,' she blubbered, 'but I love you and want to see you as president.'

'Hmmn . . . And you want the ten thousand in advance?'

'I've earned it, and Elderberry-Fyffe says I have to wait five more long years.'

'Hmmn . . . Will you swear to this in Chambers?'

'Of course.'

'Go, Miss Delaney, make yourself presentable. I shall call you shortly.'

And so the historic tragedy unfolded. The reins of office were taken by Wentworth and a resolution was put forward to award a handsome sum of money to Miss Roxanne Delaney the following month, and Elderberry-Fyffe fell through the doorway of El Paso Corned Beef.

Fable and Fantasy, page four of the *Echo*. Dylan Evans, gossip columnist extraordinaire, was hot on the trail of Chamber news, scribbling:

It is rumoured – an ugly word (if it's not true!) – that the president of the Chamber of Commerce has stepped down, perhaps vanished.

What on earth is happening at the Chamber?

Does the reader of this illustrious newsprint realise that the Chamber is two hundred and one years old?

Vikings once met on that site, trading steaks and wives and slaves in great festivity before the Norman era, burning the midnight oil. Once they burned down the Chamber. Olev the Great won a contest where Victoria and Bootle meet, downing five gallons of mead before they carted him off to Valhalla.

Queen Victoria honoured the establishment with a coat of arms, miscellaneous executives rampant on a field of doubloons.

But where is the president?

Where is that noble figure?

Is his name Elderberry-Fyffe?

Will he end up with Olev the Great on Everton Hill?

Await, dear reader, further word.

This is Dylan Evans leaving you in anticipation.

Mr Willie Bossington-Harforth was heavily into insurance, gainfully selling, not buying, recognised in the north-west as top notch in his profession and an outstanding member of upper-crust Ash-Willows Social Club into which he had introduced Camilla Finnegan, daughter of Uncle Bart.

'She has a funny accent,' commented Mrs Frobishire-Byrke.

'Must be Irish,' said Mrs Blankenforth-Angles.

'Willie seems to like her.'

'I think he's quite potty about her.'

'I have invited,' said Camilla Finnegan to Willie, 'Tom Kipper to come and look at your club on Saturday.'

'I say, old girl,' answered Willie, 'we can't do that.'

'And why not, Willie?'

'Because it's probably against club rules.'

'He's sixteen.'

'But he's not an adult, dahling.'

'I just love it when you say dahling, darling.'

Willie smiled. 'You are beguiling me,' he said.

'It's a woman's job, Willie Bossington-Harforth.'

'I suppose he can come along.'

'Good show, Willie. Oh, yes, he's bringing Tessie Salisbury with him.'

'Miss Salisbury?' Willie's eyeballs took on the shape of large ferry boats at high tide. 'She works as an office junior at the Chamber.'

'She's sixteen, too.'

'Mrs Frobishire-Byrke will boil me in oil.'

'With fish and chips, Willie?'

'Dahling, even though it is against all common sense I will allow it because I love you.'

'Will you say that again, Willie? The last part, not the first.'

So they sat and looked at each other, sipping a glass of port, smiling indulgently into a promising future, warmed by the sunshine quite unseasonable from the Irish Sea, no air raids, and rare splendour; magic.

'Lousy port,' said Camilla, 'but I love it and the company.'

We came on our bicycles, Tessie and I, pedalling up Crofton Hill to the Ash-Willows club, pushing our bikes into the parking lot which was full of ancient pre-war vehicles.

'Here they are. Wrong day,' said Camilla, looking through the window, 'but here they are. Is that the girl who works at the Chamber? She's pretty.'

'Pretty sharp, too,' said Willie.

Camilla and Willie invited us into the buffet lounge where we had gallons of tea and crunchies and delicacies we couldn't even think about at lower-crust level. It was all quite smashing.

'How is your job, Tom?' asked Willie.

'Thank you, Willie, it's fine,' I said, 'except that the boss,

Mr Fyffe, has gone into a state of great depression. No one knows why.'

Willie's eyes lit up. Not in the same way he looked at Camilla, but brightly, with purpose, quizzical, so I told him about Fyffe's fall, not from grace, but through the front door.

'I missed the last couple of meetings,' said Willie, 'so I do not know what happened.'

But I, Tom Kipper, knew someone who knew, and she was sitting at the table with us looking like a gargoyle on Liverpool Cathedral.

'It's all quite mysterious,' I said. 'Heaven knows what will happen to El Paso Corned Beef. Anyway, something happened in the Chamber.'

'It could fail?' queried Camilla.

'Signs,' I said with great drama, 'of disintegration are already showing.'

'Is he a good CEO?' asked Willie.

'He is nasty, mean and aggressive, but forthright,' I answered, not knowing where the words came from. Perhaps too much Charlie Dickens.

'There must be something you can do,' said Camilla to Willie. 'Do you want another éclair, Tessie?'

'Good cup of tea,' I said.

'Yes, I will, please,' answered Tessie.

'On Monday I will enquire,' Willie volunteered.

'But you won't be able to tell us,' I said. 'It's against Chamber regulations.'

'How do you know that, Tom Kipper?'

'Tessie told me.'

'She's right,' said Willie. 'However, hmmn . . .'

'Do something splendid, my darling,' said Camilla.

'May I speak?' asked Tessie, a tear in her eye. And so she unravelled the mystery, the plot between Miss Roxanne Delaney and Big Nose Wentworth, blubbering somewhat as she went.

'How do you know all this?' queried Willie Bossington-Harforth.

'Miss Delaney and Mr Wentworth did not realise I was in the filing room next door to her office and heard every word.'

'Damn!' said Willie.

'Wow!' shouted Camilla.

'Smashing,' said Tom Kipper. That's me.

Guy Fawkes was in nappies.

Three days later, over a cucumber and pickle sandwich, which I had to pay for, Tessie brought me up to date with the story.

'I would like to bring up before the board a matter of great importance,' said Willie Bossington-Harforth.

'You can't do that,' said Humphrey Carmichael of Carmichael's White Bread. 'You're not a member.'

'I am an associate member,' said Willie, 'controlling the insurance of this Chamber and all its members.'

The chattering died down.

'Speak,' cried Elford-Duffington of Duffington Bags and Packaging, wiping his large nose.

'A charge has been made against our valiant leader, Elderberry-Fyffe, of improper conduct with Miss Delaney.' He pointed to the secretary. 'Not one scrap of evidence has been produced to fortify this brazen accusation. Has it?'

There were rolling murmurs which to the untrained ear sounded like 'marmalade-marmalade'.

'What's your bloody point?' shouted Clark Mulford, who was half deaf.

'My point,' said Willie, 'is that Miss Delaney must produce evidence, witnesses. Do you have these, Miss Delaney?'

She was pale and trembling, her shorthand notebook falling from her grasp. She looked imploringly at Big Nose Wentworth, who was studying a Welsh spider on the ceiling.

She gave a sudden screech, a low groan, an anguished cry, some foreign words she had picked up in the Spanish bar, and scampered headlong from the room.

'Who's going to do the minutes now that Miss Delaney has flown?'

'I know the very person,' said Willie. 'Tessie Salisbury.'

'But she's just sixteen.'

'And the very best shorthand typist on Bootle Street,' said Willie.

Mr Wentworth sneaked through the back door as the Welsh spider fell from the ceiling.

'Wow, Tessie,' I said, 'you made history.'

And so it was that at ten on Monday morning Mr Elderberry-Fyffe fell through the front door of El Paso Corned Beef.

'Why,' he said in an imperious manner, though smiling, 'isn't everybody working!'

A grand thrill like a hot cheese sandwich spread through the El Paso staff.

'He's back,' said Miss Gloria Wainwright.

'He has returned,' thrilled Miss Lydia McLaverty.

'Glory be,' triumphed Mr Jones.

'Sic transit gloria mundi,' mumbled Miss Penelope Hawkins.

'I wonder if he wants a sandwich?' enquired Tom Kipper. That's me.

'And where is that lad, Tom Kippah?'

'He wants one.'

'Tell me again,' said Ma.

'You mean you want a matinee, Ma?'

'Watch your tongue, Tom Kipper.'

So I re-enacted the Great Chamber Drama, this time with Gaelic effects, for the Irish was in the blood and the spirits of the ancients ones coursed through my O'Kipper veins, all of which fascinated my ma, Mary Catherine, who awarded a bonanza portion of chocolate cake to the supreme actor.

'But what happened,' she asked, 'to Miss Roxanne Delaney who fled the scene without her job and without her money?'

'There's a rumour,' I said, 'that she's somehow mixed up in local politics. But nobody knows for sure.'

'God bless her,' said Ma, 'may the Holy Mother and St Joseph be her guardians.'

'But she's a crook, Ma.'

'Aren't we all,' she said, pouring the tea.

But they were. Her guardians, I mean. For two months later she was a member and secretary of the City Council, even though in her heart she hungered for the Côte d'Azur – and her French prince. She ended up marrying Big Nose Wentworth, a Scouse prince, his princedom supported by an adequate bar at the Chamber of Commerce on Bootle Street.

And Camilla proposed to Willie, who said, 'Jolly good show, old girl!'

It was Tessie who surprised me; she turned down the opportunity to become permanent secretary at the Chamber.

Over a cheese and onion sandwich she said, 'Tom Kipper, I'm leaving you.'

'Oh, where are you journeying to, Tess?'

'I'm joining St Theresa's Order in Walsinghamshire.'

'What, Tess?'

'I'm going into a convent, Tom. Active, not cloistered,' she added.

I felt breathless. 'How much does it pay?' I asked.

'Tom Kipper!'

When she went we all missed her terribly. And I had to go back to Betsy Braddock.

Chapter Ten

Bart's Hazard

Ye ancient olde house, Gothic-Victorian, dating back to 1842, was built for the aristocratic, upper-crust echelons of Chipton Downs. As time remorselessly passed, red-bricked working- and middle-class homes sprouted around it like mangy mushrooms. It stood its ground. It shone like a precious gem with its turrets and bays amid the tatty, crumbly, shabbily built architectural misadventures nudging elbows on its perimeter, still occupied by the same family.

Gardens surrounded the elegant structure as it aged gracefully, its spirit glowing from within, tall, elegant, graceful.

People moved to Upper Chipton Downs as their prestige and coin of the realm increased their standing, but Villa Jarrow stood still. It suddenly became empty during the Blitz; windows boarded, gates locked, it stood forlorn but still majestic, like Uncle Bart supporting the Goose and Firkin with an empty glass and empty pockets.

Then it went up for sale.

'It's almost as good as yours on Mary Lane,' said Sully, 'the one your ma stole.'

'We moved into Mary Lane,' I emphasised to Sullivan, punching his ribs, 'because of the Blitz. Ma just did a good job of negotiating with the town hall.'

'You mean she used Irish on them.'

'Whatever, Sullivan; she won!'

'Aye, Kipper, that's true.'

'They need someone to clean it first,' said my ma, banging the pot. 'I also need a new scouse pot. This one's getting rusty.' She looked at Pa, buried in *The Pickwick Papers*. 'Like somebody I know.'

'Is there any tea?' enquired the ragged-trousered philanthropist.

'That chair's going to eat him one day,' said Ma. 'Here, take him a last cup of tea.'

Betsy Braddock surprised us with an education in ancient architecture and ownership of the elegant manor.

'It belongs to my aunt; well, my Great-Aunt Esmerelda, who lives in Wales.'

'Your aunt owns the castle?' sneered Sully.

'Yes, Sullivan,' said Betsy. 'She is a descendant of the aristocrat who had it built in 1842 for his gorgeous wife, Charlotte.'

'What was his name, Betsy?' I asked.

'His name, believe it or not, was Lord Humphrey Dodington-Lloyd-Blakeley-Braddock-Jarrow. I think I've got the names right, and my Great-Aunt Esmerelda is his great-

great-niece. Something like that. There may be another great in there.'

'Wow, Bets,' said Sully, 'you're an aristocrat.'

'Don't be sassy,' said Betsy Braddock, 'or I'll have you thrown into the Bloody Tower.' She pursed her pinkish lips. 'I could get you a job, you know.' She blinked those long eyelashes at both of us.

'What job?' asked Sully.

'Cleaning the house.'

'You're kidding! Who wants to clean a house?'

'Let me tell you how much it pays.' Which she did.

'Wow, Bets, but when would we do it?'

'As soon as possible, while the job's still there. Look, why don't the three of us meet for fish and chips at O'Reilly's after work on Friday night, go up to the house, and you chaps could sleep there overnight on two camp beds in the loft. Then Saturday we could finish off the cleaning.'

'And how,' asked Sullivan, 'will you get this job for us?'

'From the estate agent, silly. I'll get him to call my Aunt Esmerelda in Bodelwyddan near St Asaph. I know she'll say yes.'

'What's she doing in Wales, Bets?'

'The Blitz frightened the you-know-what out of her, so she fled. She's eccentric. Thinks she's in the Canary Islands.'

'Sounds bloody daft to me,' said Sully.

'Eccentric is a better word.'

'Sounds OK to me; what about you, Sul?'

'Count me in. Can we get paid up front?'

'There's only one problem,' said Betsy.

'What's that, Bets?'
'It's haunted.'

The man with the silver bicycle wore a grey pinstriped suit, tie, oversize trilby hat and clips round his trouser bottoms. The bike and he just didn't fit together. He would have been better allied with a silver Jaguar. He dismounted from the bike, leaned it against the metal-railed fence of Villa Jarrow, and opened the gate with a key. I watched open-Kipper-mouthed as he walked the pathway to the front door and opened that with another.

He couldn't be the estate agent, Lloyd Davies, because I'd seen him from a distance down Raneleigh Lane putting up a For Sale sign.

I leaned my bike against the fence as he came out of Villa Jarrow carrying a painting Sully and I had looked at in the wood-panelled living room. The picture was an oil painting of Betsy Braddock's Great-Aunt Esmerelda, the one in Wales who owned the house, so I stepped up and said, 'Excuse me, sir, you can't take that picture!'

He cut me to tatters with an aristocratic sneer. 'I can, young man, and I will!' You could have knocked me down with a Morris Minor.

Balancing the picture on the frame of the bicycle he pedalled off down Courtney Drive, so I jumped on my ageing, clunky velocipede, sans mudguards, to follow him. I saw him turning left at Blackberry Place, thought I had lost him, then caught sight of him going right into Redfern Terrace. He wheeled up to No. 84 which was teetering on the edge of minuscule Newcombe Park, a green dell made for lovers.

And then I caught sight of Uncle Bart, cap angled to the north-east, silk scarf embracing adam's apple . . .

The Bird in Hand was wreathed in the fragrance of blue Woodbine smoke in the inside chambers and creepy, crawling mist tumbling in from the river on the outside. Which mattered not one jot to its indoor clientele who were riding a see-saw of emotional balance, elbows polishing the oak bar as their owners succumbed to heady English ale and Irish porter.

So all was quiet on the Mersey front.

Choirs of Scouse angels passed peacefully by, taking note of the empties.

It was Kevin O'Higgins who broke the spell as he fell through the front door from Barlow Terrace, letting in a great, creeping, rolling billow of mist and breathing hard in his ancient raincoat and tattered cap. Maginnerty pulled him inside, banging the heavy door. 'What's with ya now, Higgins?'

'You never all will believe it. I'll have a pint. Let me get my breath.'

Irish faces, expressions various, waited for the Kevin O'Higgins announcement.

'I thought someone was going to buy me a pint,' he said.

'What are you all fussed up over?' asked Maginnerty.

'Ah, you'll never believe it.'

'Try us. Buy him a pint someone.'

They knew it was worth it. He had news; sure no man can act like that without news. O'Higgins took a sip, a big sip, half a glass.

'Are you ready?' he asked.

'Give him a kick up the arse,' said Gallagher.

'He's in jail,' said Kevin O'Higgins.

'Who's in jail?'

'Bart Finnegan.'

'What?'

'Bart Finnegan's in jail.'

'That's impossible.'

Every face in the Bird looked at him incredulously.

The whole pub went quiet. You could have heard a crumpled pound note drop.

'What for?' cried Dougherty.

'What for?' gasped Gallagher.

'What for?' shouted Flaherty.

'Why?' queried Sweeney.

'Splendid,' sneered Liam McFinn the pub pessimist. 'I knew he'd get his dibs some day.'

'Oh, shut up,' said the bar lady, Blanche Fogarty. 'Speak up now, Kevin, tell us what you know. Where is he?'

'He's in the county jail on the Hill. It seems a copper nabbed him stealing an oil painting, a very valuable oil painting.'

'When?'

'Today. This afternoon.'

'Impossible!'

'Why impossible?'

'Bart Finnegan would never steal anything in daylight hours!'

'True.'

'Let's get him out.'

'If I know Bart he's already getting himself out.'

'Aye, he most probably is.'

'Wait till his dad hears about this.'

'And his sister, Mary Kipper.'

It's not easy being famous.

Aunt Esmerelda didn't come by train, boat, bus or charabanc, she took a Williams Taxi, such was her need for the utmost speed. And she came armed. Not with weapons of a physical nature but with a burgeoning avalanche of vocabulary to suit the occasion in Chipton Downs. She left the sing-song melodies of Bodelwyddan for the much more pleasurable adenoidal grunts of Scouse. They let her through without a passport as she changed her accent.

'She'll be here any time now,' said Betsy Braddock. 'She said about three o'clock.'

We all were assembled in the living room, or front parlour, of Villa Jarrow: Betsy Braddock, myself, and Sully, with a cheerful, smiling Uncle Bart accompanied by a large copper of the local constabulary coming through the front door. Then came the ruddy-faced estate agent, Lloyd Davies, fresh from having sold a sorry shack up on Grafton Hill bearing the sign 'Restorable'. The termites were smiling.

'Now,' said PC Seamus Knell, removing his helmet, wiping his brow with his sleeve and plonking himself down heavily on a finely veneered, heavily upholstered Georgian couch that groaned under his two hundred pounds, 'What's this all about?'

'Can you wait for my aunt Miss Jarrow who I believe is arriving now?' Betsy said.

The black and white Williams Taxi had coasted up Courtney Drive and was now discharging Betsy's Aunt Esmerelda. She stepped out, looking up at Villa Jarrow as she did so, wiping moisture from her eyes.

Betsy ran down the garden path. 'Aunt Esmerelda.'

Once inside Esmerelda took over. 'Now,' she said, 'who is Tom Kipper?'

Betsy Braddock held up my hand.

'Just a moment,' said PC Knell, 'I'll ask the questions around here.'

'In my house,' said Esmerelda Jarrow, 'you'll shut up!'

Uncle Bart roared applause, Betsy put a hand to her mouth, Sully and I just gawped in astonishment. She was so regal and vivacious; stylishly dressed, with a beautifully modulated voice, despite advising the local constabulary to shut up. 'Betsy, is there a spot of tea in the pot? And who will bring in my suitcase?'

I went outside and down the pathway to fetch an expensive crocodile valise, and in a short space of time we were all sipping tea.

'Now, Tom Kipper, tell us what happened.'

'It's very simple,' I said.

'Tell us.'

'Sully and Betsy and I started cleaning the house on

Friday night. Betsy had told us it was haunted and late that evening I saw a face looking through the window and thought it was the ghost.'

'And then?'

'The following day a man on a bicycle rode up to the house with a key and stole a painting of you, Miss Jarrow. He was the ghost. He wouldn't put it back, so I followed him to his house just as Uncle Bart came along. Uncle Bart took the painting from the funny fellow and was walking back here when he was arrested by the constable, who said they'd been after Uncle Bart for a long time. The constable wouldn't listen to me or Bart but arrested him on the spot.'

'And what did the real thief look like, Tom?'

'Well, he was kind of tall with iron-grey hair, large green eyes and rimless spectacles. And his accent was different, kind of la-di-da, something like my cousin Camilla, Uncle Bart's daughter.'

Sully was looking through the window, 'Wow, it's the bloody ghost!'

He was walking up the driveway, an abstracted look on his face, and entering through the front door.

'You!' shouted Esmerelda Jarrow.

'Then what happened?' asked Ma, stirring pea soup.

'She gave twenty pounds to Uncle Bart.'

'Twenty pounds? To Bart? What for?'

'For rescuing the picture.'

'Great merciful heavens! But what happened before that when the ghost walked through the front door?'

So I told Ma about the confrontation between the ghost – a Mr Percival Barrington-Sherlock – and Miss Jarrow and what had been revealed to me by the estate agent, Lloyd Davies. Some years before the war a Bridie O'Malley had lured Percival, with little resistance on his part, into an affair which resulted in a Jarrow explosion. But he was infatuated with Bridie O'Malley and they took up residence together in Chipton Downs and a flat she had on Whitechapel in Liverpool. Two years wore on until, one fine day their association began to crumble like Uncle Bart's with money.

His infatuation began to disintegrate when he discovered her relationships with younger men in the theatre and her complete disharmony with trivial domestic responsibilities like warming up a good pot of scouse. What was more, the domestic sherry bill was beginning to assume the proportions of the Prime Minister's.

She left one rainy day in November when the leaves were falling and never returned. As the days passed he became deeply regretful for his actions, admitting to himself that he still loved Esmerelda Jarrow desperately. But it was too late. The die had been cast. He took to alcohol for a while to ease the pain, knowing a reconciliation was impossible.

What he did not realise was that Miss Jarrow was still in love with him. But he never contacted her so she became bitter. Eventually the Blitz drove her to Wales. Then the house went up for sale and he ached in his heart for he badly wanted that painting.

Ma shook pepper and salt into the pea soup. 'But you

haven't told me what went on after he walked through the front door.'

'Well, the policeman – the copper – became irritated because he lost control of the situation and tried to speak up but Miss Jarrow told him to shut up again and Lloyd Davies tried to bring some order to the proceedings without success. Everybody was talking at the same time.'

'What was your Uncle Bart doing?'

'He just walked out of the door with his twenty pounds.'

'Heavens to Murgatroyd! What about Betsy?'

'She was upset because her Aunt Esmerelda was upset so she just sat down with tears in her eyes.'

'And then?'

'Ma, you'll never believe it. A great, sudden silence descended upon the house as though a choir of angels were floating slowly through. You could hear the clocks ticking, the tugs hooting down the river, but we all stood still, just looking at each other.'

'Yes, yes, go on.'

'I looked at Betsy and she looked at me. It was as though we were all afraid to speak because if we did we would be breaking a Commandment.'

Ma was transfixed, holding a pot in one hand and a large wooden ladle in the other, her Connemara eyes absorbing the precious vision.

'And?'

'Mr Barrington-Sherlock looked into the eyes of Miss Jarrow and said, "I love you, Esmerelda!" And she uttered a cry of pain as she fell into his arms.'

Ma dropped the pan. 'Glory be! Just wait till they hear about this!'

Kevin O'Higgins announced in a loud Scouse voice from the bar, 'Ladies and gentlemen and Sean McWatt, I have an announcement to make.' He raised his pint. 'That ancient king of Ireland Bart Finnegan has returned from jail!' You could hear the cheers as far away as the Dirty Duck. Even Canon Moriarty snoozing in the presbytery said to his aide, young Father Harrogate, 'Did you hear a cry of distress, Father?'

'Och, no, Canon, 'twas a cheer from that holy football team, Everton.'

'Really?'

'Probably scored the first goal of the season against Liverpool.'

The cheer raised the tatty roof when Bart walked in with some swagger, polished the bar with his bony elbows and slapped down a crinkly, mint-fresh, twenty pound note.

'One pint to me,' he said, 'and three pints to whoever gets them first.' Aye, it was an elegant gesture, ancient of days, as Maginnerty, Flaherty and O'Brien closed in on free ale.

'Did they treat you well, Bart?' asked Maginnerty.

'Nothing to complain about,' said Bart. 'An adequate supply of tea and scones, no porter, some interesting thefts of valuable merchandise. And, oh yes, a valuable souvenir.'

From his pocket he brought forth a brown paper lunch bag from which he extracted a silver object.

'Ladies and gentlemen,' said Bart, 'the police chief's cap badge!'

The laughter and applause reverberated through the Chipton Downs night.

'What's all that noise?' asked Ma, many avenues distant.

'I think Uncle Bart's back in the Bird.'

'Praise be to St Joseph.'

'Ma.'

'Yes?'

'Miss Jarrow said Praise be to Tom Kipper.'

'She did, did she?'

'And she gave me ten pounds.'

'What!'

'So I bought you a gift, Ma, from Liscardage.'

'That,' said Ma, 'is the very finest looking scouse pot I have ever seen, Tom Kipper!'

On a warm spring night, looking from the promenade of Ye Olde Spanish Inn, glasses in hand, a senior couple of *Homo sapiens*, Esmerelda and Percival, smiled at each other, fulfilling an elusive dream that had at last become a sincere reality.

A choir of angels zoomed overhead.

Liverpool, that city of great, noble courage, glimmered across the water . . .

I only wish, thought Percival, she'd stop making that bloody Welsh rarebit!

Chapter Eleven

Beans

I whistled on the Wirral landing stage. I whistled on the ferry boat, the *Daffodil*, tramping around the upper deck and up the gangplank, whistled up Water and along Dale, past clattering tramcars, down Sir Thomas Street and into the Fox Building. The sky was blue, the clouds pure, bleached white; it was Friday.

'Mr Crisp,' said Miss Wainwright, 'has the flu, Tom. You have to complete some Customs and Excise forms for him.'

I stopped whistling. 'But, Miss Wainwright,' I said, 'I don't know how to.'

'Yes, you do.'

'I do?'

'If you don't, find out.'

'What about Mr Dobbs?'

'He doesn't know.'

'Mr Hocking?'

'He's too busy.'

'Mr Jones?'

'Hasn't a clue.'

'You?'

'Too much typing.'

'But I'm only the office boy.'

'Office Junior.'

'Can I think about it?'

'No.'

'Great suffering soccotash.'

'Before he went home Mr Crisp said a CSD 240 is due at Customs today.'

Mr Crisp occupied a neat desk left over from the Charles Dickens era. Scrooge had one. It is supported on stilts, the two at the back lifting the desk or bench up into a sloping position so that papers can be viewed easily and just as easily fall to the floor, which Mr Crisp's did quite frequently, occasioning muffled expletives and oaths which Mrs Wainwright tut-tutted at.

Picking them up was also a good opportunity for him to view the secretaries' ankles.

I sat on his high, leather-covered stool and opened his desk drawers to view miscellaneous customs forms, scratching my Kipper head, not quite in bewilderment because I had become familiar with the import form CSD 240, which I had taken many times to Mr Fabian Griswald at Customs. He would balance large, horn-rimmed spectacles on the bridge of his nose and glare over them at tatty office boys and junior clerks who cringed before his majesty, but I had become so accustomed to 'Old Grizzy' that his menacing posture didn't quite have the same effect as in days of yore and he just uttered, 'Oh, it's you again, Kipper.'

Mr Crisp was very organised regarding shipments, dates, vessels, and dates of departure and arrival, keeping for this express purpose a chart of great exactitude, which I hungrily absorbed.

Mr Hocking, creeping up at my elbow, moustache bristling, said, 'You're doing a fine job, Kipper!' I had been an executive for only forty-five minutes at most, so how did old Hocking know?

I could see on the chart that five hundred cases of El Paso Corned Beef were due in ten days' time if the U-boats didn't get them and that today, indeed, was when the CSD 240 was due at Customs care of Old Grizzy.

The CSD 240 appeared to me to be a ponderous manuscript, awash with mind-boggling questions of no possible import, something as bizarre as the mystery of Edwin Drood.

I groaned.

'Good show,' said Mr Dobbs.

'You're doing well, Tom,' said Lydia McLaverty.

I sweated over the CSD 240 for over an hour and two cups of Pekoe and Black from a scalding pot.

'Miss Wainwright,' I whispered hoarsely, 'I'm going down to Customs.'

Clutching the ponderous forms I trod gingerly down Victoria Street, passed the India Building and Cunard, trod down the marble halls of Customs and Excise.

Old Grizzy was on guard. Several office boys had fallen under his sabre before my arrival.

'Oh, it's you again, Kipper.'

Mr Crisp was faultless. In his forms, that is. Grizzy knew this. But this portmanteau I carried contained documents signed by me, not Crisp. Perhaps I should have forged his signature. I placed the portmanteau on Grizzy's desk, snapped it open and produced the very last, the finest, the most inimitable flask of Flannery's Foo-Foo in the world.

'For you, Mr Griswald,' I said, sitting back.

It shook him.

It was aromatic. He put his ponderous proboscis to the flask, smiling. 'You can't get decent hair cream anywhere, Kipper. What do you want?'

'It's a gift, Mr Griswald.'

'Nobody, but nobody, brings gifts to Griswald,' he said.

'Mr Crisp sent me with the usual.'

'Hmmn . . . a CSD 240 for corned beef. Five hundred cases. Not his handwriting.'

'It's the finest in hair creams, Mr Griswald.'

'Not signed by him, either.'

'He's got the flu.'

'And signed by Tom Kipper.'

'They took me over an hour.'

'So with this jar of perfumery you are bribing me, eh?'

'Gracious, no, Mr Griswald.'

'Page two contains two errors, there's one on three, one on four and three, I think, on five. Paragraph seven is not initialled. Very poor form-filling.'

'I have a headache.'

'Go over to that desk over there, Mr Kipper, and make the necessary adjustments. I'll still be here when you're finished.'

Nobody was ever invited into Grizzy's inner sanctum.

I crept to the desk, spread out the forms and started work on the adjustments to the sheaf of CSD 240 nonsense. He was a good teacher, old Grizzy, for his pupil, Kipper, remembered his admonishments so that in half an hour I was finished.

Without turning his head, he knew. 'Bring them over here, Mr Kipper,' he said, which I did, in a hurry, licking my lips.

'Hmmn . . . Hmmn . . . Hmmn . . . What school did you attend?'

'Hard Knocks, Chipton Downs.'

'Oh, across the water. Do they speak Scouse over there?'

'In certain pubs, Mr Griswald.'

'Looks like good hair cream, Kipper.'

'It's the best, sir.'

'Hmmn . . . Call me Fabian.'

'Yes, sir.'

'This flask will last about a month. Can you get more?'

'That is the very last. But I'll keep trying.'

'Here's the papers all stamped up. Oh, yes, don't forget the beans.'

'Beans?'

'Next.'

I was dismissed.

Walking down past Cunard I felt exhilarated. But what did old Grizzy mean by beans?

I whistled my way up Victoria Street and down Basingstoke Lane to the El Paso warehouse at No. 121 to see Matthew Maginnerty and deliver him his parts of CSD 240.

'Matt,' I asked, 'what do you know about beans?'

'Great with smoky bacon.'

'Old Grizzy down at Customs said don't forget the beans.'

'Didn't he explain?'

'Didn't give me a chance to ask.'

'You got me on that one, Kipper.'

Rummaging through Mr Crisp's desk I could find nothing on beans.

'Mr Hocking, what do you know about beans?'

'Yummy.'

'Customs said not to forget about beans.'

'Don't know, Kipper. Haven't the faintest.'

Miss Gloria Wainwright was at her desk, Smith-Corona to her right-hand side containing a half-completed letter from Mr Dobbs.

'Miss Wainwright,' I said, 'do you know anything about beans?'

'Yes, I do.'

'You do, Miss Wainwright?'

'Yes. They are the edible seeds of a leguminous plant, produced in pods.' She blinked her portcullis-like eyelashes. 'They are also, Tom Kipper, inflationary to the digestion. Don't eat too many in company or they may cause such company to move to a safe distance from you.' She was smiling. We laughed together. What a sense of humour.

'What are they laughing about?' enquired Miss Fiona Healey.

'Breaking wind, I think,' said blunt Mr Jones.

'Take a letter, Miss Wainwright,' I said in imitation of the absent Crisp.

'Certainly, sir,' she said, opening her shorthand notebook.

'To Mr Fabian Griswald at Customs and Excise, etc., etc. Dear Mr Griswald, I wish to thank you personally for the most splendid assistance you gave me with documentation this a.m. We are indebted to you for services to this Junior Executive. I am quite sure that when Mr Crisp returns to duty he will echo my sentiments. Most sincerely, Thomas Kipper, Customs and Excise Dept., El Paso Corned Beef, etc., etc.'

'May I sign you off as Junior Executive, Mr Kipper?'

'Certainly, Miss Wainwright, and someday, perhaps, we can lunch together.'

She grinned. 'Don't get fresh, boss,' she said.

When I arrived home from the ferry on Friday night, Ma said, 'There's a note for you from Miss Fionna Jenkins at the chandlery.'

'What for, Ma?'

'Well, the delivery boy has taken ill in the flu epidemic and she wants to know if you can help out Saturday and part of Sunday.'

'That's tomorrow, Ma.'

'It's usually the day after Friday, Tom Kipper. She left the carrier bike.'

'That was two years ago, Ma.'

'You'll do it.'

'I will?'

'Of course. You're Irish.'

That put the lid on it. All psychological reasoning became thin, diaphanous mist; reality became a wee creature of doubtful origin sitting on the whitewashed wall of an Irish pub.

It would be exciting in a way.

On Saturday I put on my bike clips before jumping on the carrier bike to cycle down to the Charming Chandlery on Reeds Lane.

Miss Fionna Jenkins said, 'Oh, I'm so glad to see you, Tom.' She seemed distressed to me, looking vaguely in different directions.

'Are you all right, Miss Jenkins?' I asked.

'I think I'm OK, Tom. I'm going through the change, you know. Either that or flu.'

The change? What was she talking about?

That adds up to two mysteries. First the beans and now the change.

'Here are the orders to be delivered, Tom.' She put a hand to her blonde head. 'You know, I am going home.'

Into my hands she thrust a bunch of keys, mostly Yale.

Right outside the chandlery, rubbing elbows with the kerb, was her minuscule Austin. She tottered in, started the engine immediately and drove off like a Le Mans dirt-tracker.

Kipper, that's me, hadn't uttered a word in self-defence.

'Let me have some of those kitchen matches, young man, some firestarters and a quart of paraffin,' said a female voice.

'Eh?'

'Look smart, young man, I haven't got all day!' I thought she was Boadicea: sourpuss, hat wedged tight, as upright as a Coldstream Guard. 'Put them in my car outside. The Morris. Put them on my account.'

'Mrs . . . ?'

'Atkinson of the Burrows. Don't you recognize me?'

Without waiting, she stomped off. I followed her, balancing her order, to the car.

'The help these days is pitiful!' I heard her mutter as I trotted back inside.

I dialled Betsy Braddock, who answered.

'Help,' I moaned.

'Is that you, Tom Kipper?'

'No, it's St Joseph.'

'Where are you?'

'At the Charming Chandlery.'

'The one you used to carry at?'

'Hurry.'

'What for?'

'Hurry over and bring help. Bring Spuds Kinneally if you can.'

'Give us ten minutes.'

They fell through the doorway like the hordes of Genghis Khan, crowding around and plying me with questions.

'Miss Fionna Jenkins has gone home,' I explained, 'said she was suffering from going through the change, whatever that is!'

Betsy and the teenage girl she was with looked at each other and burst into laughter. Spuds and I exchanged bemused glances. 'What's funny?' asked Spuds. They laughed again.

'This,' said Betsy, 'is my cousin Rachel from Liverpool. She's staying with Mum and me for a few days.'

'Are you called Rache?'

'No, I am Rachel Griswald, Tom Kipper.'

'You know my name.'

'I know all about you from my beautiful cousin Betsy.' She smiled.

'Yuk,' said Kinneally.

'In the back room,' I said, 'is complete disorder, boxes all over the place. Can you two ladies straighten it out? And Spuds, there's a bunch of orders to take out on the bike. Can you do it?'

'Piece of cake.'

Thus recommenced the chandlery industry of Chipton Downs, order gradually oozing from chaos. Most of the clientele were ladies from middle-class homes who enquired about Miss Jenkins and laughed at me when I mentioned the change, so that I eventually changed 'change' to 'flu'.

Betsy Braddock even made tea and discovered some scrummy Eccles cakes.

It was at four o'clock that it happened. He was a large, over-sized, shifty-eyed individual, about the size of Dixie Dean, about twenty, loitering outside the front window, glancing inside, then to right and left, sniffing.

Quite suddenly he was in front of me, leaning across the counter, beading his eyes on mine, moving his left hand to grasp me by the shirt front, balling his right fist at my face.

'Give me,' he sneered, 'the money from the till. Fast!'

My Kipper feet were leaving terra firma as he pulled me up towards him.

'OK,' I gasped, my right hand seeking for a weapon to destroy him with.

He slowly lowered me down. About two inches.

'Now,' he snarled, 'open it up.'

In desperation I said, 'Would you like a cup of tea?'

Spittle was drooling down his jowls. 'Open it now, runt.'

Which was when the ladies arrived. Betsy Braddock and Rachel Griswald came silently from the store room. Usually they were in constant babble with each other, but now they were as sinister as the Ghosts of Sligo, and in their hands they each held a large kitchen mop as they crept up behind Mr Drool.

Down came the mops in a swift clubbing motion on the head of the robber baron just as I was saying, 'Would you like it in five pound notes?'

He fell across the counter, releasing me from his grip, as Spuds walked through the doorway.

Spuds Kinneally absorbed the drama at warp speed and, with the professional accuracy he had acquired by sublime observation of the art in the Academy of Hard Knocks, kicked him in the shins. Twice. I think I heard bones crunch.

We all five of us fell through the doorway into the waiting arms of PC Kelly, beefy and indispensable member of Chipton Downs cop shop.

'Well, well, well,' he said, 'what have we here; if it isn't Mr McShane. Haven't copped you for a long time. Now, I'm taking this gent to the station. Don't go away. I'll be back to take notes.'

Aye, it was a spectacular surprise, for he brought with him Filbert Joshua from the *Chipton Downs Post*, complete with camera and tripod.

Four of us stood together triumphantly in the picture, the ladies shaking their mops, Spuds and I on each side, arms raised, with the blessed Charming Chandlery on Reeds Lane as a background.

'It's time,' I said, 'to lock up the shop and celebrate with a drop of the creature.'

'They'll never let us in the pubs, Kipper,' said Spuds.

'True. True,' I admitted, 'but there is a back door to all good inns, Kinneally.'

He let us in through the back yard of O'Reilly's famous chippy, did O'Reilly, putting a finger to his lips. And in his comfy parlour we saluted each other with two pints of sparkling ale and two glasses of good Spanish sherry.

'You ladies,' I said, 'saved the day.'

Tugs hooted out on the river.

The *Chipton Downs Post* showed a large picture on the back cover, big enough for framing.

It was only a week later that I realised. 'Hey, Kinneally, in the picture you have your arm round Betsy Braddock's waist.'

Betsy sipped her tea, looked at me with those Braddock eyes and said, smiling, 'Why, Tom Kipper, are you jealous?'

When I left Mary Lane for the ferry I was whistling, for the air was fresh, invigorating, and the fearless foursome were inscribed immortally in the *Chipton Downs Post* after the scrimmage with Mr Drool at the Charming Chandlery.

But what about beans?'

Angst nagged at me the length of Victoria Street, an indefinable emotion that is bound through some obscure Gaelic bewonderment to eventually stimulate an otherwise brilliant mind or an over-impetuous nitwit like Tom Kipper. So I said to Miss Penelope Hawkins, 'Penny, can you possibly telephone Wally Wendorff for me?'

'Mr Wendorff and I are not on speaking terms, Thomas.' She continued typing.

'Eh?'

Type, type, type.

I scratched my Kipper 'loaf of bread'. 'Can you possibly, Miss Hawkins,' I asked, 'give me his number at the APO?'

She sniffed elegantly, like an aristocrat with a peasant bug, wrote the number on a pad and handed it to me.

I used her telephone.

The Yank at the other end yawned. 'Yeah?'

'May I speak to PFC Wendorff, please?'

'Is this Winston Churchill?'

'No, it's Franklin Delano Roosevelt.'

'Wise guy,' he said, laughing. 'Just a moment, Mr Roosevelt. By the way, Wally is now Sergeant Wendorff.'

'Sergeant Wendorff?'

Penelope Hawkins's eyes were rolling as her ears extended.

'Yeah. He's got buddies in the White House. Hang on.'

'This is Sergeant Wendorff,' said Wally.

'Wally. This is Tom Kipper.'

'Tom! Hey, great. Are you at the office?'

'Yes, I'm at Miss Hawkins's desk. I hope you don't mind, she gave me your number.'

'How is she?'

I didn't answer, ceasing to be a motley nitwit.

He said, 'Like that, huh?'

'Somewhat.'

'Hey, good word. What can I do for you, Tom?'

'Wally, down here at the Customs House a snotty supervisor said to me, "Don't forget the beans," but wouldn't elucidate. I have a strange feeling it's something to do with El Paso Corned Beef but no one here has a clue.'

'So you want me to phone the old feller?'

He was fast. 'Would you?'

'You bet, Tom. How's Penelope?'

I whispered, 'I think she's crying.'

'I love her, Tom.'

'Hang on.' I covered the mouthpiece. 'Miss Penny,' I said softly to her, 'he said he loves you.'

I was knocked off the stool as she grabbed the telephone.

'Oh, Wally,' she croaked, the River Mersey coursing down her cheeks. 'My precious darling.'

Mr Morgan shook his head. Mr Hocking gawped. Lydia McLaverty clutched her breast. Mr Dobbs dropped his pen. All because of inspiration, whatever that is.

He called me back in half an hour.

'Two hundred cases,' he said, 'of Brisco's Butter Beans were shipped two weeks ago, due to arrive in Liverpool on Wednesday, and today is the last day your Customs will OK entry forms. Better make it snappy, Kipper!'

'Great suffering catfish! Who did your dad advise?'

'Your CEO, that feller with the bug eyes. Fyffe.'

'Thanks, Wally! How is Miss Hawkins?' I whispered.

'Back to normal.'

'Thanks again.'

So, Mr Fyffe had had a colossal lapse of memory. He advised nobody. But nobody.

I pulled out a blank entry form and started writing faster than Uncle Bart's whippet.

'Are you going to the Mad Sandwich Shop, Tom?' asked Lydia McLaverty at my elbow. I was wrestling bureaucracy on page three.

'No, he is not,' boomed Gloria Wainwright. 'Mr Kipper is temporarily executive in charge of Customs, Miss McLaverty, and is not to be interrupted.'

Lydia McLaverty fled.

I jogged, walked, skipped down to Customs, bumping against Grizzy's desk in about half an hour and placing the CSD 240 on it.

'Ah, beans, Mr Kipper; not corned beef but beans. On the last day, too. Let me see, page one is OK, page two wrong description. Page three right ship, wrong berth, page four shipping information faulty; shall I continue, Mr Kipper? Please return tomorrow.'

'But tomorrow, Mr Griswald, will be too late.'

'Correct, Mr Kipper, but what can I say?'

'Would you, by any chance. Mr Griswald, like to know how your daughter, Rachel, is doing?'

'What's that, Tom Kipper?'

From my inner jacket pocket I took out a folded copy of the last page of the *Chipton Downs Post* and spread it out before him, the four musketeers rampant upon a field of chandlery, arms upraised in salute.

Old Grizzy was trembling. 'Rachel, Rachel,' he said more than once. 'Kipper, I never knew you knew Rachel.'

'She is cousin, as you know, to Betsy Braddock. I went to Hard Knocks with Betsy. Rachel came to visit her. Rachel is beautiful, Mr Griswald.'

It was then that he told me of his separation from her mother and the long time since he had seen either of them.

'I shall have Betsy call Rachel, Mr Griswald, and give her your number.'

'Let me have another look at that CSD, Tom Kipper.'

His approval stamp bashed the entry form, tears dropping on page three, paragraph four, line six. 'May I keep the picture, Tom?'

'Of course, Fabian.'

*

Aye, 'twas a grand morning to whistle the following day. All was quiet in the Fox Building. My spindly shanks thrust me up ye ancient steps and through the swing doors into the main office where the staff was gathering its wits together for another exciting day of El Paso Corned Beef hash.

Cries of 'Good Morning, Tom' greeted me as I whistled through to Mr Crisp's desk, where I now reigned almost like royalty. I wondered what his salary was. But I was waiting for the coup d'état, the nature of which was known to Kipper alone. So I sat at the desk of Mr Crisp with a certain document in my possession, waiting to pounce like a highwayman of the last century, or, perhaps, before. Mr Fyffe's door quivered, burst open; he advanced step by precious step into the main office, breathing stertorously, which is easy for a plump man, eyes aglow, groping for support, heading eventually for Crisp's desk.

'Crisp,' he called hoarsely, 'where is Crisp?'

'Mr Crisp,' said Miss Wainwright, 'has been absent for a week with flu, Mr Fyffe.'

'What? What?'

'Crisp has flu.'

'What? Who is bringing in the corned beef? Who is outwitting the Customs bureaucracy? Who else has such brilliance?'

'Kipper.'

'Kipper? The boy? The Office Junior? Doesn't he just negotiate the Mad Sandwich Shop?'

'Mr Kipper,' said Miss Wainwright, buffing her well-filed nails, 'is a most superior executive.'

'What? Where is he?'

'Right in front of you, Mr Fyffe,' said Lydia McLaverty.

'Are you there, Kippah?'

'Right here, Mr Fyffe. May I help you?'

'Mr Kippah, I have a terrible secret I must unfold.'

'Yes, Mr Fyffe.'

'It's about beans.'

'Beans, Mr Fyffe?'

'Yes. Two hundred cases will arrive tomorrow on SS *Crucible* and yesterday was the last and final day for filing at Customs.'

'Then it's too late?' I enquired.

'Too, too late, Mr Kippah. The consignment will be confiscated. Is there nothing we can do?'

The staff had departed their ledgers, abandoned their typewriters, let the telephones ring, left sandwiches to become moudly, and moved as one flock to Tom Kipper, that's me.

'Should these beans,' I enquired, 'arrive at El Paso, would there be a reward, Mr Fyffe?'

'Of tremendous value,' he answered.

'This,' I said, laying a Customs document in his hands, 'is the authority to pick up two hundred cases of Brisco's Butter Beans tomorrow or thereafter, Mr Fyffe.'

'What! Kippah! How did you do it?'

'St Joseph,' I said, 'and a minimum of chicanery taught me by my Uncle Bart.'

'Kippah,' he said, visibly brightening, 'you are an inspiration to us all!'

'Any chance of a raise?'

'Absolute nonsense, Kippah! Let's get those beans!'

But in my pay packet on Friday there was an increase. Not large. A Fyffe increase. Enough for more mushy peas at O'Reilly's Chippy.

Ma said, 'Will there be any chance of your acquiring some of those beans?'

'I'll give it the old college try, Ma.'

'What's bothering you?' she asked, clattering dishes in the kitchen cupboard.

'Well, when I went to the Charming Chandlery and spoke to Miss Jenkins, before she gave me the keys, she said she thought she was suffering from the change. What did she mean, Ma?'

'Tom Kipper,' said Ma, half smiling, 'sit down here. I want to tell you a story. As sure as eggs the ragged-trousered philanthropist on the couch won't.'

'What's the story, Ma?'

'It's all about the birds and bees.'

Chapter Twelve

A Bloody Good Laugh

Deep in the chambers or cellars of the building adjacent to Our Lady and St Joseph's Church, history slept. Generation after generation of priests, passing through on their ecclesiastical journeys, their spiritual missions, had left behind the imprint of their characters, the physical etching of their administrations, perhaps a ghost of personality. And wine. The cellar lay still and cobwebbed, bottles cluttered in abandoned order, layered in ancient dust, some purchased from a local vintner by Canon O'Dell twenty-something years past, unopened cases from the time of Father Toohey, who finished his blessed years in County Cork, supplies acquired by Father Michael O'Callahan on ecclesiastical impulse.

And so this treasure lingered, purchasing flavour with age, sleeping a sleep that brings a maturity of great value to the connoisseur. Unfortunately for him, the communion wine was intended for a greater destiny.

Unless, of course, it was stolen.

Fortunately, there's nothing like a small measure of chaos.

No one knew how old Canon Moriarty was. Even the gossipy housekeeper, Flora O'Toole, didn't know. Ask her and she would cluck, roll her beige eyeballs and say, 'Oh, somewhere between seventy and ninety.' Possibly even the bishop didn't know. How could he, living down there in Shrewsbury a million miles away. The canon's bicycle was an ancient Victorian structure with mudguards and a three-speed device that enabled him to pedal his craft up St Jerome's Brow, at the summit of which he would pause to look across to Spyglass Hill, the planetarium glinting in the sunshine. On rainy days the view was sombre but magnificent.

The canon would wipe his greying brow with a linen handkerchief large enough for a small breakfast table, taken from an ancient leather bag hanging on a strap that passed round his neck and under his left arm. In this bag was the 'Outdoor Collection'.

The first collection was taken at Sunday Mass after the canon gave his homily, usually based on the scripture readings. From the marble pulpit he would rumble and ramble great messages of fire and encouragement and we hadn't the faintest idea what he was talking about. Sully and I would try to occupy a bench as close as possible to the pulpit not to listen to the great orator but just to watch him, for he devoured little pills in rapid succession from atop the pulpit's balustrade, snorting decorously between each pill.

'I think they're for his asthma,' said my mother.

'No, Mary, they're for his gout,' replied Aunt Gertrude, who didn't even know what gout was.

There was always a great silence when he finished. We didn't know whether it was caused by awe or gratitude. But he never laughed. Father Francis laughed. Other priests laughed. The canon smiled, perhaps, but he never actually laughed. There was little mirth or joy in his otherwise quaint essays, never an explosion from the heart. Like those with overwhelming worldly credit or overwhelming worldly debt – wretched wealth or exhilarating destitution – it was hard for the canon to escape the shackles, the confines of mediocrity, the commonplace, the fair to middling; to rise above the middle ground. That is, until he gave thought to Potty Pete. Absent from his persona, said Uncle Bart, purveyor of all abstract thought, was a bloody good laugh.

After the last Mass he would be promptly served a lunch of Grimsby kippers, onions, bacon and fried egg, awash in cholesterol, by the imperious housekeeper, Mrs Flora O'Toole, drink two cups of strong tea and prepare for the Outdoor Collection.

When he was much younger he was six foot four, but he had shrunk to a mere six foot two: sparse bony frame, an ocean of pure white, wispy hair, trouser bottoms held tight by large black bicycle clips.

He consulted the notebook from the bag tied to his side and pedalled with ecclesiastical urgency to his first house. 'Good afternoon, Mrs Mulcahey,' touching his hat. 'Outdoor Collection.'

'The teapot is waiting for you, Canon.'

'No tea, thank you, Mrs Mulcahey. Just the collection.'

In three hours he drank seven cups of tea.

At three o'clock he would wobble back to St Joseph's next to the Academy of Hard Knocks, for the bike was willing but the shanks were weak, needing, without a doubt, a wee drop of the creature.

Life is short, said the poet (I think it was O'Bannion), the days are numbered (his bookkeeper), fifteen minutes is all the glory you get (Uncle Bart), so that one fine, blazing June day, Canon Moriarty parked his velocipede, took off his bike clips and said, 'There's got to be a better way than this!' He almost forgot, but not quite, that many Merseyside moons before he had whispered, 'Here I am, Lord!'

So the following Sunday he ventured out on a damp, dirty, dismal, murky June day for the very, very final Outdoor Collection, which was when he was eased off his bike by a large push from behind as he rested atop St Jerome's Brow, his bag was wrenched free and the 'Brow Thief' fled downhill with agile step through ancient moss-covered tombstones, clutching the very last, most honourable Outdoor Collection.

'It contained,' said Canon Moriarty to Inspector Callahan, 'two hundred and thirty-three pounds, fourteen shillings and sevenpence exactly.'

'Are you sure of the amount?' asked the inspector.

'It's in the book,' said the canon, 'which I keep in my pocket.'

'Do you also keep a record of souls saved in the

same book?' queried the inspector, late of the Bird in Hand.

'It depends on whether you're employing derision or irony,' chuntered the canon, sharp as a brick of Cheddar cheese.

'Dear me, now I'll have to tell it in the box,' simpered the inspector.

'If I let you in,' countered the canon, smiling a benign smile reserved for absurd crackpots wearing brass buttons.

Of all the triumvirates to be pulled together in one comprehensive whole, this was combination X. Who pulled those names from the hat? That night, the firewatchers were Dooley and myself and someone we had left far behind in our conscious being when we quit Hard Knocks six months ago for *Echo* and commerce, so that Thursday night at seven, when we met as scheduled in the commons room, Pops seemed diminutive in stature but just as comfortably assertive as in days of yore.

'Good evening, boys.' He slipped out a cigarette from a package of Players Weights, lit it from a silver lighter and, catching us in his gaze, said, 'Would you like one?'

Six months ago if we had been caught with a Woodbine behind the girls' lav he would have delivered six with his springy bamboo cane especially imported from Brazil. For such was justice at Hard Knocks. The Romans never had it so good.

Dooley took one, I didn't. Dooley was in heaven. Smoking fags with Pops Devereaux!

'Do you boys know how to work a stirrup pump?'

We shook our heads.

'Let's go out into the schoolyard.'

We picked up the pump and a galvanised bucket on the way.

A brass tap stuck out from the side of the gym and from this we filled the bucket with cold water. Pops said, 'Now all we do is place one fork of the pump, like this, in the bucket, take aim with the nozzle and pump like mad. Let's try it.'

So Jim Dooley aimed the nozzle while I pumped.

A slim jet of no great dimension shot about twenty yards at infrequent intervals, then stopped as I ran out of breath.

Dooley said, 'Are we to put out bloody fires with this?'

'Perhaps we just squirt it on the bombs?' I asked.

Pops smiled, scratched his balding but noble head. 'This piece of equipment was invented by an idiot. Don't quote me, boys. However, I have a telephone in the commons just in case a big one hits us. The stirrup pump is just to water the weeds, I think.'

'I've got a better water pistol at home,' said Jim Dooley.

Our sleeping quarters consisted of a fairly large room furnished with three coconut mats, pillows and blankets. Pops took off his shoes with a Pops Devereaux sigh, pulled up a chair and took out the *Echo* after he had put on the tea kettle.

'Do you mind, sir,' I asked, 'if we walk around the school grounds?'

'Oh, no, carry on. Just don't steal anything.'

Just before twilight enveloped the Academy of Hard Knocks, spreading its fingers into its frescoes and gables,

Dooley and I climbed over the outer railings and let ourselves down noiselessly into this most forbidden territory, for it was Sunday and the Academy slept.

We stood motionless, gripped by a feeling of awe and wonder, overwhelmed, for in an empty schoolyard ghosts and goose bumps lurked in the shadows.

'Let's go and steal something,' whispered Dooley. We did, but it was unexpected.

We sped on errant wing between the junior school and Pops Devereaux's office, into the stretch of the darkening back playground, our feet echoing softly to a splendid adventure. 'This way,' I breathed. Over the ancient brick wall capped with sandstone, tiptoeing down the grey alley between the priest's house and the church. A figure moved ahead of us, crouching, startled, then shambling away. 'Who's that?' asked Dooley, grasping my arm.

I didn't answer because I didn't know and I was scared out of my wits.

'Maybe it's a ghost.'

But we both knew the ghost was running away so we didn't – we just stood there breathing like fire engines. It was Dooley who moved first, I creeping along after him. 'He's left something on the ground.'

In the grass verge, next to a casement window level with the ground, was a cardboard box half full of large wine bottles left in disorder by the fleeing shadow. The rectory door banged. Light spilled out into the darkness for a brief moment. Footsteps fell on gravel going away towards the big iron gate.

'I think it's Father putting the cat out.'

'We can only take one each,' said Dooley. 'They're too heavy.'

'Which way?'

Bolder than two impoverished cat burglars we walked out through the big iron gate, down Switchcross Lane, through Poet's Alley. 'Let's take them to my place,' said Dooley. 'We have a shed and my ma won't know.'

'And I've got a good customer for these,' I grinned.

'Worth two bob,' said Sully.

'Two and six.'

Slipping like skinny wraiths through the Mersey gloom, we deposited our bonanza before slipping back to fight fires with Pops Devereaux who was still ploughing graciously through the *Liverpool Echo*.

'What is happening to this country?' asked my mother, handing Uncle Bart a cup of tea in one of her best Wexford china teacups.

'That was the largest Outdoor Collection ever,' said Bart. 'They say that Brinsley McCabe, the bookie, had a very fine day at Chester Races, had a drop of the creature in him and gave the canon one hundred and fifty pounds, more than he gave his wife, Moira, who is still presenting him with some good advice.'

'Generous to a fault,' said my mother. 'By the way, where on earth did you get that fine red wine?'

'On the black market. And I got it for only one and three, Mary.' Bart grinned at me.

'I'm going over to confession, Ma,' I said.

'I sometimes think that boy is going to be a priest,' I heard her say to Bart as I slipped down to the Dell to meet Sully.

'Let's drink to his success, Mary,' said Bart.

Confessional days always seemed to be sombre going in and quite illuminated coming out.

You could hear the silence in St Joseph's. The benches were old, smooth kneelers polished by an army of penitents' knees, creaking ancient, sinful history, warm and encompassing, so much like the bar at the Bird in Hand.

What can surpass a good honest vacuuming of the soul to Him who saved – and it doesn't cost you a penny?

'Potty' Pete Pendennis was before us and behind was Mrs Maggie Maguire, who kept nudging Sully who nudged me. Canon Moriarty prayed in the box, mused when concentration deserted him, thought of the Irish joke told him by Father Harrogate, refused to think about money – the great enemy.

'Father, forgive me for I have sinned,' said Potty Pete with what sounded like a simper crossed with a chuckle. 'I stole, Father.'

'Yes, my son, what did you steal?'

'Two hundred and thirty-three pounds, fourteen shillings and sevenpence.'

The silence outside the box travelled by spiritual measure inside the box. For roughly ten seconds.

'You what?'

There was no answer.

'Are you there?'

'Yes, Father.'

'Tell me,' sighed the canon, 'what did you do with the money?'

Sully and I slipped in to see Father Harrogate, because he seemed to smile at our sins, even though we saw but an elbow leaning and a hand covering the silhouette of a face.

'Father,' I said, 'I stole a bottle of wine.'

'Tsk tsk. You didn't drink it, did you?'

'No, Father, I sold it.'

'Sold it? For how much?'

'One and three.'

'Hmmn . . . You know you have to make reparation?'

'Yes, Father.'

'You know that means giving it back?'

'I gave some to charity.' He was chuckling. 'I gave threepence to Potty Pete and put sixpence in the poor box.'

'That leaves sixpence to go.'

'Yes, Father.'

'And you're thinking about that?'

'Oh, yes, Father.'

'Three Our Fathers and three Hail Marys. Ego te absolvo. In Nomine Patri, et Filii, et Spiritu Sancti, amen.'

Outside the sun shone brightly on Switchcross Lane.

Absurdly young, Father Francis Harrogate took over the Outdoor Collection on his motorbike, a sleek Triumph

Tiger, exploding with power, pouring petrol fumes and carbon monoxide, all of which were quite intoxicating to Potty Pete, who tended the flower gardens, first the hyacinths then the monoxide. Members of Our Lady's Guild say they saw him dancing in the flower beds. Purely hearsay, of course. Mrs Quigley pursed her wise, Irish mouth. 'Ah, the good Sisters of Our Lady of Charity brought the lad up well. Knocked some sense into him with a big stick they did, his origins being a great mystery.'

The canon was not amused.

'Can you not use a bicycle or your feet, Father Harrogate?'

'Ah, 'tis faster on the Triumph, Father, and the faster you go the faster increases the collection.'

'You're from Killarney, Father?'

'Every Irish part of me.'

'And you've this English name, Harrogate?'

'It's from the Normans, the ones who conquered the English before we did. I just may be related to the Conqueror.'

'Well, don't drive too fast. And watch Mrs O'Dell. She'll slip a drop of the creature into your tea.'

'Yes, Father.'

Mother Superior Constance Mooney mothered, without benefit of clergy, over five thousand children so they say, orphans, the great unwashed, living on the edge of the village within twenty minutes' walk from the beach.

The convent chapel of Our Lady of Charity, a humble

abutment to the main building, was splendidly utilitarian, quite un-Gothic.

Father Francis Harrogate, after his first appointment as assistant pastor to St Joseph's (and the Academy of Hard Knocks), spat gravel from the tyres of his Triumph Tiger as he ploughed into the minuscule parking lot each Sunday to say Mass, cassock billowing behind, smiling his Tipperary smile. Not one jot like Canon Moriarty who arrived in sedate fashion by car, or occasionally his beloved bicycle, saluted by the orphans, blessed by the sisters.

The sky was blue over the Mersey estuary one Sunday morning. There had been a raid by the Luftwaffe the night before, but the damage was minor: the Bird in Hand lost an outhouse, no ale was spilled, and Uncle Bart heaved a sigh of relief and blessed himself. So Canon Moriarty pedalled over, freewheeling with great dignity into the lot.

He heard the sisters' confessions after Mass, then allowed himself to be cajoled into the kitchen for tea and crumpets with Mother Superior Constance Mooney. Sunshine glinted through a window facing out towards the Irish Sea, spreading its benevolence on the dining table.

The canon looked forward to this part of his day, a time to relax, to clink his teacup in its saucer, perhaps sigh, smile benignly. It was possible for only one thing to disturb the even tenor of his day and that was if Mother Superior brought up the taboo subject of money. The canon hated the stuff. Much of his time as pastor of a parish was taken up with counting money, money they had and mostly money they didn't have.

'I don't count up spiritual values any more,' he would say sadly, 'I count up money.'

'Let me speak to you about money,' said Mother Superior.

The canon dropped his china cup into its china saucer.

An inaudible wail escaped his lips.

'It is hard to believe how gracious the good St Joseph is,' she said, leaning forward to capture his ear. 'Last Wednesday evening an anonymous donor pushed into the letter box a package of notes and coins. May the Lord be praised! It was almost the identical amount we needed to pay off the debts. Canon, you will never believe how much it was!'

'Yes, I will,' he said.

'You will?'

'It was two hundred and thirty-three pounds, fourteen shillings and sevenpence exactly.'

Mother Superior Constance Mooney gawped with uncharacteristic bewilderment at Canon Moriarty. 'How did you know that, Father?'

'St Joseph,' said the canon, blessing himself, 'St Joseph. Now I must be going.'

Mother and two of the sisters escorted him through the kitchen and into the playground, Mother Mooney still gazing with rapture at the canon. He clipped his trouser bottoms.

'Would there be anything else, sisters?' he asked.

'Well,' said Mother Mooney, 'he also left three cases of wine. The labels look quite old. Not much value. I wonder what I should do with them?'

*

On the crest of St Jerome's Brow the canon looked across the rolling, green plain to the planetarium on Spyglass Hill.

'I think,' he said to himself, 'I'll hand this job over to Father Harrogate.'

He freewheeled down the hill laughing to himself, or so he thought, but it was with the greatest gusto so that people on St Jerome's Brow, that quiet Sunday night, heard him and smiled, for all the world loves a bloody good laugh.

Chapter Thirteen

The Etruscan Vase

It was a vase of most creative design brought back from the Far East by Sergeant Major Augustus Reckitt early in the century. The vase vanished somewhere in the wake of the May Blitz of 1941 when the Reckitt family moved lock, stock and barrel, minus vase, to Quebec, Canada.

They also jettisoned most of the accidental paraphernalia picked up by a family in any class of society over a given period of that mortal enemy, time.

Wee Jimmy Reckitt even left behind his bike, his roller skates and a picture of Winston Churchill scowling.

The item they never, ever wanted to see again was the crater, for the bomb was of singular, large dimension meant for the Liver Building or Cammell Laird's shipyard, or maybe the Dirty Duck.

The Anderson air raid shelter housing the Reckitt family of two adults, three offspring and an ancient dog teetered mercifully on the brim of the crater, the family and the shelter unharmed and undamaged, a major miracle.

'Hey, Kipper,' said Whacker Doyle, 'let's go over to see the crater on Marmaduke Crescent. They say it's the biggest ever made.'

'So I hear. They say Jimmy Reckitt left his bike behind.'

'Oh, yeah, minus a wheel and a seat.'

'Never gave much away, that feller.'

'I wonder if he took his brain with him.'

Betsy Braddock, Whacker Doyle, Gobs Flanagan and I all cycled over to Marmaduke Crescent on Saturday morning when we were not taking the ferries to our jobs in Liverpool. The crater was enormous, the biggest we had ever seen, perfectly round as though deliberately created in that design, the shelter dug in, lopsided, to its circumference. All was quiet on the Crescent, except for the dog scratching away in the dirt down in the cavity.

'What's he after?' asked Betsy Braddock.

'Maybe the missing wheel.'

'I think it's an ancient Roman artefact.'

'Or an ancient Roman.'

'It's a vase,' said Betsy Braddock.

We all slithered down the slope of the crater to see what the ragged dog was pawing and pulling at, all of us except Betsy who stayed up top to direct operations.

'It's a vase,' said Whacker.

'I think there's a wheel sticking out here, too.'

'Jimmy Reckitt's not in there, is he?'

'Nah, he's in Quebec chasing French girls.'

'What about these boots?'

'Can one of you boys bring up the Roman vase?' asked Betsy.

'The queen has spoken,' said Gobs Flanagan.

There were stashes of bricks, ancient of design to us, stones heaped one on top of the other, multi-coloured seashells, a pungent aroma. Suspense seemed to hang in the abyss, a warm and then cold feeling, the sound of faraway battle, time, despair, laughter; a pit of something known, unaddressed.

I stood still, trying to capture obscure mysteries.

'Tom Kipper, are you going to bring up the vase?'

'OK, Betsy.'

The ancient dog had yelped his way to the top and vanished down Marmaduke Crescent.

'It's beautiful,' she declared, cleaning off soil sticking to its rim.

'It's made in Hong Kong.'

'I'm going to keep it.'

'No, you're not.'

'Why not, Tom Kipper?'

'Because it's mine.'

The vase was unbroken even after the bomb. It has a waist above the main, rotund body which expanded upwards to fluted leaves of alabaster for enclosing flowers. Two handles curved graciously out and then bent downwards to the waist like the arms of a graceful lady.

'It belongs to all of us, Tom Kipper.'

'Well, OK, Betsy.' I said this because the germ of an idea,

the inkling of creativity, a most mischievous abstraction, was forming in my impish, Irish mind.

We cycled home through the park, autumn leaves decorating the trees, carpeting the lawns and playing grounds. 'Hey, Bets, let's look at the pond, see how the ducks are doing. Do you want me to carry the vase?'

She looked archly at me. 'No, thanks, Tom Kipper.'

'Bets,' I ventured, after we were seated on the duck pond bench, 'do you remember the lessons we learned on Roman history at Knocks? And the fact that the Romans occupied Chester, just eighteen miles away, also various locations in North Wales?'

She nodded, clutching the vase. 'So?'

'Well, they must have travelled a great deal on Merseyside, maybe even to Chipton Downs, even to Marmaduke Crescent.'

'And?'

'Perhaps they left a vase there.'

'This vase, Tom Kipper, is made in Hong Kong.'

'Yes, I know, Bets, but remember that creative class all you girls took in pottery and you smeared plaster of Paris all over the classroom and Pops Devereaux got madder than a hatter?'

'Yes.'

'Well, if you worked creatively on this vase with my help we could turn it into an ancient artefact, spread the word and have fun.'

'Spread the word?'

'I have a buddy at the *Chipton Downs Post*. We could

take a picture of the Etruscan vase and he could drop it on the editor's desk.'

'Ridiculous!'

'It could work.'

'Tom Kipper, you're bloody wonky!'

'Hmmn . . . you wanna go home?'

'Wait till my Ma hears about this. She'll laugh her Irish head off!' said Betsy Braddock.

The following day, Monday morning, on the *Daffodil*, Betsy Braddock said, 'My ma did laugh her Irish head off. Thinks it's a fantastic idea, Tom Kipper.' She was grinning in a great, Irish fashion, for the wee people, from Limerick perhaps, had tickled her fancy. 'Come on over tonight,' she said.

When we had creatively finished the vase, it looked older than the steps of the Cackling Hen in Chester, but still retained its utter style and dignity. Mrs Braddock said, 'Have another mince pie, Thomas, me boy.'

Filbert Joshua was on duty at the *Chipton Downs Post* when I gave him a call from El Paso Corned Beef, telling him about the Etruscan vase from Marmaduke Crescent, but not about Hong Kong. 'I'll have a photo in a couple of days, Filb; will let you have a copy.'

'Smashing, Tom,' said Filbert Joshua, 'might make a good story for the *Post*. I'll ask the editor, Mr Kilpatrick. He's always ga-ga for a good story.' Thus spread the juicy news on errant wing.

On Friday a breathless voice said to me over the El Paso phone, 'Have you read the *Chipton Downs Post* this morning, Tom Kipper?' It was Betsy Braddock.

'Not yet.'

'Our vase is on the cover page.'

'The cover page?'

'Yes, with the picture!'

'Wow!'

Which was an exclamation uttered also by the renowned archaeologist Sheridan Twistleton, President of Cheshire Roman Artefacts, a man hungry for recognition in his field and arch-enemy of Filbus O'Leary, always hungry for cheeseburgers, and president of Liverpool's 'Roman Forum' of Merseyside. Swords drawn in the Coliseum of Liverpool Stadium they'd have sold a zillion tickets. Without lions. 'Miss Mahey,' shouted Twistleton to his secretary, 'we're going to Chipton Downs tomorrow.'

'It's your wife's birthday tomorrow, sir.'

'Damn.'

'Sir.'

'Yes, Miss Mahey.'

'Have you read today's *Liverpool Echo*?'

'Who has time, Miss Mahey, to read trashy newspapers when the Roman world is in jeopardy?'

'The same story as was in the *Chipton Downs Press* is in the *Echo*.'

'What! Now you tell me. That meddling fool, Professor Filbus O'Leary, will be drooling at the jowls. Tell my wife we'll be having lunch tomorrow in Chipton Downs, or maybe Liverpool.'

Filbert Joshua, honourable employee of the *Post* and capitalist to boot, had slipped out of the back door, taken the ferry to the Pool, lied his way to the editor's desk of the *Echo* and slipped the black and white photograph under Sean Sheehan's Gaelic nose. 'A Roman artefact,' he said, showing him also the *Chipton Downs Post* of yesterday.

Money changed hands. The presses ran wild.

Page two read:

Archaeologists and historians are racing with all speed to a crater in Chipton Downs formed by a large missile dropped by the Luftwaffe on Marmaduke Crescent. Ancient artefacts, such as the Etruscan vase pictured above, were discovered by young people excavating the area. Roman legionaries camped in various parts of Merseyside. The young people, it is rumoured, were assisted by a shaggy dog named Grip. Keep watching this page for an exciting and historical update.

Thus raced Professor Sheridan Twistleton from Chester to Chipton Downs in his Jaguar and Professor Filbus O'Leary from the Lake District in his shabby green Ford.

'Anything unusual happen to you over the weekend, Tom Kipper?' enquired Mr Crisp at El Paso offices, stacking papers for me to take to Customs.

'Not much, Mr Crisp,' said I. 'Saw a giant crater left by last week's raid.'

Mr Crisp adjusted his rimless spectacles. 'Saw an article in the *Echo* about that. A couple of history societies searching for a vase and can't find it. Say it may be worth a pound or two.'

'Oh?' My ears pointed skyward.

'Yes. It must be at least two thousand years old.'

'How much,' I said to Mr Crisp, taking the Customs papers from him, 'do you think it may be worth?'

'Who knows, Tom. Hard to say. Beauty is in the eye of the beholder. In this case, two tatty, totty professors can't even find it. Maybe five pounds, maybe five hundred or ten thousand.'

'Holy catfish!'

That night I said to my ma, 'Ma, is beauty in the eye of the beholder?'

She sliced the loaf on the board with a bread knife salvaged, it seemed, from the cutting edge of a revolutionary guillotine. Given a mask, she'd make a most splendid executioner.

'What are you talking about, Tom Kipper?'

'Ma, you're always asking me that question.'

'I ask it because, young man, that busy Kipper mind of yours is generally up to no good, cooking up something of a most radical nature.'

'Trust me, Ma.'

'Your father said that to me once. Look at him now.'

Pa was absorbed in non-locomotive energy, deep in the arms of Morpheus, creating ways of doing nothing. He snored gently, destroying the capitalist system.

'Did you miss him when he was in Italy, Ma?'

Her face softened. The guillotine became silent. 'Ah, yes. I did. Now, what was your question?'

'Well, if I owned something and I knew that it was worth, say, just a couple of bob, but someone wanted to buy it from me for a lot more but didn't know its real value, would it be OK?'

'OK to what?'

'Sell it for the overpriced amount.'

Mary Catherine Kipper pursed her lips and looked at me with those all-encompassing grey Connemara eyes. She was about to deliver judgement but she didn't, for racing through her humorous, mystical self was an Irish imp, one of the wee people who smiled at her from the Blarney Patch.

'Tom Kipper,' she said very gently, 'I trust you. Do what you think is best under the circumstances, but speak to St Joseph before you do.'

Aye, she was a saint.

In Betsy Braddock's parlour that night she told me about a man who said he was an agent or assistant to archaeologist Sheridan Twistleton who had knocked on their front door looking for information regarding an Etruscan vase. Her mother, Megan Maria, had answered the door, told the enquirer she would look into the matter and yes, it was OK to call back.

'They're not going to get my vase,' said Betsy. Her mother shrugged her shoulders.

'It's our vase, Betsy,' I bravely volunteered.

'That's nonsense, Tom Kipper.'

'OK, Bets. Your poor mother can just make do with that old washing machine.'

Two pairs of exquisite Braddock eyebrows lifted in grand unison.

'What are you talking about, Tom Kipper?'

'That's what my mother said. Listen. That vase's real value is about ten bob, if that. If there should ever be an auction for this creative object attended by professors of Roman, Greek, Byzantine or pure Scouse cultures who had other ideas of its value we could make quite a few pennies. I mean pounds.'

'You're crackers.'

'You said that last time, Bets.'

'Oh,' said Megan Maria Braddock, shaking her head, 'I can make do with the same leaky old tub.'

'Ma,' said Betsy, 'you're as bad as Kipper!'

'Chief,' said Foreman Mortimer Kilpatrick, 'they've erected a fence round the chasm.'

'What?'

'Over on Marmaduke Crescent.'

'A fence?'

'It's actually stakes, white stakes, about a foot apart stuck in the rim of the crater and hung with red ropes and a large sign reading 'Keep Out' by an archaeological company from Chester.'

Chief Engineer Pagan Shaughnessey of Chipton Downs scratched his head. 'You mean to say a fly-by-night outfit from Chester, that bloody Roman ruin, had the confounded audacity to trespass on Chipton Downs property and erect signs?'

'Yes, Chief, but that's not all.'

'Oh?'

'A similar organisation from the Pool has been sniffing around. Remember Filbus O'Leary?'

'That bloody Irish nutcracker!'

'I thought you were Irish, too, Chief.'

'There's Irish and there's Irish, Mr Kilpatrick!'

'Well, he's been seen and heard looking for an Etruscan vase found in a bomb crater by a dog and some teenagers.'

'Holy Moley! Get the lorry out, Mr Kilpatrick. We're going for a ride.'

Finder's Keepers, a pub of inestimable value, flowing with the Mersey tide of pilgrims at the Pier Head, enjoyed a mixed clientele, for seafarers, passengers, cops, villains, lovers, politicians, pariahs, outlaws, attorneys and even plumbers passed with great thirst through this noble establishment, emerging poorer but refreshed.

At the rear of the building is a room dedicated to clients who wish to meet for all manner of purposes, even those below drinking age, such as Tom Kipper.

'Uncle Bart,' I said, 'you will have to dress up a little.'

'Aye.'

'And change your accent.'

'Trust me.'

'Ma said I can't use that expression.'

'She'll never know.'

By means many and devious and honest, there assembled in that historic room and pub Professors Filbus O'Leary of

Liverpool, Sheridan Twistleton of Chester and Bartholomew Devereaux-Pepys of Farleigh-Wallop. Also present were Betsy Braddock, her mother Megan Maria and myself, Tom Kipper.

All the assembled held an alcoholic beverage in contoured glasses except for we tatty kids with lemonade.

'Cheers,' said Professor Bart Devereaux-Pepys, his bowler at an angle.

'You're from Farleigh-Wallop, Professor?'

'Always,' said Bart, slurping half a pint.

'Is that in the Cotswolds?' asked Professor Twistleton from Chester.

'Always has been,' said Professor Bart. 'Not far from Great Snoring.'

'I did not know,' enunciated Professor O'Leary of Liverpool, 'there existed a Roman History Archaeological Unit in the Cotswolds, Professor.'

'It's an agency,' said Bart, not knowing what he was talking about and not actually caring after two Guinnesses from Finder's Keepers.

'An agency?'

'Yes, for Bath.'

'Bath?' Professors O'Leary and Twistleton exchanged glances for, although enemies in mortal Roman combat, they wanted no foreigners from Bath excavating their precious Roman viaducts.

'And now to business,' I said, setting down my lemonade glass firmly on the oak table. 'Miss Braddock, may we have the exhibit.'

Betsy set the cardboard box on the table, extracting from it the Etruscan vase which she unwrapped.

'Magnificent,' breathed Professor Twistleton.

'Glorious,' gasped Professor O'Leary.

'Superb,' said Professor Bart. 'Is there any more Guinness?'

'Please do not handle the exhibit too roughly, gentlemen,' I said.

It passed from hand to hand.

'It is identical to one discovered in a shaft of the Roman walls in Chester over a hundred years ago. Must be of the Byzantine period.'

'No. No. It is Greek in origin,' said Professor Twistleton to Professor O'Leary.

'Looks archaic,' said Professor Bart. Everybody looked at him, including myself. Megan Maria Braddock, down two gin and tonics, started to laugh.

'Miss Braddock,' I said, indicating Betsy with a nod of my Kipper head, 'is the proud owner of this artefact and wished to retain it for her future grandchildren. However, she heard the call of sacrifice. Right, Bets?' Betsy nodded her head gravely. 'Now, gentlemen, who will start the bidding at ten thousand pounds?'

'Two pounds,' said O'Leary.

'Three,' said Twistleton.

'Ten,' said Professor Bartholomew Devereaux-Pepys.

'Eleven,' from O'Leary.

'Twelve,' from Twistleton.

'Twenty,' from Professor Bart, who was broke.

The three of them looked at each other, arose as one man and moved, still standing, to a corner table.

'Gentlemen,' said Twistleton, 'this is insane; this precious object has no monetary value.'

'None at all. It's an object of history,' muttered O'Leary.

'I'll give thirty pounds for it,' said Bart.

'You people from Bath are utter cads,' said Twistleton.

'Capitalist,' breathed O'Leary.

Bart said, 'Fifty is my maximum,' stepping to the bar for more Guinness.

Twistleton wiped his brow. 'Very well.'

'Ditto,' said O'Leary. They moved back as one man to where we were sitting.

'Fifty-one,' said Twistleton.

'Fifty-two,' said O'Leary.

'This,' ground out Twistleton, 'is my final offer. Sixty.' He mopped his brow.

O'Leary hesitated. Bart nodded to me without benefit of audience.

I banged the lemonade glass. 'Taken,' I said, adding, as Bart had advised, 'This sale is now over, gentlemen. No degree of validity is guaranteed by the owner or the sales department.'

Professor Twistleton's eyes glowed as he counted out sixty crinkly pound notes. I think he was crying. O'Leary was gnashing teeth, glaring at Twistleton, at me, at the vase.

'Give Bart ten,' I whispered to Betsy Braddock.

'We're going home now,' said Betsy, taking her mother's arm and slipping fifty pounds into her handbag. 'See you later, Mr Kipper.' She smiled. 'I think we'll take a taxi.'

Gulls wheeled overhead crying at man's inhumanity in eating all his lunch.

'Mr Kilpatrick,' asked Chief Engineer Pagan Shaughnassey, 'is the bulldozer well oiled and conditioned?'

'Aye, Chief.'

'Take it down to Marmaduke Crescent with an assistant, maybe two, and wait for me.'

'Aye, aye, Chief.'

His bloodshot eyes glistened, shone. 'Look at that, Professor O'Leary, magnificent perfection. Let us transport ourselves to the artist.' He lifted up the vase to the light. 'Think of the ability to mould with such imagination, such clarity of vision. No crude vigour here. Perhaps he considered the divine form of his Etruscan loved one.'

'Bottoms up,' said Professor Bart.

'I'm catching a ferry back to Liverpool,' said the aggravated, perturbed, disconsolate, distressed, infinitely peeved Professor Filbus O'Leary.

'Stay one more moment,' requested Professor Sheridan Twistleton of Chester. 'Enjoy another review of our glorious possession and, perhaps, an ale?'

'Good idea, Professor,' said Bart of Farleigh-Wallop.

O'Leary scowled. 'Just one,' he murmured.

Glasses refurbished they lifted them in salutation, which was when, in a movement of completely accidental occurrence, O'Leary's foot trod on that of Twistleton at the rail of the bar. Twistleton in a reflex action moved his body in the direction of the River Mersey, his right elbow twisting out of its normal orbit to gently strike an ancient vase standing on the bar. It teetered on the edge. Twistleton grabbed and missed. Two thousand years of history took a final flight.

The barman, Seamus Doyle, said, 'Tsk tsk, gentlemen,' and moved with professional speed with his pan and brush.

'Don't touch it,' screamed Twistleton, 'that vase is two thousand years old and priceless!'

But Seamus Doyle had already picked up the base, the pedestal, which he was examining with some obvious curiosity.

'It sez here,' said he, 'Made in Hong Kong.'

'Tell me again,' said Ma, absorbing all data for the benefit of the Mince Pie Gang of Aunts Madge and Florence, Clara Garrity, Zelda Sweeney and Maureen Mulvaney, meeting that evening at Mary Lane, where her heart is.

She was talking to Bart, who was lavish with detail.

'There's a Guinness or two in the cupboard, Bart.'

'Aye, Mary, one for me and one for Tom Kipper.'

'He's too young to imbibe, Bart!'

'A wee drop, Mary.'

She nodded reluctant assent. 'Just that.'

'Professor O'Leary,' said Bart, 'took the ferry back to Liverpool grinning like a Cheshire moggy and Professor Twistleton, wishing to salvage an iota of his prestige, journeyed back to Marmaduke Crescent to discover Chief

Inspector Pagan Shaughnassey bulldozing the entire area, even burying the fence that was left of number eleven into the crater.'

'And,' said Ma to Uncle Bart, 'Tom Kipper had a hand in all of these shenanigans?'

'Aye,' said Bart, 'he's one of those rare human beings who realise that beauty is in the eye of the beholder.'

'Hmmn. I must ask,' said Ma, 'about the beauty in the eye of Mrs Braddock's new washing machine!'

Chapter Fourteen

The Flying Spoon

The Spotted Dog down on Hackins Hey, nudging elbows with Dale Street in central Liverpool, was almost hidden from sight, for it had steps leading down from Hackins which were a legacy from its former years as a gentlemen's club. Its handsome interior entertained articled clerks by day and scurrilous Scousers at eventide as shadows fell mysteriously and quite quickly behind the town hall and the historic Liver Building.

In daylight hours conversation was a boring symphony of legalese and trite innuendo, while at night it became almost dangerous, depending upon whether you opted for Liverpool Reds or Everton Blues.

Good advice would be to always speak Scouse, never in a posh, clipped accent from that 'across the water' place, Chipton Downs. Birkenheadese was tolerated, but speak Chipton and you were deader than last years' wet *Echo*. The pub was half-timbered and red brick on the outside but steeped with haunting mystery through its creaky timbers and ghostly staircase leading to rooms as aged as the peeling Victorian wallpaper, musty, silent, keeping their grungy secrets. Nobody knew anybody else who had walked up that staircase.

So far the Luftwaffe had failed to burn it down. It also had a football team which played in the Liverpool City Centre League with forty-four other pubs, having a weekly Saturday morning playing schedule, the greatest achievement of the entire season being to win the Flying Spoon Cup. Evening Scouser inhabitants of the Spotted Dog gloried in that cup. It had last been won by them shortly after World War One, black and white snapshots of eleven men with skinny legs and funny boots hanging behind the bar, but now, in this 1941/42 season, they were to meet the Goat and Compass pub from Paradise Street in the glorious final.

'We'll beat the bloody tar out of them!' declared the captain, Cedric Maloney of the Spotted Dog. 'The cup will be rightly ours!' You could hear the cheers in the town hall.

They lost two goals to one.

'What's all that noise, Hawkins?' queried Lord Mayor Fitzgerald-Pilkington.

'I think they're murdering another inhabitant of the Spotted Dog, sir.'

'Oh. yes. The Dog. Hmmn . . . Who?'

'I think it's the captain of the football team.'

'Hmmn . . . ?'

'They lost to the Goat and Compass in the final of the Flying Spoon Cup.'

'How sad. Is there any more tea, Hawkins?'

At the Goat and Compass, inhabitants of that Paradise Street palace were gargling their evening quota of Walkers ale in celebration of a year's ownership of the Flying Spoon Cup and weeping into the bargain, for the cup had disappeared.

'It was here,' said Bannister O'Brian, 'on this glass shelf on Saturday from noon until nine and then it vanished.'

'Stolen?'

'Of course it was stolen. But not for money.'

'Nazi agents?'

'Just the same. Maybe worse. Spotted Dogs!'

'But they lost.'

'They think they won.'

'But that's grand larceny. Have you proof?'

'No,' said Bannister O'Brian, 'but we'll get it. We shall have our revenge!'

Betsy Braddock's elder brother, Leonard, was an habitué of the Goat and Compass, even though he lived 'over the water', for his lunch breaks had taken him from time to time into its panelled interior to quaff a quart of Tetley's with its varied and colourful clientele, and so, inspired by other number-crunchers, he visited in the eventide and became a staunch member of the football team, even promulgating after two ales that he was a close confidant of Dixie Dean.

'Did you tie his shoelaces?' sneered Jackie Collagan, the pub's conscience.

It was Betsy Braddock who told us about the vanished Flying Spoon Cup in the youth hostelry adjacent to Hard Knocks Academy.

'How could such a smashing trophy just disappear?' asked Sully.

'My brother Lenny is very distraught about it,' said Betsy. 'He talks about nothing else.'

'Sherlock Holmes could get it back.'

'Well, he and Watson have gone to the Big Copper in the sky.'

'Perhaps we could pray to Sherlock.'

'Sherlock is not a saint, silly! Maybe *we* could get it back.'

'We?'

'We three,' said Betsy. 'According to Lenny, the captain of the Spotted Dog stole it.'

'What? The cad!'

'On the Saturday that it vanished they were in enemy territory – the Goat and Compass – which was packed with football fans in great clouds of tobacco smoke and they must have just reached over and taken it off the shelf.'

'Then let us,' I, Tom Kipper, said, 'become Humphrey Bogart Private Eyes and move into enemy territory too. We'll call ourselves the Flying Spooners!'

'Smashing,' said Betsy.

Thus was hatched a plot, more dashing than the defeat of the Armada, more splendid than the Conqueror's 1066 and all that, of greater effervescence than a Churchill Havana, more elusive than Maid Marian giving the big eye to Robin, more stumbling than Guy Fawkes.

'I shall wear one of my ma's Victorian dresses,' said Betsy.

'You won't be involved in this, Bets.'

'Why not?'

'You're a girl.'

'There are women detectives, you know.'

'Only in books, Bets.'

'Don't call me Bets.'

The mid-Victorian dress borrowed surreptitiously by Betsy Braddock from her mother's expansive if ancient wardrobe had seen better days, but eloquent clothing for women was in very short supply so that whatever could be salvaged from mothballs was eagerly appropriated. The dress reached almost to her feet, edged with intricate frills, as were the sleeves touching her wrists and the high collar. All girls reaching beyond their teens liked to wear their mother's shoes, and Betsy shod herself in a polished black sheen with enamelled buckles. Perfumes, scents from other years clung faintly but faithfully to the dress. The hat was a massive creation of layers, bows, folds and sweeps, adorned with imitation fruits, blossoms, and feathers which covered the upper head and sides with all-consuming ownership. To complete the ensemble was a short jacket in muted but glorious colours and a handbag of beige with a large silver clasp which closed on love letters not to be read by children.

'Holy smoke – you look like Lorna Doone!' said Sully.

*

Cleaning lady Mrs Corrina (Corry) McLaverty said to cleaning lady Marsha Cogarty, 'We're doin' the Spotted Dog tonight, luv.'

'I think it's bloody well 'aunted,' responded Mrs Cogarty.

'Then let's get in there and out just as soon as he shouts "Time, gentlemen, please", although I've never seen a gent in that place.'

'There used ter be back in the old days, they say.'

'Really? There won't be any now. They lost the final in the Flying Spoon, you know.'

'Crikey!'

Late afternoon and evening stole in, rolling a carpet of light fog up Water Street and around the town hall, and crept stealthily along Hackins Hey, lingering for reasons unknown around the Spotted Dog. Two men and one woman loitered on the corner of Hackins Hey and Water Street, all three shorter than average in stature, all three with high button collars, the men wearing trilby hats pulled quite low over their foreheads and the woman wearing an outsize bonnet festooned with various plastic fruits and curious paraphernalia from the Victorian era.

One of the men hissed through his oversize raincoat at the woman, 'Go away, Bets!' but she moved not one iota.

The three of them moved in concert through the main door into the most accommodating bar. Players Weight tobacco smoke thicker than a Tory lament festooned the Scouse occupants.

'Good evening, gentlemen,' said the large barman, 'what is your pleasure?'

'Two pints,' said Sully from the depth of his shaggy mac.

'Smashin' ale,' said a skinny Scouse nearby, spitting in the sawdust which wasn't there.

'Two pints, gentlemen,' said the barman, Clancy Rafferty, looking in the direction of Betsy Braddock. 'The lady will have to move into the Ladies' Lounge, I'm afraid.' He pointed into the blue smoke.

'Do you have a compass?' queried Sully.

Clancy said, 'That will be two shillings. Please ask the lady to move.'

Betsy whispered, 'See you later, Tom,' and slipped through the smoke.

Sully gave the barman two shillings in sixpences. 'Who won the cup?' he asked.

All heads turned to Sully's shaggy silhouette.

'Don't ask questions like that,' said Clancy, 'or you'll lose your head!'

'OK,' said Sully. 'Any good air raids lately?'

Sully was looking for trouble.

Penelope (Penny) Maloney said to Betsy Braddock, 'Do you know at the end of the war they're going to do away with trams?'

'Will we get bicycles?' asked Betsy to keep a correspondence flow.

'Buses,' said Penny. 'Can you imagine, we shall never again hear tramcars grinding up the hill from the Pier Head or see sparks flying from the overhead cables or passengers falling off the tram steps into Dale Street? It will be a piece of history gone.'

'Glory be!' said Betsy.

'Oh, you poor dear, you must be tired at your age standing up; come and sit over here. And you've got nothing to drink. Would you like a glass of white wine? I think it's from Australia or New Zealand. Not the best, but there's a war on.

'I'm Penelope Maloney,' she continued when she came back from the bar, extending a hand. 'Just call me Penny.'

'Braddock,' said Betsy Braddock, wondering why she was telling the truth. 'Call me Betsy.'

'Here's looking at you, Betsy,' said Penelope Maloney, extending her glass. They sipped and were quiet for a moment.

'You know, I shouldn't be calling you Betsy, I should be calling you Mrs Braddock. How many children do you have?'

'About eight, I think.'

They laughed with the greatest mirth together, for there was an instant collection of mysterious forces that drew them into binding harmony within the thinnest stretch of time, guardian angels tying the knots.

'How old are you? Wait, I should never ask that question. However, how old are you?'

They laughed again.

'Eighty,' said Betsy.

'Impossible,' said Penelope Maloney, 'although I can't see your face properly.'

'The doctor said I've got to keep warm.'

They sipped West Coast Australian wine.

'Did you hear the story,' asked Penny, 'about the old lady who put strychnine in her husband's tea and poisoned him to death and showed no remorse? Well, when she got before his honour, he said, "Mrs O'Flaherty, you poisoned your husband to death and you showed no remorse?" "Oh, yes, I did, your honour." "Oh, Mrs O'Flaherty, and when was that?" "Well, your honour, it was when he asked for a second cup!"'

Their laughter brought the barman over.

'Who's the lady, luv?'

'It's Mrs Braddock from Birkenhead. She's eighty and got eight kids. More than we have. Betsy, this is my husband Cedric Maloney. He's the captain of the football club.'

'Who won the cup, young man?' asked Betsy from her Victorian armour.

'Don't ask that question, Betsy,' said Penny.

Cedric Maloney walked away, stamping his boots as he went.

'I hear the cup disappeared.'

'Oh, yes. The Goat and Compass won it but it disappeared the same day they brought it back to Paradise Street in triumph.'

'Disappeared?' Betsy was all ears. She gave a ten shilling note to Penny for more drinks.

Penny was beginning to swim in her own sardonic sense of humour with the aid of the nectar of the gods. 'Oh, the damn thing is just behind the bar, here. They think they own it, should keep it, it's theirs. You know the way men are, they're all bloody barmy!'

'Behind the bar?'

'Yes, with all the corkscrews. Back in a moment, Mrs Braddock, I must visit the Ladies.'

She tottered off towards a distant door in the south-east corner and in the same instant Betsy realised the lounge was almost empty, the few occupants in comfortable corners solving Liverpool's problems, discussing the price of a good flask of the creature and enquiring how comfortable was your air raid shelter. The eighty-year-old lady moved on feet of sixteen to the rear of the clunky mahogany bar under which she dipped to surface with the Flying Spoon Cup. Very quickly it disappeared under her voluminous Victorian dress and she trod wearily in hunched eighty-year-old fashion to the door leading into the men's bar.

'I've got it,' she whispered to them as she passed by me and Sully. 'See you outside.'

Startled, we dropped our warm pints as Clancy Rafferty shouted, 'Time, gentlemen, please.'

The grey mist was beginning to swirl on Hackins Hey.

'Where is she?' asked Sully. We had searched each corner and embrace of the street without success. 'Silly twit has got herself lost. Perhaps she's in the town hall.'

Betsy was embracing the Flying Spoon Cup under her dress and trying to prevent her hat from falling over her eyes just as the cleaning brigade of Corry McLaverty and Marsha Cogarty trod briskly through the doorway with mop and pail and bandannas on their heads and temper

224

tantrums tied in a neat bundle. The haven Betsy hurried to was the Gents, large, unoccupied, skylights blowing cold Mersey air from the Irish Sea. She rearranged her dress and hat and the Cup, trod wearily back into the corridor, bumped into a pail and mop, placed the Cup in the pail, shouldered the mop, opened the door into Hackins Hey and fell into the loving embrace of Sully and me, Tom Kipper.

'Where the heck you been?' ground out Sully

'Where's me bloody bucket and mop!' shouted Corry McLaverty.

But the triumvirate moved ghost-like at extraordinary speed down Water Street in the direction of the grey-green River Mersey, churning on its banks in impatience at the tides.

'Bets, you're fantastic!' I said.

'Don't call me Bets, Tom Kipper.'

The pub was silent. The Victorian wallpaper slept. Inanimate objects just stood or lay there in the Ladies' Lounge like bric-a-brac in the war zone after an air raid, deadly in their non-committal absence of activity, seeming to be objective personalities but devoid of movement like my dad, Joseph Prendergast Kipper, sunk deep in his voluminous armchair with his buddies Marx and Engels, who were deader than a week-old Manx kipper.

Penelope Maloney sipped her Chardonnay, still looking with great intent at her husband, Cedric, who had his feet upon the highly sheened mahogany table.

'Soccer,' she said to him, 'Cedric, is not the be-all and end-all of life, is it?'

An absence of response made her believe he was thinking it over.

'Is it?' she repeated.

'The war is moving to a conclusion,' he said.

'Utter nonsense, complete and utter nonsense,' said Penelope. 'Answer my question, Cedric.'

Cedric sipped his porter.

Gangs of Scousers at 'Time, gentlemen, please' had quit for Bootle and Everton and the streets, melting like Scouse shadows. All was quiet on the Hackins Hey front. 'The Flying Spoon Cup is really ours, luv. Look at that picture behind the bar. In the middle is me uncle.'

'They say he drank too much.'

'War nerves. He fought on the Somme. Transferred to Paris. Chased a lot of French girls, you know.'

'You Maloneys do a lot of that. Anyway, what's all this got to do with the Cup? You lost. The Goat and Compass won. Give it back.'

He slurped porter. 'I can't.'

'Can't what?'

'Give it back.'

'Why not?'

'It vanished.'

'It's behind the bar, darling.'

'No, it isn't. Take a look.'

She slipped wraith-like behind the bar, eyes widening to orbs as she scrutinised the empty shelves. 'What happened, Cedric?'

'Last night when you were floating on a ocean of

Chardonnay like a ferry boat in distress, the Flying Spoon Cup vanished into thin air.'

'Goat and Compass?'

'No. They're honest people in that pub, my darling.'

'Do you understand the word, Cedric?'

'What word?'

'Honest.'

'Penelope, you're putting the screws in me tonight. I'm an honest chap. Finish your glass. Have another. Sing, or something.'

'You owe them an apology.'

'I was waiting on that.' He raised his glass to heaven.

'Why me, Lord?'

Hackins Hey slept . . .

Over on Paradise Street they brooded.

The Goat and Compass was unusually quiet even though the evening clientele were all present and correct, wearing cloth caps and tweedy jackets, but the silence was ominous, trembling underfoot and in the stained timbers, the tremor before the earthquake.

'We should burn the bloody place down,' said Padraic Costello in a loud, grating baritone.

He was referring to the Spotted Dog, for all those present knew they possessed illegally the Flying Spoon Cup in sinister embrace, probably drinking from it over there at Hackins Hey.

'While you're doing that, we'll take care of the women over there!' mouthed Mrs Darcy Flanagan.

The volcano was primed. The rumbles were increasing in volume. And than Cedric Maloney of the Spotted Dog walked in with his wife, Penelope, hanging on to his arm.

This was the arch-enemy, the vicious, diabolical, abhorrent, monstrous, heinous, barbarous, venomous, sinful captain of the Dog, who had appropriated with malice aforethought the Flying Spoon Cup, and he had walked as bold as brass into the enemy camp.

Penelope trembled as hostile, female eyes tore her to shreds, tatters, food for Grip, the dog.

The assembled company were so aghast that silence reigned for a historic moment, which is when Cedric Maloney said, 'Ladies and gentlemen of the Goat and Compass, I have come to apologise!' The floor creaked. No one spoke.

'I have come to apologise for taking the Flying Spoon Cup without due cause. The cup rightly belongs here at the Compass, who won it handsomely. It is with great regret that I recognise the terrible error I made!'

Penelope squeezed his arm.

'But where's the bloody Cup?' shouted Darcy Flanagan.

A thousand eyes, all hostile, bored into Cedric Maloney. How could he tell them it had disappeared? How?

At that moment the doors crashed open to admit the Flying Spooners: Betsy Braddock, Sully and myself, Tom Kipper.

'Here it is!' shouted Betsy, holding the silver trophy aloft, and the massive roar of applause shook ye ancient timbers of the Goat and Compass, reverberating through Paradise, Victoria, Lord and North John Streets, so that Lord Mayor Fitzgerald-Pilkington enquired in the town hall, 'What's going on down there, Hawkins; is another resident of the Spotted Dog being guillotined?'

'No, sir, something quite infinitely more gruesome. I think they're drowning an enemy agent in a very large vat of scouse.'

'Is our brave constabulary aware?'

'I believe they are at their posts in the Goat and Compass checking up on the matter, sir.'

'Hmmn . . . Is there any tea, Hawkins?'

It was quite a historic moment when Cedric Maloney and his blushing wife, Penelope, were hoisted up on to the main bar of the Goat and Compass and toasted by a grateful enemy.

In the quiet that ensued, Penelope took Betsy Braddock into her arms and said, 'Your grandmama was wonderful. She was shopping in the city and dropped in to the Spotted Dog for a drop of light refreshment. Eighty years of age, she said – magnificent. We never stopped laughing. She had to leave suddenly as the sun was going down. You know, she was sweet. She should never have been in that area at her age, but she had a kind, friendly disposition you don't get much of these days. Couldn't see her face properly in that stupid, dingy pub, but she was a lady.'

She stopped talking for a moment; not too long, for Penelope Maloney was a talker: create then vocalise in the same instant.

'You know,' she said, looking at Betsy Braddock, 'somehow or other she reminds me of you.'

Betsy Braddock just smiled.

Irish imps grinned.

And Tom Kipper, that's me, wondered . . .

Chapter Fifteen

'Peaches' O'Grady

'Have you ever been taught about William the Conqueror, now?'

Sully and Betsy and I looked and smiled at one another.

'But of course, Dad.'

'Well, let me tell you about the La Salles, a history that is either hidden or obscure.'

Dad was never like this. He was the one who was either hidden or obscure. All eyes were glued on him. 'Is there any tea, Maria?' he asked Ma, who was ironing a pair of his tatty underpants. She looked puzzled. Probably as puzzled as the day he proposed before going to Italy to win World War One.

'A fine people were the La Salles, from Le Havre in Normandy. Historians say they were vintners and absorbed far too much of their own produce. But who can trust historians?'

He sipped his tea. 'When William the Conqueror decided to invade England in 1066 he called upon all Norman families of noble heritage to join him. If they didn't he cut off either their plumbing – which is pretty bad in France – or their tonsils. No anaesthetic. William didn't mess around.'

I whispered to Ma, 'Hey, Ma, what's going on?'

'So Pierre the Elder, as they called him, was sent to represent the La Salle family. He put the cork back in the bottle and sharpened his sword. His ma, Consideratum La Salle, gave him a good breakfast of kippers and porridge before he boarded the exquisite vessel, *Davignon*, for the voyage from Calais to Dover. All the ships were magnificent in their full sail, and the men, the gallant Norman seamen, the fine Norman sailors, full of Chardonnay and Stella Artois, their mistresses waving to them from the quayside. Maidens of the same historic outlook were waiting for them at Dover.

' "Hey, we got it made here," said Pierre La Salle.'

'What did he mean by that, Dad?'

'Well, he meant that there were easy moorings for the ships. Anyway, the captain, Rougasch, chided him: "Don't you have a fiancée in Paris, Pierre?"

' "Let's hope she doesn't have opera glasses," said a vagrant deckhand, who was given forty lashes, which was written in history, although it is not recorded in discretionary manuals. Not far away, north-west, lay the peaceful land of Ireland, which has not much to do with 1066 and all that.

'The invasion wasn't a piece of cake. However, the

wretched enemy, men full of Scottish ale, didn't stand a chance against the Conqueror.

'King Harold historically caught a Norman arrow in his eye on a low ridge north of Hastings, fired by Pierre La Salle who won a medal and an assortment of ale in the Men's Club.

'William had a good old time dividing up the kingdom. Pierre La Salle was granted Chester and as far as he could reach. It was a good estate. He was knighted.

'In Chester he walked the Roman walls and said, "Hey, you Norman chaps, we can do better than this!" However, in Chester were a plethora of fish and chip shops.'

Betsy and Sully and I said in unison, 'But there were no fish and chip shops; this was 1066!'

Dad adjusted his wire-rimmed glasses, eyebrows bristling like English ivy crawling over the hedge. 'How do you think that England managed in that historic period without fish and chips?'

His argument went over our heads but into our hearts.

'Now, let me tell you, after the Conqueror came six Henrys, six Edwards, a couple of Richards, the Magna Carta, the Battle of Agincourt, the Wars of the Roses, the Reformation, a few Georges and Marys. Not to mention pubs. Pierre La Salle went to his maker, leaving in his wake about ten kids.'

'Kids?'

'I mean children.'

'Carry on, Dad.'

'The La Salles were labelled by the monarchs as Keepers

of the Realm throughout the ages until the Irish started giving them a pain in the . . .'

'Gluteus maximus?'

'Who told you that?'

'You did, Mr Kipper.'

'As I was saying, the king sent a La Salle, Maximus Ensuras, to Ireland to quell a rebellion about the price of ale. The La Salles at the time, by royal prerogative, were known as Keepers for they were the keepers of law and order, very aristocratic chaps.'

'And they went to Ireland, Pa?'

'Straight to Dublin, to keep order.'

'Did they settle in with the Gaelic peasantry?'

'Settle in? The first thing Maximus Ensuras La Salle did was look for an Irish pub in order to get a legitimate feel for the land he was "keeping", to ensure he had the peasantry under control.'

'So there were pubs, Mr Kipper?'

'Aye, lassie. Not the pubs we see now, but real pubs, where the beer was free and Irish maidens danced till dawn.'

By this time Ma was scorching his drawers with the hot iron. 'So,' she said, just to be part of the bedlam, 'what happened to the La Salles?'

Smoke drifted up from Dad's underwear.

'Maximus Ensuras became beloved of the Dublin populace. Every night he shouted "Free beer" at the O'Kelly tavern, sending the bill to the king, until he eventually absorbed the loving kindness of the Gaelic spirit and became known not as "Keeper" but, as fluently as the peasantry could manage with all that free ale, as "Kipper".'

It was a blinding revelation. It spread through my being. Dad was an O'Kipper. Dad was really Irish. Ma didn't realise that. Only me and the dancing Gaelic spirits.

'Dad,' I shouted, 'you're Irish!'

'Aye, Tom, me boy,' said he, 'Henry VIII wouldn't believe me. Perhaps not your own mother. But I'm a broth of an Irish boy. I am an O'Kipper!'

His drawers went up in Irish flames. Spirits danced across the Irish Sea . . .

Mrs 'Peaches' O'Grady, stalwart member of the Mince Pie Gang, who had called in for a cuppa, was the one who laughed the loudest at Dad, exuberantly clapping her hands in approval of his most definitive history of the ancient O'Kipper tribe. I suppose, really, it was only later that she told me why.

A week passed.

Meanwhile the history decided upon by impervious mankind trundled on across Europe in its Hun boots. Methods of bringing the world to perfection by human desire and efficiency washed wretched shores, except on Merseyside where a Scouse spirit sang mostly off key in the Bird in Hand, the Dirty Duck, Greave Dunning, Flanagans Apple and the Speckled Hen, and Uncle Bart ruled like a noble knight of great heritage.

'Give me another stout, Charlie,' he said.

'Have you got the money, Bart?'

'No. But you have.'

*

His sister, Mary Catherine Kipper, said, 'Whatever happened to Mrs O'Grady?' next time the Mince Pie Gang were assembled.

'She couldn't have been affected by the bombing last night, even though one end of the Commons was destroyed, because Gloria Parham told me at church it was not the end where Peaches lives,' said Zilda Sweeney all in one breath.

'Aye, but you can never trust that Gloria Parham,' said Clara Garrity. 'Now, I've managed to acquire a bottle of port.' She slapped it in the table centre where it glowed, gleaming Spanish cheer from Madrid.

The gang looked pleased. All members were primed with a slice of jolly gossip, waiting their turn to take centre stage, bask in five minutes of glory, sip aromatic sherry, nod the Gaelic head with worldly knowledge, purse the lips, sniff appropriately perhaps.

'It was a bad raid last night. Two ships were sunk at Garrison dockside.'

'Tilbury Avenue was hit,' said Francine O'Toole.

'Where's Peaches?' asked Ma.

Nobody knew.

'Tom Kipper,' said Ma, 'why don't you and Betsy go over to the Commons to see if she's all right.'

Betsy said, 'OK, Mrs Kipper,' before I could answer. Girls are so pushy.

The ceiling had been shattered to tatters by the blast, the roof stripped of its Welsh slate, so that the weak sun slanted through to the bedroom, causing the fallen pollen to glisten in ghostly fashion, throwing a grey blanket of powdery ash across the large bed.

I tripped at the top of the flight of stairs, kneeling in the debris.

'Twerp,' laughed Betsy Braddock as she stepped over me.

'Not funny,' I said. 'Where's the dog?'

'On the bed, I think,' said Betsy.

Johnnie Walker was on the bed at the bottom end, showing his canine teeth and growling in his throat, which meant 'You're trespassing!', but he was glad to see us. He looked fierce, but hungry, tail wagging.

'There's a person in the bed,' said Betsy.

'What?'

'There's somebody lying in the bed.'

There was. A small form. Hands gripping the outer cover, pollen illuminated by a weak Scouse sun drifting down like falling snow.

'I think she's dead.'

'Betsy, you're bloody daft.'

'Come along. Take a look.'

She was tiny.

Fallen debris lay across the outer cover of the bed, a counterpane of vibrant hues draped across her recumbent form. She looked peaceful even in that sombre, melancholy light.

A picture of the Sacred Heart in a brassy frame was suspended crookedly on the wall over the bed, looking down on her.

'I think you're right, Bets. I think she's dead.'

Johnnie Walker growled.

We stood looking down at her.

It was Mrs O'Grady all right, she whom the Mince Pie Gang called Peaches. I had seen her many times at the Mince Pie meetings; she never said much, she was just there, a humble but sparkling member of the gang, for fortune takes us on errands that are unexpected, to deliver gifts we did not know we possessed, and the gang had missed her, the gilt-edged presence of her gentle ways. The world would miss Peaches O'Grady. Betsy and I moved closer.

'Hey, Bets, let's say a Hail Mary for her.'

'OK.'

We had both thought we would recoil or at least be abashed in the presence of death. We bent our heads.

'Oh. Hello, Betsy,' she said.

I don't know what happened to Betsy Braddock. I just fell backwards into the fire grate with assorted bricks and plaster.

It seemed a fortnight before I regained my composure even though it could not have been more than five glorious minutes.

She was blinking those grey, Connemara eyes just like Ma's and the smile was still there.

'Are you all right, Mrs O'Grady?' I asked like a one hundred per cent nitwit, ninny and nincompoop.

'Water,' she said.

'Betsy, get water,' I shouted.

She had disappeared down the stairs somewhere but trundled up through the consequences of World War Two with a cup of water which she administered gently to Mrs O'Grady.

'I am going,' I said to Betsy, 'for help. Stay here. I shall return with the speed of light.'

PC Shally Burke, whom I collared on Crabapple Drive, moved in like a number four bus in his elevenses with a torch and all the efficiency of the force in his bearing, a cool copper, a bobby, a Sir Robert Peeler.

'She's alive,' he said, taking out his notebook.

'She won't be, Mr Constable,' said Betsy Braddock sarcastically, 'unless you move your enormous boots and telephone medical people.'

He fell down the stairs into the kitchen.

Clatterthorpe General lay peacefully on the far side of Mount Royale College on the hill, which housed in the daylight hours young teenaged ladies who gave their teachers much essential reason for seriously considering Shakespeare's indulgence, 'To be or not to be?'

Boys, on the other hand, could be slaughtered by their teachers, their bodies brought to submission by iron fist and metal rule. Boys just caved in; girls prospered in adversity, which is the obvious reason why they should be flying the Spitfires instead of Johnny Johnson and 'Legs' Bader.

Betsy and I visited Mrs Peaches O'Grady at Clatterthorpe, ignoring the injunction from the head nurse: 'Don't stay too long!'

Peaches looked quite angelic. Another lady, Mrs Willows, occupied the same room.

Through their one large window they could see the historic River Mersey, fussy tugboats plying the grey waves, the Liver Buildings towering in utmost majesty over its waters, half the docks burned to cinders by the glorious Luftwaffe, flags flying, fish and chips ruling the waves. There'll always be an England while Scouseland survives.

'It's so wonderful to see you both,' said Peaches. 'Come and sit over here.'

We sat, one on each side of the bed.

'Both of your mothers have visited me bringing mince pies and apple pies that I can't possibly eat, so I want you to take them with you. Go down on the Esplanade, gorge yourselves and the pigeons.' She laughed. What's she doing here, I thought?

We talked about the gang and the way they missed her, said a prayer together, and then she said, 'Underneath the stairs at number thirty-seven is a small box with brass latches, a case really. It's behind a bureau, a chest of drawers. Do you think you can bring it to me in the next few days?'

Impetuously I said, 'I'll bring it tonight!'

Which I did, Betsy Braddock as my aide-de-camp.

'What are you taking in there?' grouched the head nurse, nostrils flaring. Looked like our dog, Grip. With flu.

'A suitcase full of secret documents from Winston Churchill.'

'Come back here.'

But we were gone.

Mrs Peaches O'Grady opened the small suitcase as she sat up in the bed.

'I should not really have asked you to pick up the box,' she said, 'but I was suddenly overwhelmed with a desire, a need, to see and feel some objects and to show them to you both.'

There were two military medals from the Great War still looking brand new, one of gold hue, the other silver. She took them from the box.

'Won by Harry,' she said gently, 'in the last war; you know, the one they said was the war to end all wars.'

Both Betsy and I held them in our hands, some mystery from the past giving them weight, substance.

'They're heavy,' I said.

'Harry never held them,' she said simply.

We sat in silence.

'He was killed at the Somme.' She didn't cry. Tears from the past had cleansed her fragile heart. 'Now,' she exclaimed brightly, 'here is something you may never have seen.'

It was wrapped ever so carefully in clear paper, kept flat in a large envelope, a black and white photograph of girls and boys, early teenagers, seated on long benches facing the camera. Nobody was smiling. All were sitting to attention.

I suddenly recognised the room, the hall, for it was St Joseph's Academy of Hard Knocks.

The photograph was very clear considering its age, from a pre-war year. 'That's the big hall at Hard Knocks,' I said.

'Indeed it is, Thomas.'

The boys were sitting on benches on one side, the girls seated primly on the other.

'Now,' said Peaches O'Grady, 'recognise anybody?'

'That's you,' I said, pointing to a wee lassie small in stature at the end of the bench.

'Wrong, Thomas, that's Marge Muldoon who was even smaller than me. That's me, there, in the middle, with the funny hairdo.' She paused. 'Now who do you think that is?'

I followed Peaches' crooked finger to an almost smiling figure, who probably got into trouble because obviously you weren't allowed to smile. Might ruin the film.

'It's Ma,' I said, as gently as I was able.

'Aye, it's your mother all right, Tom. Prettiest girl at the school. Now I'm going to tell you a secret, but you must never tell anyone, not even your dear, dear mother, Mary Catherine Kipper.'

Betsy and I glanced at each other. 'But of course, Mrs O'Grady,' I said, crossing my fingers.

'These three boys were all absolutely crazy about your mother.' She pointed to three of the boys, one after the other. 'And that last one, his name was Greg, was head over heels even after we all left school. He was not from Liverpool but from the south, the south of England, near London, and he became very wealthy. If your ma had married him she would have become Lady Gregorious Whitney Carstairs and lived on a large estate.'

'But she married Dad, Joseph Prendergast Kipper.'

'Who didn't have a penny,' said Peaches, 'but she was quite crackers over him.' She closed her eyes. 'Your pa came upon the scene out of nowhere singing an old popular song: "Be sure it's true when you say I love you. It's a sin to tell a lie . . ." and Mary Catherine fell for him hook, line and sinker. So did I for that matter. But never tell your ma. My Harry came along and just filled his place. Or perhaps I should have raced after Gregorious Whitney Carstairs.' She had a faraway look in her eyes. 'Well, there you are, Tom and Betsy, the memories of an old fossil. Now, what are you going to do?'

'The first thing will be to eat your mince pies.'

'But of course. Just in time. Here comes Canon Moriarty.'

The canon was a piece of history. He was as neat and clean as a new kid at Hard Knocks but his clothing was of ancient heritage, hanging, it seemed, in great shrouds around his tall, gaunt physique. The ladies loved him, almost adored him, for he exuded permanence; you knew who you were speaking to, and his authority, gentle, compassionate, somewhat whimsical, of oddball humour, was a rock upon which you could build your own unstable thoughts and regrets. When he picked up the Second Collection you always gave him sixpence more than you intended. Moriarty was stability.

We crept out, Betsy and I, to leave them alone, for Peaches needed to confess her sins. Heavens knows where she found them!

'So, you were a hero, Tom Kipper, rescuing a lady in distress, you and your sister Betsy.'

'Betsy's not my sister, Mr Crisp.'

'Oh? Who is she?'

'Well, Betsy's just around; you know, like a kind of well-worn er . . .'

'Pair of boots?'

'Well, not exactly.'

'Hmmn. Sounds like your secretary, without pay. Tell me more about Peaches O'Grady.'

'She's in Clatterthorpe General Hospital. Comes out tomorrow, I think.'

'Good Irish stock, eh!' said Mr Crisp. 'Anyway, Tom, back to business unfortunately. I would like you to go down to the Cunard Building and drop off these documents. No hurry. You can do it on the way to the ferry going home. Take off early.' He continued humming 'Mademoiselle from Armentières'.

There was something disquieting about Betsy's being like a well-worn pair of boots.

Did he say it or did I say it?

Walking down Raneleigh Street to the Cunard I started thinking about Betsy Braddock in a new light. She was a nuisance sometimes. Always there. Mostly cheerful. But did I need an aide-de-camp? Admittedly I could not have rescued Peaches without her assistance.

I bet she comes over to number six Mary Lane tonight with her ma to the Mince Pie Gang meeting, I thought. Peaches O'Grady would be back again, too, filling out the assembly with her smiling, cheerful demeanour, her quiet, solicitous benignity, that radiance. She'd get a hero's welcome from the crusty old and ancient members, telling her not to dismay them again by her nonsensical absence.

Aye, it was all quiet on the Mary Lane front, nudging shoulders with ye ancient St Thomas More Cemetery, our benign playground, the church spire piercing the blue sky with its cirrus cumulus threatening from the Irish Sea. I trod through the front door into the parlour singing 'Rule Britannia' for no obvious reason.

All was quiet. The Mince Pie Gang were in good order around the oval table, which was covered with a square, multicoloured cloth, but no one was talking. The world had closed down. All members cradled a drink. Betsy was seated with Dad over in his den. And she was crying. No one spoke.

Peaches' chair was empty. I knew she must be there, but the chair was empty.

'Ma,' I said.

'She's gone, Tom.'

'Peaches?'

'Died in her sleep. This morning. I was with her.'

'How could she die, Ma?' I cried.

'Heart failure. Heart failure brought on by the shock of the air raid.'

How can people die, I thought. They are here one minute and the next they are gone. Two people died in our own street when their house disappeared, but I didn't know them. Betsy and I knew Peaches. Where was Betsy? She got up from the couch and we hugged one another, she blubbering away like a babbling brook. At that moment I slapped myself for thinking of her as a well-worn pair of boots.

'Hey, Bets,' I said, 'let's go down to Marmaduke Place for some ice cream.'

I hugged and kissed Ma, and Betsy and I went down the steps into Mary Lane.

Which was when the air raid siren wailed dismally across Merseyside for three lousy Heinkels, we discovered later, two of which landed or plunged into the Irish Sea.

I took Betsy's hand to go back inside Kipper Castle. Not one gang member had moved. I knocked on the table, gently, with my knuckles.

'Peaches O'Grady,' I said, 'told Betsy and me to always keep on smiling!'

The assembled company all looked at each other, raised their glasses in unison, and said with ever widening smiles, 'To Peaches O'Grady!' There was general laughter. Nobody went to the shelter.

And way up there somewhere in the vaulted heavens, Peaches was with a heavenly Mince Pie Gang, all Irish, with wings of wondrous proportion to match their hearts, led by St Patrick himself.

'I don't remember, Tom Kipper,' said Betsy Braddock, taking my arm as we walked the terrace, 'Peaches saying keep on smiling.'

'Neither do I,' I said.

Chapter Sixteen

Ephesians?

We took our places the way we used to do in our schooldays. Betsy Braddock, Sully and I sat in a pew just below the marble pulpit where Canon Moriarty would sermonise, between each paragraph snorting pink pills which Aunt Emma said were for his gout. He rounded his Donegal vowels with a great Gaelic shaking of the larynx. Sully and I would imitate him afterwards, much to the annoyance of Betsy Braddock who was prim and proper and averred strongly that it was disrespectful.

'Most pastors,' said the canon, chomping a pill, 'do not care to expound upon St Paul's letter to the Ephesians, in which he writes that wives should be subordinate to their husbands, but who are we to say that scripture is in error? I ask you – who?' He looked over his pince-nez at his audience, a wry smile upon his Donegal lips. Almost a chuckle. Ladies would assault him verbally later on in the parish hall, even though they loved him.

'Perhaps,' he said, 'I should say no more about the matter.'

Mrs Flora Maginnerty in the seventh row on the left put an elbow in Sean Maginnerty's ribs and said, 'Good idea, Canon!'

All the congregation laughed.

Father Francis Harrogate wasn't the main celebrant at the nine o'clock Mass but he was on the steps of the church chatting exuberantly mostly with young parishioners who really liked his style, his soft Irish accent and his friendly grin.

'Tom Kipper,' he said over the heads of his audience, 'I need to talk to you. Can you hang on?'

I nodded yes, wondering why.

'Listen, Tom,' he said afterwards, 'as you know there will be a big celebration in the hall on Saturday the eighth and I've written a play – well, it's really a short humorous sketch – and I need you in it.'

'Me, Father?'

'Yes, you. Headmaster Devereaux said that when you were next door at Knocks' – he smiled – 'you were in a couple of plays.'

'Well, yes, but Father . . .'

'It's very short, Tom, and you will know most of the other actors.'

'But Father . . .'

'Tom, it will help raise funds for a copier, a new

typewriter, a filing cabinet and other items needed for the school magazine. You were editor, weren't you?'

'Yes, Father, but . . .'

'Good show, Tom. Meet you next Wednesday night in the school hall at seven.'

And that's how I, Tom Kipper, became the Sympathetic Undertaker in an eponymous comedy, no less.

They were all older, the rest of the cast, much taller, towering head and shoulders over the diminutive Kipper, a pimply Irish kid not long out of Hard Knocks, but they needed me. Why was this? Father Francis Harrogate said, 'Try this on, Tom.' It was a black coat, as though from a dress suit, draping my Gaelic bones like a shroud, sleeves down past my fingertips, the body falling somewhere between my gluteus maximus and the floorboards.

'Perfect fit,' said Father Francis.

It was a rehearsal. I had thought it would be one of many. But there was just one.

'This hat,' said Miss Harringay, who was in charge of wardrobe, 'should suit you fine.'

It was a top hat, salvaged perhaps from the refuse of the twenties, discarded by Fred Astaire, falling over my Gaelic head like a brass bucket.

'It used to belong to the canon,' smiled Miss Harringay.

'It's big enough to take a bath in,' I ventured.

'Now the story goes like this, lads,' said Father Francis, and we began the rehearsal.

Seamus Flynn and Matt Brannigan, in their twenties, dressed as elderly Irish sisters, shawls about their shoulders, black lace draped around their heads and tied under many chins, festooned in midnight black gowns, were rocking on either side of the fireplace, lamenting the demise of their Grandpa Quigly, who was lying on a stretcher at the edge of the stage, and anticipating the fine wake they would have for him.

But Grandpa had not yet expired, for he was bemoaning his fate on the stretcher, which was propped up at four corners by large literary volumes.

At this point, the Sympathetic Undertaker – myself, Tom Kipper – would bounce in, shouting, 'And now to business, ladies! The first thing we must do is measure him up!' I had to carry in with me an extremely long tape measure over which I tripped many times, telling the ladies how thirsty I was.

Bottles were produced. 'Are you thirsty?' was the perpetual cry.

The corpse, who was still alive, would be toasted, fine man that he was.

Grandpa Quigly would interrupt the overdressed Sympathetic Undertaker so that many times I would shout, 'Quigly, if you're not careful I won't bury you!'

'See you on Saturday,' said Father Francis. 'You're doing well, Tom Kipper. Regards to your mother.'

'Listen, Ma,' I said, 'the canon said that wives must be subordinate to their husbands.'

'I heard him,' said Ma, banging big pots like church bells.

'Can I ask you a question, Ma?'

'Depends what it is.'

'OK, Ma, I'll describe it and then you can tell me if I can ask it.'

'You're looking for a box behind the ears, Tom Kipper.'

'I'm sixteen, going on seventeen.'

'Hmmn . . . And born with the spirit of contradiction!'

'Shall I ask it?'

'Aye, go on.'

'Are you subordinate to Dad?'

'Explain yourself.'

'Well, Ma, if Dad tells you to do something, do you obey him?'

'You're looking for trouble, Tom Kipper.'

'It's in the book. The canon said so, Ma.'

She threw a saucepan into the cupboard and then wiped her hands on her apron. I thought she was going to toss me in after it. The gauntlet had been thrown down. Aeons of Irish blarney and resilience surged in her Scouse blood.

Fire from the Post Office blazed in her eyes.

'Tell me, Tom Kipper,' she said, 'to whom was St Paul writing?'

'The Ephesians, Ma.'

'Then they, young man, were the people he intended the message for!'

Ma's logic was spellbinding. I looked at her in awe. She was almost a genius. Wait till the canon got a smack in the kisser with this one. Women the world over would rejoice.

I said humbly, 'Thanks, Ma,' and stumbled out into Mary Lane.

*

It was called the Pot Luck Game and it had absolutely nothing to do with casual consumables. It cost sixpence, a tanner, to buy a ticket; it was a lottery, a raffle, a sweep. A tanner got you a ticket and millionaire aspirations.

Organised by the SVDP Society for the benefit of the school, it gave fifty per cent of the proceeds to the Academy of Hard Knocks, the other half being the prize. Which was growing fast.

Once a month a duplicate raffle ticket was drawn from 'the hat', the metal kettle holding them. Should the ticket not have been sold, the prize was carried over to the following month. Six months passed. Nobody won it. It grew like Irish blarney. The *Chipton Downs Post* carried the news to its growing number of readers, including Ma, who said, 'It's over a thousand pounds.'

It was 1943; you could buy a house for that. Maybe not a Rolls.

News, good and bad, travels faster than Uncle Bart's imagination, and he scratched his head in bewilderment. 'Nobody wins it you say and the money's there, standing still, doing nothing?'

Ma banged the oven door on an outsize custard pie. 'It's in the Bank of England, Bart. Even you can't beat the Old Lady of Threadneedle Street!'

That night a bomb fell on the bank. All the funds were saved and rushed to another branch. Bart just shook his head.

*

Mrs Lavinia Bright-Chalmondeley, upper-crust bastion with her husband, Sinclair, of the Ash-Willows club, adjusted her pince-nez on her bony nose to peer more closely at the Chipton Downs newsprint. 'They say, Margo, that it's approaching two or three thousand.'

Mrs Margo Trotter said, 'Isn't that church hall at the other end of town near the Pier Head?'

'I believe so.'

'Do they have parking, Barton?' she asked her husband.

'Must have, dahling. They say it's quite civilised.'

'Do they have a bar?'

'Must have. Mrs Lavender O'Connor says it's the best in town. Buffet too. Might be worth dropping in.'

'I was thinking the same thing. What about it, Betty?'

Mrs Betty Garrison-Smythe said, 'Barrington could take us there in the Rolls.'

Saturday would be a melange of upper, lower and middling classes of society. All thirsty.

Ma was going; Betsy Braddock, Conks Murphy and Whacker Doyle were attending. Even I bought five tickets ahead of time.

Mother Angelica of the Holy Trinity had been invited as an honoured guest to draw the ticket from the green kettle at eight p.m.

In the afternoon members of the SVDP and sisters of the Holy Trinity were tearing duplicate tickets from rolls to pop into the big drawing kettle. 'You can help out, too, Tom Kipper,' said Dotty Deveraux, secretary of the society.

So Betsy Braddock and I joined in filling up the pot.

Among the parishioners were two ageing Irish ladies, seemingly tottering out of the Old Testament, Clara and Josie Rafferty, diminutive creatures, one two years older than the other, avid churchgoers, living in a crumbling, minuscule house with a leaky roof and an ancient washing machine, of quite sparse income, most cheerful personalities in spite of their surroundings down Pinafore Lane.

Charitable societies visited them from time to time, helping them shore up their heap of sticks they called home. It still leaked. What they really needed to be blessed with was a complete upgrading of the Swallows' Nest, as they called it.

'If we could just win that raffle,' muttered Josie, buttering breakfast toast.

'Good money after bad,' said Clara. 'Besides, tickets are sixpence each which is out of our range. The good Lord will provide.'

'I wish he'd provide a new roof.'

In their seventies, going on eighties, they received a small measure of social security from parsimonious Tory bureaucrats with gold watches in waistcoats, and eked it out a copper penny at a time, occasionally a threepenny bit. Porridge was a staple.

Mother Angelica and the sisters were busy on one side of the tableclothed bench selling tickets and putting duplicates in the kettle. Ma said to Clara and Josie Rafferty, 'There's two tickets here for you ladies.'

'Oh, we can't afford them, Mary.'

'They're a gift from the Ladies' Guild.'

Mother Angelica zipped off two tickets to give to Ma to give to the Rafferty sisters, who were twittering away and moving their feet like roofing pigeons.

As Mother Angelica sat down on the other side of the trestle table she accidentally knocked off a roll of tickets with her sacred elbow. Sir Walter Kipper immediately went on his bony Irish knees to reach under the ample tablecloth to recover the tickets, but Mother Angelica was faster than Uncle Bart's maths. As I picked up the heavy, brocaded cloth I saw her on her knees putting a ticket into a wee chest pocket in her habit.

Back on my Ralegh feet I said to Betsy Braddock, 'Let's go and have some tea, Bets.'

I kept the incident in my heart; the Scouse intellectual vibrations of my Kipper brain were very slowly working on the ticket tucked into the holy habit under the table . . . which began to sound like a Dirty Duck tavern story.

Mother Angelica was like her name: an angel, devoted to her prayer life, an inspiration to her adoring sisters, a protector and charitable guide to the poor. In an unguarded moment she had once said to a dispossessed parishioner, 'If you can't afford it, take!' which sounded like Uncle Bart down at the Dirty Duck. After Guinness.

Me, Flynn and Brannigan were extra early for the performance.

'Let's get a pint,' said Seamus Flynn.

'Where, Flynn?'

'At the Bird in Hand. It's just down Switchcross Lane.'

Matt Brannigan scratched his big Cork chin. 'You know,' he said, 'that's a good idea. We've got more than an hour.'

I, Tom Kipper, didn't say anything. I felt I was being marshalled into a river of blessed, all-consuming emotion as we trod the cobblestones to the Bird.

The noise was frantic and deafening until you fell into it and then it was loving and consuming and shrouded in Woodbine and Players Weights smoke, a holy blue shroud that hid my diminutive Kipper figure this side of the bar.

'He's too young,' said Brannigan.

'Then give him half,' said Flynn.

'Cheers,' I said, for the very first time in my life. It floated down like the secret mists of Gilhooley.

'Well, well,' said Uncle Bart, not a great deal taller than I, holding up the bar with two Dublin elbows. 'Tom Kipper!'

'Hi, Uncle Bart.' I smiled.

'You're in the skit,' he said.

'I'm an undertaker.'

'What?'

'Father Francis twisted my arm.'

'I'll be over.'

'Cheers, Uncle Bart.'

'Keep low, Tom. The coppers are everywhere.'

'In the Bird?'

'Everywhere. Do you want to see someone you know very well?'

'Here?'

'Yes. Just look over there.'

Which I did. Through the Woodbine smoke and the magic

of the moment, I beheld Grandpa Finnegan on a bench, porter in hand, cloth cap angled on noble head, white silk scarf circling neck, a widow on each side. King of railway-track coal. Three generations, profoundly imbued with Scouse. I sipped the Guinness. 'He's an English king,' I said.

'An Irish king,' said Bart.

'Time to go,' said Brannigan, far above me.

I slurped the Guinness. 'See you later, Uncle Bart.'

In the changing room at the side of the stage, Miss Harringay fussed over costumes with great accuracy. I was attired in the long morning coat and top hat when a bottle of pale liquid was thrust into my hand by Seamus Flynn.

'Father Francis left supplies,' he said. It tasted like lemonade but kind of bitter. I sipped again and the bouquet rose to meet me.

Flynn and Brannigan were already on the stage.

'You're on, Tom.'

Pencil and clipboard were thrust into my hands as I was propelled towards the curtain and so I entered, Guinness raining in my head.

The hall was like a can of squishy, human sardines. I could see Conks Murphy, Whacker Doyle and Fred Magee in the front rows, Ma, Aunts Madge and Florence, Zilda Sweeney, then all the rest was shrouded in darkness.

'And now, ma'am,' I shouted, as I jumped through the curtain, dragging my tape, 'shall I measure him up?'

Then I stood still. Ten thousand voices roared applause. The blood stirred within me like the Mersey at high tide. Oh, this was poetic.

The deceased, Hugo Castillo, lying on a stretcher supported by volumes at the edge of the stage, moaned, 'Mercy! Mercy!' for he had not yet been elevated to Gaelic heaven.

The two old biddies sitting round the fireplace, looking for a financial bargain, said in chorus, 'It's a thirsty night for an undertaker,' and produced a bottle of pale ale, which I sipped from.

'Now to business,' I shouted, my black coat festooning my skinny bones, the hat like a steeple. 'It just might be expensive.'

And so the two old biddies and the Sympathetic Undertaker financially see-sawed with delight and pale ale while the deceased, Grandpa Quigly, cried for mercy at the edge of the stage.

Tom Kipper, resplendent with Guinness for the very first time in his exuberant life, shouted at Grandpa Quigly, 'If you're not careful I won't bury you!'

To this very day I wonder why I added emphasis by jumping on top of the corpse lying on the edge of the stage, for the spirit was upon me. So was the corpse.

With several cries, the bed, the corpse, the volumes for legs and the Sympathetic Undertaker fell into the audience.

Everybody in the world was laughing, splitting their sides as we picked up bodies and books and blankets before climbing back on stage.

'It was great, colossal success,' said Father Francis the following day, while my Kipper bones ached with a mysterious throb.

'You have no fever,' said Ma, holding my head; 'must be the change of seasons. Of course you fell off the stage again after the play was over.'

'I did?'

When Father Harrogate's hilarious skit came to a happy end we all retired to the expansive hall with the small dance floor, bar and buffet next door.

'Is everybody happy?' grinned Father Francis.

Above the noise that followed he announced, 'And now we will draw the winning ticket for the big Pot Luck.'

'How much?' shouted Quigly (the deceased).

'Nineteen hundred and sixty-five pounds,' shouted Father Harrogate.

'Great Holy Moley,' said Bart Finnegan.

'Our very special guest,' said Father, 'is Mother Superior Angelica who will endeavour to pull out the winning ticket. Nobody has done this successfully for the past six months so hang on to your hat, Bart Finnegan, it just may be you. Could we have a roll of the drums, please.'

Bart blessed himself. The drums, played by whipper-snapper Danny McCarthy, started rolling.

Mother Angelica, a beautiful smile on her benign face, advanced to the podium, lowered her right hand slowly into the kettle, which was brimming with tickets, down to her wrist, and slowly pulled up a slip of paper which she handed to Father Harrogate.

Father took the ticket, looked at the number and announced in grand Irish fashion, 'And the winning number is five, seven, three, one. Five thousand, seven hundred and thirty-one.'

A great babble of voices arose.

'Does anyone have the ticket?'

A great silence. Nobody had the ticket. Was it all going back into the pot? Was it?

'Please look at all your tickets.'

We all looked. I, Tom Kipper, was four million numbers away.

I was close enough to see Ma lean over to Clara and Josie Rafferty. 'Look at your tickets,' she was saying.

They hadn't even looked, standing there looking like two amiable sheep ready for a pot of scouse.

Then they looked and Clara said to Josie, 'I think we won.'

'They've got the ticket,' shouted Ma in a most un-Ma-like fashion. 'Glory be!'

It was handed to Father.

'Ladies and gentlemen,' he announced, 'and Bart Finnegan, the winners are Clara and Josie Rafferty!' The applause was heard down at the Mersey Docks and Harbour Board and there was great rejoicing for five minutes, and then the air raid siren went off and parishioners fled for shelters or braved it to their homes.

The flock scattered.

'What is the greatest of all the Commandments, Tom Kipper?'

'To love God.'

'And next?' She banged the pot.

'To love your neighbour as yourself.'

'Very good. Tom. Now, are you happy?'

'Hmmn . . . Is it OK to do like Robin Hood and give to the poor?'

'Well, Friar Tuck seemed to think so.'

'So,' I said, 'if, by pure accident, the wrong winning ticket for the Pot Luck raffle was pulled out of the kettle last Saturday and the prize was given to the right person it would be exactly the same as loving your neighbour as yourself?'

Oh, it was a great, humongous Gaelic sigh she uttered as she stopped all her activity and studied me. One hand went to her left hip, the other to her chest.

'What on earth are you talking about, Tom Kipper?'

I gave her my very best beguiling, innocent smile I'd picked up from my brother Vincent.

'Charity, Ma,' I said.

'Is there any tea, Maria?' asked my dad from the volcano of his leather armchair.

'Heavens to Murgatroyd! Give this cup of tea to Aristotle.'

Dad said as I handed him the cup and saucer, 'Ah, tea!' which is what he said every hour.

Ma looked at me again and then went back to the pot.

I could see her Connemara mind churning over like gooey treacle.

'Tom Kipper,' she said, 'are you referring to the fact that old Clara and Josie Rafferty won the Pot Luck raffle out of sheer good fortune?'

'I suppose so, Ma.'

'Well, are you or are you not?'

'Yes, I am.'

'Well, young man, think of it this way. If Friar Tuck was in the place of Mother Superior you saw under the table everything would be all right, right?'

'I suppose so, Ma.'

'Don't suppose.'

'Yes, it would be.'

'Then there's no problem. Love your neighbour.'

'Ma.'

'Yes?'

'And you gave her the arrow for the bow?'

'Tom Kipper!'

'Just an idea, Ma.' I smiled.

'This doesn't have anything to do with the Ephesians, does it?'

'No, Ma.'

'Thank the Lord and St Joseph for that.'

'I love you, Ma,' I said, before I stepped out into Mary Lane.

Ah, she was the queen of Connemara.

Chapter Seventeen

Traitor's Gate

Upper-crust Chipton Downs groaned beneath the weight of its money, a cumbersome responsibility for those ladies at the club in their resplendent diaphanous gowns, sipping Epernay champagne not available to lesser mortals in World War Two, but trickling through sparkling pastures of bounteous higher-class Chipton Downians.

'Isn't that Partington McLeesh talking to Francine Maginnerty over by the west window?'

'I do believe it is,' answered Mrs Blankenforth-Angles. 'They say he's brilliant.'

'They also say he's daft as a brush.'

'Heavens, Helen, where did you pick up such an expression!'

'From my cleaning lady, Mrs Lavender O'Connor. She brings me titbits of news from Seacombe.'

'You mean gossip.'

'I suppose so in a way, Joanna, but it's really news these days.'

'I wonder what the eminent psychologist and Francine are talking about.'

'Money, do you think?'

'What else?'

'The juvenile patient,' said Partington McLeesh, 'must not undergo a painstaking exploration of childhood experience but be made aware of his own neurosis.'

'Let me tell you about Duncan,' said Francine Maginnerty, which she did.

'You mean this boy Duncan wants to hold up a bank with a water pistol? Hmmn . . . tell me more.'

Francine filled him in.

'How terribly interesting,' said McLeesh. 'A classic case of distorted perception sabotaging an innate need. Let him do his will.'

'Wow,' said Francine Maginnerty, 'wait till Brendan hears about this!'

'Yes, indeed. Give him the water pistol. Allow him to hold up the Bank of England. Rid him of his inhibitions. Do they have any more of that champagne?'

'You mean Duncan should be allowed his will?'

'Of course. That fellow Freud was a nice chap but he should have realised that therapists should intervene directly.'

'Do you like the champagne, Mr McLeesh?'

'Most splendid. Call me Partington.'

'Call me Francine.'

'Are you Irish?'

'Isn't everybody? Wait till I tell Brendan what you said.'

'Do it slowly, Francine.'

'Why, Partington?'

'Well, you know how policemen are.'

'Do I?'

Later that evening Francine said, 'Darling, I have something to talk to you about.'

'Is it about money, my sweet?'

'No, actually it's about water pistols.'

'How interesting. I do like these mushy peas.'

'I spoke to Partington McLeesh at the club and the Pogelthorpes are coming to dinner tomorrow.'

'With a water pistol?'

'Don't be silly, my sweet. It's about Duncan.'

'You mean,' said Chief Inspector Marcus O'Brian-Pogelthorpe, raising his wine glass, 'you want to let this whippersnapper hold up the Bank of England?'

'Aye.'

'With a water pistol?'

'Aye.'

'Mrs Maginnerty, are you listening to your daft husband?'

'Oh, yes. He's only half daft, he's also cracked and demented, quite unhinged. Drinks a lot.'

'And he's chief inspector of the Chipton Downs constabulary?'

'Has delusions of glory,' said Mrs Francine Maginnerty. 'Do you like this port?'

'I do. Did you acquire it locally?'

'Contraband. Brendan had to confiscate a liberal quantity.'

'In Chipton Downs? It belongs to the county?'

'It was generally accepted that the consignment would deteriorate if left too long in the sun.'

'But it's been raining.'

'It was a brave decision to make.'

'And he drinks a lot?'

'Irish. Shocking husband. What about the hold-up in the Bank of England?'

'Out of the question.'

'Would you care for another measure of this excellent port?'

Chief Inspector Brendan Maginnerty of Chipton Downs said, 'Marcus, old chap, a psychologist friend of mine from Liverpool advised that at some point in negotiations with a juvenile who is mentally clambering into adulthood it just might be advisable not to lay down the law but to let the patient have his own way.'

'With a water pistol?'

'With a cricket bat or a spear. The means is just part of the psychological trauma. The great mentor, Partington McLeesh, advised that it circumvented hostility in the patient, obscured opposition of dissenting factors, leased stimulation to reasonability. McLeesh was the master.'

'You've been reading too much. Would you pass the contraband?'

'I think it would be great fun,' said Carla O'Brian-Pogelthorpe, slurping port like black and tan.

'No more port for you,' said Marcus, smiling at her over his glass. 'What do you think, Francine?'

'Daft, but splendid.'

'Now, do we know which side of the river he'll hit?'

'We'll let you know. My chaps in Chipton Downs are pretty sharp.'

'Well, air raids seem to have almost ended, so a bank hold-up with a water pistol should be just tickling the ribs. Do you know this boy, Brendan?'

'He's my nephew.'

'Ah, now we're getting down to brass tacks. What's his name?'

'Duncan Mahoney. Attends Hard Knocks.'

'Hard Knocks?'

'St Joseph's. It's called Hard Knocks.'

'Yes, I will have another drop of that fine port.'

It seemed they were all babbling at once, voices interchanging, a semi-musical, low-key cacophony of sound, wrapping soft social dialogue, amusing all four of them at the thought of Duncan Mahoney and his water pistol robbing the Old Lady of Threadneedle Street, being given fake five pound notes by a smiling teller. It was absurd.

It was saucy, silly, slap-happy, slapstick psychology interlarded with Gaelic whim, fantasy, comic proportion, and farce; and four Irish hearts took it to their bosom.

Within a short space of time they had forgotten who was going to tell whom what.

Duncan Mahoney's mother, Brenda Mahoney, nee Kelly, said to her barmy offspring, 'We're going to Lewis's

Department Store and the ice cream parlour on Paradise Street if you're a good boy.'

'May I take my water pistol, Ma?'

'Yes, but don't put any water in it. Do you hear?'

'Yes, Mother,' returned the deranged lad, with his fingers crossed. After all, what's a pistol without water? St Joseph tut-tutted in his chambers.

The fragment of Scouse Threadneedle history came to being when El Paso Corned Beef treasurer Mr Hocking said, 'Tom Kipper, before you hit the Mad Sandwich Shop today would you make a deposit at the bank for me, there's a good lad.'

The judge wore a wig.

Duncan Mahoney, aged twelve, kept looking at the wig with curious fascination. His mother, Mrs Brenda Mahoney, wore a wig, and until this moment Duncan had harboured the unconsidered Duncan belief that only women donned hair from a scalp other than their own.

Judge Cargill, seated at his dais, with an assistant on either side of his sparse body, seemed to Duncan Mahoney like a wee privet hedge sticking up over a big wooden fence, wearing large, horn-rimmed spectacles.

His honour Judge Clarence Cargill was sensitive about his appearance, touching his wig, frequently pushing the large glasses back up his shiny nose, and he did not miss for one moment the vacant, precocious stares of this miserable nostril-exploring juvenile who would not stop staring at his grey wig.

'The accused,' said PC Rafferty, sniffing, 'entered the

Bank of England on Dale Street with a weapon hidden on his person with the intention of robbery.'

'With violence?' questioned his honour.

Rafferty hesitated.

'Well, Police Constable?'

'Your honour, with whatever violence the weapon would provide.'

'And what was the weapon, PC Rafferty?'

'A pistol.'

'A pistol? A pistol, you say?'

'Yes, your honour.'

'With bullets, Constable?'

'With water, your honour.'

'A water pistol? You are referring to a water pistol?'

'Yes, your honour.'

His honour seethed under his large wig. He tapped his pen on the mahogany dais. 'What charges, Constable, are being brought against this juvenile?'

His honour already knew the charge for it was written in exaggerated police scrawl on the blotter in front of him, but his judicial intellect logically reasoned there must be more to meet the eye than was conveyed by the three words inscribed there.

'Disturbing the peace, your honour.'

'Hmmn . . . Disturbing the peace.' He swivelled his chair so that Duncan Mahoney obtained a much better view of the honourable wig. 'This young man,' he pondered judicially, 'shot water from his pistol on to the teller and that's "disturbing the peace"?'

'It was between the eyes, your honour, as in a western-type moving picture show.'

'Tom Mix?'

'Tom Mix, your honour?'

'As in a Tom Mix picture, Constable.' His honour was smiling broadly, for he just loved Tom Mix. 'Perhaps, PC, you are not acquainted with Tom Mix?'

The PC shut up, chose acquiescence. He knew he was drowning in a sea of water pistols.

'Tell me, Constable Rafferty, how was the accused apprehended?'

'By Tom Kipper, your honour.'

'Tom Kipper? Not Tom Mix? The plot deepens.' He was enjoying his own superb sense of humour. 'Now who is this Tom Kipper?'

'I'm Tom Kipper,' I said, standing up from my chair in the front row of the juvenile court.

'Come up here, Mr Kipper, if you don't mind.'

I trod up to the minuscule magistrate.

'Now, how old are you, Tom Kipper?'

'Nearly seventeen, your honour.'

'Nearly seventeen, eh?'

'Yes, sir. May I ask you a question?'

'Certainly. What is it?'

'How old are you?'

There was a grim silence. It crept around the court like a thief in carpet slippers.

Judge Clarence Cargill's assistants, one on either side, gasped; a gargling noise issued from the one with big ears, the one on the right. It was like asking the king of England what time he picked his nose.

The judge leaned back in his upholstered throne, his eyes opening wide, then his lips. 'Ha, ha, ha, ha, ha, ha!' His shoulders shook with quaking mirth. His wig fell sideways and then to the floor.

'Ha, ha, ha,' shouted Duncan Mahoney, pointing a grubby finger at the wig.

'Ha, ha, ha!' said the judge's two assistants, and then the court went into an uproar as legal assistants, constables, secretaries, parents of criminal offspring, and the offspring themselves dissolved into laughter, holy, genuine laughter which included myself, Tom Kipper.

When it had simmered to a soft whisper. Judge Cargill wiped his eyes, looked at me and said, softly, 'Seventy, Tom Kipper. God bless you.'

He tapped some papers edgewise into uniformity on his desk top. 'Tom, tell me,' he said, 'how you apprehended Duncan Mahoney.'

'Well, sir, I happened to be in the bank making a deposit.'

'For yourself?'

'No, sir, for El Paso Corned Beef Incorporated.'

'And where are they located?'

'Sir Thomas Street, sir.'

'A fine Liverpool street. Were you hit in the Blitz?'

'Not the office, sir, but we were hit at home.'

'Oh, yes, and where is that?'

'Chipton Downs.'

'Oh. yes, across the water. Is the family in good shape, Tom?'

'Yes, sir. Me ma – I mean my mother – took us all to a new house after the bomb dropped and we're still living there.'

'So, you apprehended the boy Duncan. How did you do this?'

'I tripped him up, your honour, and I'm sorry I did.'

'Tell me why you're sorry, Tom.'

'He's only twelve, sir, and what he did was excusable because of his age. When I was twelve I was quite daffy, and I jumped into every chance I could think of to be silly.'

'And you're not that now?'

'Much less, I think.'

'Then tell me, why did you trip him up?'

'I don't know, sir. He was running past so I stuck out my leg and the coppers got him.'

'The coppers?'

'The police, sir. Some of them are as daft as Duncan.'

'Ha, ha, ha, ha, ha,' chuckled Judge Clarence Cargill.

'Ha, ha,' said his assistants.

'So, Tom, what punishment do you think I should administer to the accused?'

'None, your honour.'

'None, Tom?'

'Well, I think he should apologise, and be given a good telling off and a smack in the kisser by his mother'

Duncan started to cry. He ran from the bench to his mother, who smothered him in her arms while he blubbered that he was sorry.

'This case,' said his honour, banging his gavel, 'is closed! OK, Tom?'

'Yes, sir. It wouldn't have happened if it hadn't been for Chief Inspector Pogelthorpe.'

'What? Are you talking about the Liverpool city chief of police?' People slowly resumed their seats. All eyes were beamed on to the judge. I felt that I was falling into a chasm, a great yawning chasm, with no footholds, no way to clamber out.

'It was the Mince Pie Gang, your honour.' I fell deeper. 'Me ma's Mince Pie Gang.'

'A gang of mince pies?'

'They meet once a week on the Hill.'

'The Hill?'

'Mary Lane. Chipton Downs.'

'A gang? Controlled? Unruly?'

'No, your honour. They are a group of mothers who meet every week.'

'With the chief police inspector of Liverpool?'

'No, your honour.'

'Explain, Mr Kipper.'

'I heard Clara Garrity telling Mrs O'Toole that she had heard from Zilda Sweeney who was told by Inspector Pogelthorpe's wife, Carla, that the psychologist, Partington McLeesh, had advised Francine Maginnerty that it would be in the better interests of a juvenile to let him have his way.'

'Let him have his way? What way?'

'To hold up the bank.'

'With a water pistol?'

'Er . . . yes, sir.'

'Oh, ho, ho, ho, ho, Chief Inspector Pogelthorpe from Gradge wants tatty kids to hold up banks with water pistols, and the Maginnertys of Chipton Down apparently agree! We're in the absolute middle of a war to end all wars and our constabulary are playing with water pistols!'

I fell deeper into the pit.

'Oh, ho, two chief inspectors with water pistols and that crackpot psychologist McLeesh who doesn't know what day it is. A very fine kettle of fish, indeed! Mrs Mahoney, please take your boy home. Talk some sense into him. This court is now closed. Tom Kipper, come with me!' The gavel banged.

'I don't know any more, Judge.'

'Come with me anyway.'

'I think it was Professor Partington McLeesh's idea.'

'That absurd nincompoop! Tell me more, Mr Kipper!'

'I don't know any more, your honour.'

'Come into my chambers.'

I was falling into an abyss. I could not find a footing, a handhold. Where oh where was Betsy Braddock now that I needed her?'

'I must use the rest room first, your honour.'

'Hurry. Then come to chamber number one.'

I waited breathlessly, then slipped out into a Liverpool eventide on beautiful Dale Street wrapped in a glorious mist. There was no moon.

Dylan Evans, on page four of the greatest newspaper in the world, the *Liverpool Echo*, awash in most splendid, illustrious gossip, plunged into personality disintegration with great élan.

Policemen [he wrote in his column *Fable and Fantasy*] organise peace and stability in our communities. The very last occupation in which they should be involved is holding up banks, particularly with water pistols, or encouraging such criminal activity. However, it has been revealed that law enforcement officers of the most elevated rank, on both sides of the river, have found it a worthy pursuit in which juveniles should be instructed, supported, no less, by a most illustrious national psychologist. With water pistols.

As with Tom Mix?

There's more, dear reader. Stay tuned.

'It was startling to poor Carla,' said Maureen Mulvaney, sometime VP of the Mince Pie Gang.

'Carla who?'

'Carla Pogelthorpe. She's the wife of Chief Inspector Pogelthorpe of Liverpool. A close friend of our Francine Maginnerty in Chipton Downs.'

'Both policemen's wives,' grouched Cathy Sullivan.

'Both fine women,' interjected my ma, Mary Catherine Kipper, who didn't even know 'poor Carla'.

'Then what happened?'

'There was a traitor.'

'A traitor? You mean like Lord Haw-Haw?'

'Aye. Somehow he gave the information to all and sundry.'

'So the poor boy was picked up as a traitor?'

'No, no, no, silly! He wasn't the traitor. It was whoever gave the information to the legal authorities, to Judge Cargill of all people.'

'You mean the Hanging Judge?'

'Oh, is that what he's called? Then the news leaked to the press. The *Echo*. That columnist, what's his name? Dylan Evans, was probably in the courtroom. I never read him myself.' She sniffed.

'It's not like our *Chipton Downs Express*.'

'If he's caught will he hang in the Bloody Tower?' asked Zilda, sipping at her glass.

I shrank behind the couch.

Oh, what a snake in the grass I was, a treacherous back-stabber. Judge Cargill had not really twisted my arm and I had mentioned the names of two chief inspectors and the world's most vaunted psychologist, Professor Partington McLeesh.

The bells were tolled in the Bloody Tower by ancient ghosts of despicable traitors . . .

'Mr Crisp,' I said, 'in the Bloody Tower how are traitors executed?'

'Hanged,' said Crisp.

'Occasionally they chop their heads off,' said Mr Hocking, folding his *Liverpool Echo*. 'Could you pass that tea pot?'

I'm a traitor.

A betrayer. I betrayed the Mince Pie Gang. I was no

better than historic figures of the past consigned through the Traitor's Gate into that massive, grim, stone edifice, the Bloody Tower.

Going home to Chipton Downs on the ferry boat *Iris* did not buoy my spirits. In my fantasy ships were sailing south to London full of traitors bound for the Thames.

'What's wrong with you, Kipper?' asked Betsy Braddock at my elbow.

'I'm a traitor,' I said.

'A traitor? What are you talking about, Tom Kipper?'

'Sit down, Betsy,' I said, 'while I tell you a tale about a hanging judge and a traitor. That's me, I'm the traitor.'

So I told her. She sat and listened to my grim narrative which I espoused with mournful visage, sighing miserably at appropriate junctures. She was very quiet. We said goodbye at the yellow bus stop.

'See you tomorrow, Tom,' she said. kissing me on the cheek, eyes glistening.

Late that evening as I lay in my bed with the sheet over my head, Scouse stars twinkling in the sky which I did not see, Guy Fawkes said to me. 'Hello, Tom. Nice to see you here. What time's your execution?'

I groaned.

'Hey, Tom,' said Guy, 'don't worry. It's not so bad. One moment you have your head, the next you haven't. Would you like to see mine?'

I groaned further.

'Is there another Tom here?' asked Thomas More.

'Over here, Sir Thomas,' said Guy Fawkes.

'Nice to see another Tom,' said Thomas More. 'Been here long?'

'Too long,' I said miserably.

'Leave the poor boy alone,' said Anne Boleyn. 'Hello, Tom. Are you English?'

'Mostly Irish, I think.'

'There are more English ghosts here. Mostly men. Many of them nice chaps. Why are you here?'

'I'm a traitor.'

'Welcome to the gang.'

'I think I'll sleep now.'

'Goodnight, Tom.' She sounded like my ma.

The river was choppy the following morning, the Liver Buildings a princely tower over the stately Mersey. I trod the boards up the gangplank, walked to El Paso Corned Beef Inc., slunk like a traitor through the Traitor's Gate.

'Good morning, Tom,' said everybody to me, or so it seemed, as I sighed my way to my creaky old desk.

'What's wrong with Kipper?' asked Mr Pembroke, the new assistant cashier.

'Teenage blahs?' ventured old Hocking.

'Ha, ha, ha,' twittered Miss Gloria Wainwright. 'Have you read that Taffy scribe Dylan Evans today? Written about the juvenile court again!' My eyeballs fell out. I grabbed the paper. 'Look, even Tom's reading it!'

Inimitable scribe, Dylan Evans, splashed page four with unforgettable drama:

What is psychology, you may ask, and frequently muse about in a vacant five minutes in this almost post-Blitz era.

And well you might ask!

Does this mental science eliminate, create, absorb human activity and drama? Did the great master Shakespeare (reliably rumoured to be from Bootle) thread his personal psyche into the fabric of his characters, minuscule or giant in proportion? Am I disturbing you, dear reader?

Did the witness at the juvenile court last week follow Partington McLeesh's teachings when he unveiled the advice of this famous psychologist that young people should be allowed a much greater measure of freedom?

Freedom to stick up a bank, the Bank of England, that noble institution, with a water pistol?

Why are you smiling, dear reader? Of great interest is the investigation into the background of Partington McLeesh. Reliable information reveals he is not affiliated with any mental health organisation or clinic in the United Kingdom, nor does any scholastic institute honour his name or memory. And yet he prevails.

Or he did.

Conversation with him by telephone was brief. He said he was taking a holiday (vacation was the word he used) in the Canary Islands. Then he hung up.

However, his seemingly absurd (or ponderous)

exposé of juvenile behaviour has stimulated excited commentary in the world of psychology.

At a recent meeting, attendees were asked what they thought of his advice regarding the treatment of juvenile rebellion.

The answers threw new light on the subject. They were: idiotic, bloody daft, comedic, brainless, insane, hogwash, asinine, crackers, demented, unhinged, potty, loco-in-the-cabeza, mental blackout, something snapped, loose screw, he should be in the meat wagon, non-compos-mentis, barmy, bonkers, cuckoo, fatuous and bizarre.

Take your pick, dear reader!

But there are two sides to every coin. The exposé created by the young man in the juvenile courtroom – we think his name was Skipper – was brilliant, for Skipper knew the absurdity of the premise and in his own unique way brought it to light.

Water pistols indeed! Thank you, Skipper, for setting certain wheels in motion, upsetting an absurd applecart of sheer nonsense.

You are the invisible force of reason.

That's all for today, dear *Liverpool Echo* readers. Stay tuned for the next Dylan Evans Expose in *Fable and Fantasy*.

I folded the paper.
I'm the 'invisible force of reason'.
Wow!

'Hello, Betsy,' I burbled into the telephone, 'I'm the invisible force of reason.'

'What on earth are you on about, Kipper?'

'Can we have lunch?'

'You pay?'

'Of course.'

'Twelve thirty at Scrummy's?'

'See you there.'

And so the tale unfolded over deep fried fish and chips. There wasn't anything else. They were delicious.

'Tom Kipper, how is it you always survive?'

'I do?'

'Yes, you do.'

'You know, Ma says exactly the same thing.'

Betsy looked at me in that unflinching Braddock way, slight smile, big, brown, glowing eyes. What's in her emotional psyche, I thought, taking a cue from Partington McLeesh.

'My spies tell me,' she said, shaking her auburn head, 'you've been seeing a lot of Diana Partington every morning on the ferry boat.'

'Eh? Diana? Oh, yes she always seems to be on the same run. Wonder why that is.'

'Do you know what you are, Tom Kipper?'

'What's that, Bets?'

'A traitor.'

'Bets, surely you josh?'

Chapter Eighteen

Harry Mitty's Tripe

Three years ago, in 1940, in the pre-Blitz era, Cooley Maguire lived in Willington Close, not far from where we lived before the bomb dropped.

He was a bookie for the district, registered at the town hall in his colourful profession, somewhat small in stature like Uncle Bart, although not of the same artistic leaning, for Cooley loved the game, the fierce spark of chance, as long as it leaned in his favour, and the money, librae, solidi and denarii (LSD), was poured across his threshold in Willington Close by small, medium and large speculators with coin of the realm to cover stakes from one shilling to one hundred pounds.

For the art is long, change all-consuming.

His missus, Molly Maguire, ruled No. 114 Willington Close. Their only child, Joey, was the same age as me, Tom Kipper, but never seemed to socialise in 'the yard', that is, the schoolyard, the way other kids like Sully and me and Hacker Doyle and Gobs Flanagan did, for we fitted together like mouldy kippers in a tin can, while Joey Maguire dressed more neatly than us and didn't shed his kicking-shins blood the way we did. However, he was the best spitter in the school. He was champion.

Betsy Braddock said he was a horror and disgrace. We envied him but didn't particularly like him. Betsy though he should be fettered in the Bloody Tower. After torture.

The bookie business boomed, frantically, interrupted by the Blitz although not quite altogether, you understand, for wagers, small and medium, were often laid on how many Heinkels would be shot down by Spitfires in Merseyside at war.

Horses and riders thundered on the turf, horseshoes tearing into the ground, spraying out grassy clods of Aintree. Riders crouched low in the saddle breathing encouragement and threats in the horses' ears.

Spectators, bettors and bookies followed with opera glasses and adenoidal grunts, or shouts of high, explosive excitement.

'Paradise is coming from behind.'

'Paradise?'

'Paradise!'

'That mangy nag couldn't jog on Egremont Beach!'

'Wow! Isn't he about thirty to one?'

'Paradise is a girl.'

'How can you tell?'

'She's frothing at the mouth.'

'Come on, Paradise!'

Cooley was sweating. Paradise was an outsider.

Paradise just can't win. Should such an historic event happen, Cooley would go down in Aintree history as a bookie buried in bets at thirty-one to one.

'Come on, Splinter,' shouted Cooley Maguire, which was unusual for bookies, for bookies were calm, reserved, dignified, not of loquacious disposition, inhuman, detached.

No bookie would ever scream like Cooley Maguire.

Paradise romped home slathered in lather and money.

They say Cooley Maguire's tears caused an extra swell on the Mersey.

He was carried out. Mrs Cooley stopped smiling.

At No. 114 Willington Close the silence was broken only by bettors knocking down the front door for their money from Paradise.

On the evening of that fateful Tuesday, when mist blanketed the quiet surface of the Mersey between tides, and shoals of herring surfaced for a sly peek at the Liver, a short figure dressed in black, trilby included, trod across the boards of the ferry building in spectre-like gloom, face obscured by a grey scarf knotted at the nape of the neck.

In the figure's hand was hefted a large calibre .45 revolver from World War One, perhaps the Boer War, for it was ancient, antiquated of design, more like a cannon than a revolver. Just to lift it was an effort.

'Stick 'em up!' he said.

The revolver was pointed at Alice Aspinall, the bookkeeper, Bradley O'Toole and Belinda Fahey.

Alice dropped the tray of money she was holding like burning chips on to the desk.

'Put all the money,' said the stick-up man, 'into that bag or I'll fill you full of lead!' Just like moving pictures from America. 'Now hand it to me.' Which Alice Aspinall did. Then he was gone like a wraith, a spook, a Mersey phantom.

'He just slammed the door and was gone,' said Belinda Fahey.

'What do you think about all this, Mr O'Toole?' asked Inspector Crawley.

'I thought I was in America in a bank hold-up,' said O'Toole.

'Describe him to me, Mr O'Toole.'

'Well, he was short, not tall, just a wee man.'

'Dressed in black,' said Alice.

'Wearing a black trilby hat,' volunteered Belinda, 'and a mask.'

'Did he have an American accent?'

'Oh, no, he was a Scouser just like you and me.'

Inspector Crawley looked bleak. He never liked to think of himself as a Scouser. He had an impeccable, upper-crust, Ash-Willows accent; Scousers were the people he arrested. After all, he had the dignity of the force to consider.

There is a square in the city of Liverpool brightly named Harlequin. It has on two of its outer edges a small theatre and a large, prosperous department store with most splendid dormer windows.

Early-morning trade in the mostly cobbled courtyard is conducted from colourful barrows, large and small, attended to by cloth-capped men and aproned women who bustle buoyantly about their produce like bossy wives in the kitchen while the husband snores a-yet.

I walked through Harlequin Square from time to time to envelop myself in its mystery, for you felt as you passed a Dickensian aura of *Oliver Twist* and *David Copperfield* and *Sketches by Boz*. After passing into Lord Street you felt back in the real world of the Blitz.

But it was not called Harlequin Square by all and sundry (sundry, perhaps) but Harry Mitty Square, for Harry rode a barrow of tripe like none other in the universe.

Female office workers, department store attendants, would absent themselves even during working hours to descend upon Harry Mitty for his tripe, succulent, squishy, smelly and splendid. His barrow emptied by one o'clock each day.

'Tom,' said my ma on one occasion, 'bring home some of Harry Mitty's tripe.'

I groaned.

'Ma,' I said, 'this means I have to pick it up in my lunch hour, store it in the office, take a ferry and a bus, and come home, carrying Harry Mitty's tripe.'

'So?'

'Ma, it's almost an indignity.'

'Good word. Bring it home.'

'But, Ma!'

'Do I give you breakfast?'

'Yeah, Ma.'

'Dinner?'

'Yeah, Ma.'

'Do you have to bring home the bacon and eggs, make the scouse?'

'No, Ma.'

'But you don't want to bring home Harry Mitty's tripe?'

'Aw, gee, Ma.'

'Don't use those American expressions in this house. Bring home the tripe.'

I spoke to Betsy Braddock about it, for she worked in the elegant department store abutting Harry Mitty's Square.

'So,' said Betsy, 'your mother wants you to bring home tripe?'

'Yes, Bets, can you imagine it? A young executive like me having to hawk tripe through the city.'

'I bring home Harry Mitty's tripe twice a week.'

'You do?'

'Tom Kipper, what kind of person are you? Your poor mother slaving in the kitchen and you don't want to help her!'

'I don't?'

'Well, will you bring home the tripe?'

'Aw, gee, Bets.'

'Boys! Tom Kipper, I personally will get your mother's tripe from Harry and bring it to her.'

'Hmmn . . . Won't that get me into trouble?'

'I certainly hope so!'

Harry left Liverpool shortly after that and the Scouse bard was right when he said there were two sides to every story, for Harry has merged into legend before his time. Three years ago, before the Blitz, Mrs Lucy Mitty told her husband Alfred, 'The boy's different. He has enterprise.'

'He has, my arse,' replied Alf, turning to page four of the *Express*, which he studied. 'Have you noticed,' he continued, 'the ferry building was stuck up by a highwayman?'

'A highwayman?'

'Well. Some sort of gangster.'

'What did he steal? Do you want some more of this tripe?'

'All the day's takings for ferry tickets, hundreds of pounds. Yes, please, luv. And it was on the other side of the water.'

'The Wirral?'

'Aye.'

'I thought they were posh and civilised over there.'

'Well, after he took the money he said thank you.'

'A gentleman thief. Perhaps he's a Robin Hood.'

'He had a Scouse accent.'

'Who doesn't?'

They heard the kitchen door close softly.

'Ma, Dad,' said Harry Mitty, 'I have made a momentous decision.'

'Aye? What is it, lad?'

'I'm going into business.'

'I told you he had enterprise,' said Mrs Lucy Mitty.

'What's the business, son?' asked Mr Alfred Mitty.

'Tripe.'

'Tripe?'

'Aye, Dad, the tripe you're eating right now.'

'Where are you going to get the tripe from and where will you sell it?'

'A secret supplier in Bootle who gets it from Llanfairpwllch. I'll sell it in Harlequin Square from a barrow.'

'That'll take money, Harry.'

'I've got the money.'

'When will you start?'

'Tomorrow. Could I have some of that tripe, Ma?'

How can you advance in years when you're a teenager? The world stands still. You are a hero. If not locked in historic embrace, you stand out like Valentino, Jack the Ripper, Henry the Eighth, Cesar Romero, Julius Caesar, Plutardinos or Mickey Rooney. You stand still. You will always be a teenager.

That is, until you're seventeen and people in the office say, 'Another year and you'll be in the army, Tom.' Then you grin like a Cheshire Cat without cheese.

One of the ladies in the office, Miss Penelope Hawkins, made me an apple pie, quite large, crusty pastry, bulging with old green pippins, drowned in black market sugar with cream layered like Tory promises on top.

'The Germans have heard about you already, Tom Kipper,' said Mr Hocking. 'You'll be just in time to give the Führer a kick in the gluteus maximus.'

'That's the arse,' said the unpoetic Mr Jones.

'Have some more pie, Thomas,' breathed Miss Winters. I was now her assistant, working in Bills Payable with her in the morning and in Customs with Mr Crisp in the afternoon. Miss Winters was in her early twenties, smothering me with solicitude whenever I sat on a highlegged stool in her department. At that time she always purred like a self-satisfied moggy. With fleas.

Mr Crisp in Customs had watery eyes and blond hairs growing out of his ears, but he was absent-minded, poetic, forever scratching, sneezy, as ancient as a Hun promise, and of a most amiable disposition.

His over-large jacket drowned his pudgy body and drooped over his seat so that the four stool legs looked like his. He smelled heavily of aftershave, pipe tobacco and Walkers Draught. He didn't always know I was there, prattling away merrily as he filled out forms in triplicate with a leaky ballpoint pen at the speed of a Messerschmitt 109E.

'There's the battered fuselage of a Heinkel on Winston Hill,' said Sully. 'It has German markings on it.'

'Hey, let's go up there on Saturday and have a look at it.'

'And take some sandwiches.'

'I'll bring those,' said Joey Maguire. 'Come to think of it, Mother has many acquaintances on the Hill.'

Ye Olde Tea Shoppe in the village was a favourite place for teenagers and older mums to yak and gossip and tell stories, sometimes tinged with the truth, or at any rate slightly factual.

It was built of red and pink sandstone on Reveller's Row just off the Main Street near the Pig and Whistle. The tales and stories and reminiscences exchanged there on rainy afternoons and early evenings were not always tinged with the truth, but they were colourful and entertaining. The teller was always listened to, for in the telling his or her personality shone forth so that later in the day the audience could say, 'What a crock!' or 'Wow!' or 'Poppycock!'

So Sully said, 'Three years ago today a highwayman stuck up the ferry building and stole the day's takings. They never caught him. It was in the *Post* "On this day . . ." section.'

'Maybe it was a woman.'

'Women are not highwaymen,' said Betsy.

'I think he was a Yank.'

'No, he was a Scouser. With an accent.'

'Never left a clue.'

'Or a footprint.'

'Apparently he said thank you when he took the cash.'

'Hey, I've just had a thought.'

'How unusual, Sully,' I said.

'Not funny, Kipper.'

'Maybe,' said Sully, 'it was Harry Mitty.'

'You're joshing,' said Betsy.

'Could be. Didn't he set up around then? We'll never know, though, now that he's gone to New York.'

'Philadelphia.'

'Where did they get that name!'

There was a silence. Rain pattered on the lace window

looking out on to Reveller's Row. The Tea Shoppe's cat, Quincy, meowed.

'It was me,' said Joey.

'No, it was me,' said Betsy.

'How about Dixie Dean?'

'Lord Haw-Haw.'

'No, it was me,' said Joey again. He wasn't smiling.

The doorbell tinkled as a slim teenage girl entered, carrying a trim beige and silver handbag, dark, curly hair peeking out from under a white bonnet, blue eyes looking apprehensively around until she saw Joey. Then she smiled and I almost fell in love – until Betsy lowered her eyebrows and pulled her mouth down in most splendid Braddock fashion, and I assumed my benign face again.

'This is my sister, Melinda,' Joey said. 'Melinda, meet the gang.'

'Very interesting,' murmured Sully.

'Melinda, we were just discussing Harry Mitty.'

'A wonderful man.'

'I told them.'

'You did?'

'I don't think they believed me.'

'It's true,' said Melinda.

'What's true?' I asked.

'Joey held up the Ferry Accounting Department with one of Daddy's old pistols and stole that money.'

'What?'

'He still has it. Harry Mitty advised him to return it one way or another but he still has it. He didn't want the cash for himself but for Daddy, who lost everything on a horse called Paradise three years ago. But two weeks later Joey still had the money and Daddy had a reversal of fortune.'

'On a horse?'

'Bizarre.'

'Bizarre?'

'Everybody put their socks on Bizarre in a big race over in Chester and the horse stopped en route to chew the hedge. He threw the rider, Harry Magee, and he is now immortalised.'

'Bizarre or Magee?'

'The horse.'

'So Joey still has the hold-up money?'

'Well, he does not feel, shall we say, comfortable giving it back himself, so he wants Tom Kipper to do it.'

'Me?'

'Are you Kipper?'

'Yes, I'm Kipper.'

'Do you mind? He said you're a hero.'

So it came about that evening, in Mary Lane, I said to my ma, 'Will you do it?'

My ma, Mary Catherine, rolled her grey Connemara eyes. 'You want me to what?'

'Go to the police station.'

'Tom Kipper, way back in the history of the family there was a crockpot, a dreamer, a fruitcake, a bizarre eccentric named Lancy O'Toole and even he wouldn't go to a police station. It's contrary to Gaelic natural law. All police stations are run by the English.'

'Dad's English, Ma.'

'Yes, but he surrendered.'

'Ma, Cooley Maguire is Irish.'

'But we're doing this for Joey Maguire. Right?'

'Yeah, Ma.'

'So Cooley Maguire, his father, will never know.'

'St Joseph will.' That stopped her.

'Thomas Kipper,' she ground out, 'you should have been a politician like your father.'

'Is there any tea?' enquired the recumbent form in the leathered depths.

But it was Betsy Braddock who took the money back, cool as a cartload of Harry Mitty Square cucumbers.

'I found it on the number four bus,' she told the teller.

'Just a moment. May I have your name?'

'Certainly,' said Betsy, 'but please hurry, I have to catch the seven forty-five if it's not been bombed.

She smiled at me as she boarded the *Daffodil*, for she knew what had happened the last time I was in the Craven Arms police station and Chief Inspector Flanagan never forgot a face, particularly a Kipper face. On the top deck she said, 'Do you know who Harry Mitty married? An American woman from the Red Cross.'

'Must have been quite a charmer.'

'People keep asking for him in the square. They've erected a monument to him.'

'To Harry Mitty?'

'Yes. Hey, do you have time, Kipper, to take a quick peek

in the square before you disappear into El Paso Corned Beef?'

'Sure, Bets. Come on.'

It was most splendid, a glimmering brass edifice.

He went down in Scouse folklore as the Man Without a Shadow, for only saints don't have shadows. Betsy Braddock believed it. 'Surely not, Betsy. You don't believe a human being ever existed in this world who didn't have a shadow?'

'Aye, 'tis true,' breathed Betsy Braddock.

'Bets, surely you're kidding?'

'It's true, Tom Kipper. I remember now that every time I went to Harry Mitty for tripe he never cast a shadow.'

'That's because there was no sunshine. No sunshine, no shadow.'

'You know, we've been having rain now for about six months, Tom Kipper, but every so often the sun has shone.'

'Aye, but it's been always later in the day when we were walking to the Pier Head and Mitty packed up his barrow every day at one o'clock.'

'Tom Kipper, I know what I saw.'

'You mean didn't see.'

But Harry Mitty was gone, off to somewhere in Philadelphia. We don't know how it came about, but a bright stone block was placed in the centre of Harry Mitty Square and an upended brass replica of his barrow erected on top. And underneath the barrow were inscribed the immortal words:

In Liverpool's fair city
Lived the great Harry Mitty,
A hero he was of unusual type.
Now his ghost wheels his barrow
Though he cast not a shadow
And all of us hunger for Mitty's great tripe.

We looked at Harry Mitty's barrow and it had a shadow, even if Harry didn't.

So Harry lives on in perpetual glory, for folklore survives from one generation to the next, almost becoming fact, although reason would have us believe it is an illusion. His tripe, however, does not.

'Hey, see you on the ferry, Bets.'

It was the Scouse and the tripe that did it.

Both of them are delicious, particularly if brought to absolute perfection of bouquet and taste by me ma, Mary Catherine.

'May I have some tripe, Ma?' I asked, most humbly, after consuming about four gallons of beatific scouse.

She looked at my skinny frame. 'Where do you put it all, Tom Kipper? No. You're already swallowed a gallon of scouse. Do you want to look like your father?'

'Dad's skinny, Ma.'

'Hmmn . . .'

So I chomped down deliriously, which is, of course, the reason I dived into a great, mysterious chasm of Gaelic hysteria as my head hit the pillow, for I was swimming in the office of El Paso Corned Beef and I could hear a thousand voices say, 'Another year and you'll be in the army, Tom . . .'

Which is time, for I had seen seventeen Scouse summers.

'Aren't you going to say anything to me, Tom Kipper?'

'I'll write, Bets.'

'That's it?'

'See you on my first leave.'

'Oh, Tom Kipper, you worm.'

'Worm?'

'You're hopeless.'

'Hopeless?'

'Pathetic.'

'I am?'

'Tom Kipper, say something meaningful.'

'Meaningful? Hey, the train is moving. Why are you crying, Bets?'

'Don't you know, Tom Kipper?'

'Eh? Oh, yes, Bets, I think I love you.'

'Think?'

'I do. Yes, I do love you, Bets.'

The sun burst through the Mersey fog.

She was smiling.

I was laughing.

Somewhere a foghorn sounded.

A brand new Scouse day was dawning. In Liverpool.